THE
GOODNIGHT
SONG

ALSO BY NICK HOLLIN

Dark Lies

THE
GOODNIGHT
SONG

NICK HOLLIN

Bookouture

Published by Bookouture in 2018

An imprint of StoryFire Ltd.
Carmelite House
50 Victoria Embankment
London EC4Y 0DZ

www.bookouture.com

ISBN: 978-1-78681-433-3
eBook ISBN: 978-1-78681-432-6

For my family

PROLOGUE

TWO YEARS AGO

Nathan follows his partner DI Katie Rhodes under the police tape and through the front door of the long-abandoned school. Ahead of them is a damp corridor, paint peeling from walls that would once have been covered in posters and artwork, adding colour, life. It's an old comprehensive, nothing like the expensive college Nathan's mother's multi-million selling novels paid for him to attend, but something about the place does seem familiar. Might he have been here before? No. He would remember. Along with his imagination, his memory is key to who he is and what he does. No matter how often he might have wanted it to, his memory has never failed him.

'Careful,' says Katie quietly as they reach a doorway that leads through to a large room. 'I hear it's pretty bad.' Nathan stops and looks at his partner; she's never showed such concern before.

'Steven Fish,' she says. 'His body was discovered early this morning by kids who rang in and didn't want to leave their names.' Nathan can see why when he tentatively peers into the assembly hall and sees several smashed windows and a wealth of graffiti. He takes careful steps towards the crime scene in his paper suit and paper shoe covers, but his balance is slightly off and he bashes his shoulder against the door frame as he enters the next room. Again, Katie looks at him with concern.

'Do you want to take a few minutes?' she says, stepping across and blocking his view of the area where he knows the body will be.

'I'm fine,' he says defiantly, sidestepping her to give himself a clear view.

The body of Steven Fish has been strung from the climbing bars on the wall, his arms outstretched, fingers wrapped around the uprights. You'd think he was alive and mid-ascent, were it not for the two fingers that have been snapped back, and for the cut where a knife has been dragged up from his ankle to his neck. And then there's the head that's been hacked from his shoulders, sitting propped upright on the floor, the eyes – still open – staring straight at Nathan from an enormous pool of blood. Nathan can feel his own blood thumping violently in his throat and chest. He crouches down, feeling increasingly unsteady, and sees that, running across the badly scratched floor of the hall, are lines of a different liquid.

'Water,' says Katie, following his stare. 'They think he was part-drowned in the toilets, over there, before being dragged across.'

Nathan rises and takes a step closer to the body. He pushes out a long breath, then draws it slowly back in, working through the tried and tested process that allows him to detach from the reality and consider what might have been going through the killer's mind as they worked. Normally he waits for Katie to share all the evidence she's so carefully gathered, but he seems unable to wait on this occasion; he needs to be there straight away, to dive into the details and use his imagination to re-enact the killing in his mind.

The connection is instant. He feels a powerful wave of emotion taking him over. On previous occasions, there's always been some part of him still fighting for control, but that defence isn't there; this time there is no resistance. It's as if a drug has entered his system and there's nothing he can do. Not that he wants to do anything. In fact, there's nothing in the world he wants more than to go with this ride, wherever it might take him.

He feels a jolt. With his eyes closed and his mind as open as it's ever been, it takes him a moment to realise what's happening. A hand has grabbed his arm and is dragging him away from the body and out of the thoughts and feelings that he was starting to love. He wants to shout out, to tell whoever it is to leave him alone, but the move is so sudden and so violent that there's nothing he can do until he's outside the school, in the bright sunshine, staring into Katie's eyes.

He plays back the events leading up to this swift departure and realises that he had been smiling broadly as he stood over the headless body of Steven Fish. This wouldn't have been obvious to most people in the room, not beneath the face mask he'd been wearing, but the fear and disgust on Katie's face tell him that he's not fooling her.

'It's over,' he says, peeling off his paper mask.

'What is?' asks Katie.

'All of this.' He gestures back towards the crime scene, but the sweep of his arm takes her in, too. And it's this realisation that almost drops him to his knees. Their partnership is finished. 'I need to go away,' he says, with greater urgency, already taking a step towards where they've parked the car.

'Where?'

Nathan considers this and realises that for now, there is only one essential requirement. 'Where nobody else is.'

CHAPTER ONE

The anonymous, unfiltered truth about crime and the criminal justice system

I know it's almost six months since the inquest in the Cartoonist murders finished, but much like the press, I keep coming back to the case. I want to get it straight in my mind, but there's just too much that's happened, too many unanswered questions. I've tried to break it down to the most basic facts, to see if that's helped. I'm not sure it has, but perhaps it'll trigger something for you:

- Nathan Radley. The best criminal psychologist the police have ever had. Incredible memory. Remarkable imagination. Nobody gets inside a murderer's head like he does. But at what cost to his mental health?

- Christian Radley. Nathan's twin. The Cartoonist. The one mind Nathan couldn't get inside until several people had already been killed. How could Nathan not have known?

- Steven Fish. One of Christian's first victims, and the case that sent Nathan into hiding almost two years ago. He told the inquest it was simply a breakdown, but what was the real reason he ran? Did he see his brother's work in that crime? Or did he see his own potential to do the same?

- DI Katie Rhodes. Nathan's long-time police partner. I'll leave it to the tabloids to speculate on how much more they might be to each other. She's the woman who brought him back from hiding and helped him track his brother down. She's brilliant. Flawed. And now, thanks to Christian's final act, she has scars down her once-beautiful face. Will she ever recover from what she's been through?

- The journal. Nathan's darkest fantasies, written as a deeply troubled teenager. Traces of his mother's literary skills. Traces of his brother's murderous desires. Its being leaked to the world just after the inquest is the most likely reason that Nathan and Katie felt the need to run off and hide again.

- The missing journal pages. Perhaps the thing that intrigues me most. Who took the four pages out of the journal? Was it Christian? Was it Nathan? Nathan says he can't remember what was on them. Is he lying? What secrets might those pages hide?

- The future. Where are Katie and Nathan? How can the press not have tracked them down already? Are they ever coming back?

CHAPTER TWO

ONE MONTH AGO

'They might have forgotten,' says Katie, pressing her face up against the window, staring out at the hillside behind their stone cottage.

'They'll never forget,' replies Nathan, seated at the kitchen table, his hand wrapped round a glass of white wine.

'Plenty more will have happened in the world since we left.' She takes a large swig from her glass and moves over to the sideboard where the radio had once been. The day they'd moved in it had gone the same way as the television and the phone, ripped out by them and broken beyond repair so they couldn't change their mind about shutting themselves off from everything.

'I prefer not knowing,' Nathan says quietly.

'What's happened to that famous imagination of yours?' says Katie. 'Have you managed to shut it down completely?' He turns to look at her, still surprised whenever she snaps at him like this, even though it's becoming more and more frequent of late.

'If you want to go back to London, then we can. I'll just deal with what happens. Or you can go back on your own. It's not your journal they've read. Not your thoughts.'

'We're in this together now,' says Katie. 'Forever.'

Nathan feels the warmth of her words at last, and can't help but smile a little. 'And we'll find a way to work it out.'

'You're right,' says Katie, matching his smile. 'Sorry, I'm just having a bad day.'

'Anything I can do to make it better?'

'You could find me something more exciting for dinner than pasta,' she says. 'I don't think my stomach can take any more.'

'I know what you mean,' says Nathan, with a sigh. 'Maybe we can risk a delivery. We could ask them to leave it up at the end of the drive. I'll hide behind the wall and wait till they've gone.'

Katie laughs. 'Ordered how? And paid for with what?'

'We've got some cash.'

'But no phone. And no internet. Maybe I could walk half a mile up the hill and wait for the shepherd to pass on his quad bike, and when he gets close I could throw fifty quid and a shopping list over, tell him I've got some sort of psychiatric condition that means I don't like being seen.' As she says this she lifts a finger to one of the scars on her cheek, and Nathan remembers the flash of the cameras on the steps outside the courtroom at the inquest, how she'd buried her face into his side to hide them.

'You make our situation sound ridiculous,' he says.

'It is ridiculous.'

'It's necessary. The first time anyone recognises us, it's over. The world and his wife will be on our doorstep in under an hour.'

'Do you really think we are that significant anymore?' asks Katie, before adding quietly, 'I certainly don't feel significant.'

'It won't be forever,' says Nathan. 'When things have calmed down, and we're better, then maybe—'

'What do you mean, better?' she asks, cutting him off. 'I'm fine.'

'Yes, but...' Nathan doesn't go on. Mentioning his concerns over her recent mood swings will only make them worse.

'Even if we've both gone a bit crazy,' says Katie, 'how on earth would we even know? Who do we have to compare ourselves with?'

Nathan shrugs to acknowledge her point. 'Just try and remember who you were before.'

He watches as Katie's hand moves down to her stomach, not the point on the side where the knife went in, but the centre, which she softly strokes. 'I'll never be that person again.'

Katie is pacing backwards and forwards in front of the window, reminding Nathan of a caged tiger he saw once with his family when he was a boy. A sad zoo. And a very sad memory. Then suddenly she stops, a grimace on her face.

'Are you okay?' he asks, rising from his chair.

'No,' says Katie, doubling over and falling sideways against the wall, her hand now pressed firmly into her stomach. 'I'm not sure I am.'

'I have to go!' Nathan says, crouching down next to where she is curled up on the bathroom floor. She's been like this for more than an hour, vomiting, gasping and groaning, pleading with him to stay, telling him it's all right, that *she's* all right. She's holding her stomach in the exact place where his brother Christian had plunged a knife eight months before. There had been a lot of blood that day, but this is almost worse, not knowing what's going on inside her, no way of knowing how bad it is, how long she might have.

He stands up and slaps his trouser pockets for the hundredth time, cursing their decision to get rid of their phones. If only they'd thought to keep a mobile for emergencies. 'I'll run to town,' he says, grabbing his trainers, still covered in mud from the two hours he spent running up and down the hill at the back of their cottage earlier that morning. His legs are tired, but he'll have no problem covering the five miles to town, and if he gets lucky he might spot a car and be able to flag it down. He bends over and places a hand on her forehead, pushing back the strands of sweaty hair and feeling the heat. 'I won't be long.'

'Wait!' she cries, through gritted teeth. 'If you have to...' She groans again, and curls into an even tighter ball. 'There's a house.

This side of town. A yellow front, a blue Saab in the drive. He's a doctor. He can keep a secret.'

Nathan hardly has time to wonder what secret she's been keeping from him in this place where they know no one. 'I love you,' he says, then heads for the door with one last glance back, trying not to think it might be the last time he sees her alive.

He arrives at the yellow house in half an hour, his legs almost giving under him the moment he starts to slow. He thumps a sweaty fist against the front door, relieved to see the Saab is there and desperately hoping that its owner is, too. It takes what seems like forever before the door is opened and a slightly stooped, balding man who looks to be well into his seventies hurries forward at the sight of Nathan about to collapse through his doorway.

'Are you okay?' he says.

Nathan is so short of breath he can barely answer, but he forces the words out with a rasp. 'You have to come with me. Please.' He expects to be asked more questions, for more time to be wasted, but the old man simply nods and reaches for a set of car keys.

*

'Food poisoning, most likely,' says the man Nathan now knows to be Dr Richard Evans, rising slowly from where Katie is curled on the floor of the bathroom.

'More likely a rejection to eating the same food over and over,' she groans.

'So it's nothing to do with…?' Nathan nods towards the obvious scar on Katie's side. The doctor had said nothing when he'd prized away her hands and lifted her top, gently pressing his fingers against her skin.

'I think not,' he says. 'What she needs is rest and plenty of fluids. If you want a second opinion, then I can drive you to the hospital. It's only—'

'No.' Nathan cuts him off sharply before covering his tone with a smile. 'I mean, no thank you, doctor. And thank you for coming out here. You must know why we don't want too much attention.' He turns his face away from the doctor, although he's certain he must already have been recognised.

'You'd be amazed at what I don't know,' says Richard, matching his smile. 'And what I don't want to know. All that's important to me is that your friend here,' he gestures towards Katie, 'is okay. So if you don't mind, I'd like to pop back for another look tomorrow. I'm guessing you don't have much in the way of medicines?' He glances briefly back at the nearly bare rooms he'd rushed through to get to the bathroom. 'I'll bring you a few things.'

CHAPTER THREE

ONE WEEK AGO

Katie laughs so hard a small wave of the wine in her glass sloshes over the edge and drops to the decking. Looking down at the stain, she gasps, as she's reminded of the last time she saw a pool of red on the floor like that, and her hand moves automatically to her stomach. When she looks up, she sees that Nathan and the doctor have also stopped laughing and are staring with concern.

'Are you all right?' asks Nathan.

'Why shouldn't I be?' asks Katie, more sharply than she'd intended.

'Sorry, it's just, after…'

She follows his eyes down to her stomach and pulls her hand away. 'I'd forgotten about the poisoning,' she says, although that's not what she'd been thinking of.

Nathan looks down at the wrist where a watch would once have been. 'I guess it must have been a good month ago now.'

'A very good month,' says Katie, 'thanks to Richard.' She raises her glass and takes a large enough swig that there's little chance of her spilling any more. 'You saved me.'

'I didn't do anything,' says the old doctor, sipping his own wine. 'It was just something you ate.'

Katie reaches out and scoops up a wedge of rich cheese. 'And thanks to you, I've been eating far better ever since.'

'We both have,' says Nathan, through a mouth half-filled with delicious cold meats, delivered by Richard that morning.

'It's been nice to have the company,' says Richard. 'I was getting a little lonely in my yellow house. People forget about us oldies.'

The smile on Katie's face slips again as she thinks back to the fleeting conversations she had with her dad in the care home before he died. His Alzheimer's had robbed him of the ability to understand what she was saying when she visited, and all she had really wanted to let him know was how sorry she was that they didn't talk more when they'd had the chance; sorry for having been so wrapped up in her police career.

'They're fools,' says Katie. 'To miss out on all that life experience.'

'They're lucky,' it's Richard's turn to look uncomfortable, 'not to have lived it.'

Katie sees the sadness in the old man that only occasionally breaks to the surface of his kind, wrinkled face. 'Maybe it's our turn to try and help you. If you're ready to share?'

'After all, we've already shared our story,' says Nathan. 'Or rather, the papers have.'

'Actually, I wasn't joking when I said I didn't read the papers,' says Richard. 'And I barely watch the television. I read fiction, mostly, and of late I also talk to you.'

'So you genuinely don't know who we are?' asks Katie.

'I know exactly who you are from our conversations. And okay, yes.' He sighs. 'The outside world is almost impossible to avoid, no matter how hard I try, and so once or twice I might have heard mention of people who sound very much like you when the news comes on the radio.'

'And you're not scared?' says Nathan. 'You don't believe what they've said about me, about what I must be capable of, because of my twin brother's crimes?'

'No,' says the doctor. 'Working in London hospitals for so many years I learned not to make judgements about people. I just accepted them as they were and did what I could to help.'

'And is that all we are?' asks Katie, setting her wine glass down heavily on the table, hearing the snap in her voice return. 'More patients for you to try and heal?'

'Of course not,' says Richard, his old face tightening as he looks away. 'You're friends. My only friends.' He swallows hard and starts to knead his hands together. 'My story is nowhere near as dramatic as yours, but the ending…' He gestures towards the empty landscape outside the window. 'You're not the only people who have run away, you know. I've seen a lot of terrible things. I still see them, sometimes, at night.'

'I know what you mean,' says Nathan, nodding.

'PTSD,' Richard says. 'That's what I had. Self-diagnosed and self-healed, in part, by coming here and shutting myself away.'

Nathan nods again. 'How long did it take?'

He looks down at his pale, wrinkled hands. 'Far too long. Please don't make the same mistake as me. There's so much good out there. So many wonderful people to meet. I mean, if you hadn't been ill, I'd never have met you two.'

'You're going back?' asks Katie.

'Oh no,' says Richard, looking to the window again. 'This is it for me now. I have all I need right here in Wales.'

'I think we do, too,' says Nathan, looking across at Katie, who finds she cannot match his smile. 'I can't think of anything that could drag us away.'

CHAPTER FOUR

TWO DAYS AGO
BLOG: Seeing Red

The anonymous, unfiltered truth about crime and the criminal justice system

OMFG. You will never believe what just dropped into my inbox. I'm not sure I believe it. I know, I know, I'm obsessed with this case, have been writing about it ever since it became news, but you never really expect to be *involved*. It could be a prank, of course – you'll have to judge for yourself – but from the brief investigations I've just done it seems real enough.

I'm probably not making any sense. Hardly surprising, given the amount I've had to drink. I know it's morning, but I had no choice. I needed something to calm me down. I just can't get my head around what's happened. I believe I've just received a scanned copy of one of the missing pages from Nathan's leaked journal. It's one of his fantasies, one of the crimes he lived out in his head then put to paper. I keep thinking I should go to the police, but you, my loyal readers, are the only people I trust. And so, I'm trusting you with this:

It's like art. Although not nearly as boring as the classes at school. And the knife doesn't feel clumsy, like a paintbrush, it feels like it's meant to be there, like it's an extension of me, of my true self. I twist it under the light, enjoying the brilliance of the surface

I've polished for hours in anticipation. Back then I'd imagined this moment over and over, but this is the real thing, the chance to finally make my mark. Ha, I quite like that. I might share it with my victim when he wakes from the blow to the side of the head I gave him.

He'll struggle, but there's not much point with the ropes around his wrists and ankles, but he'll figure it out for himself soon enough. And I need him to use up some of his strength before I push his head down in the bath.

He'd better wake up soon, the water is getting cold. I want it at 37 degrees, the temperature of blood. He's close. I can tell, because his breathing is quite ragged. I hope I didn't get carried away too early on. I couldn't resist peeling some skin off his back in advance, just to see what it felt like. I wonder what it will feel like for him? He'll tell me anything, of course, even though there's nothing I want to hear. He'll think there's a reason. He'll think that I'm sane.

I'm not going to hurt him for too long. That's not why I'm doing it. It's really all about the ending. And what an ending! How clearly I can picture that last long, single stroke, along the ankle then up the back of the leg, over the buttocks and back and across the now skinless shoulder to the neck. I'd like it to be smooth, but my hand keeps shaking with all the excitement. I can't wait for all that blood. There might even be a scream, to match the one I'm already hearing in my head.

He's not coming round. I am. The fantasy is leaving me, along with the urge. But there's still enough to convince me that I cannot stop what is going to happen. It might be months, it might be years, but this will be more than just words.

More than just words. I reckon it's one of the crimes Nathan fantasised about, and it certainly sounds like it was written back when he was in his late teens, but I can't help thinking about the similarities between this and the Steven Fish murder. I mentioned Fish in my last post: he was one of the cases that Katie failed to solve when Nathan had run away to Scotland. He was the *reason* Nathan ran away to Scotland, because, as he revealed at the inquest, he couldn't cope with the evil of that crime.

Steven Fish was part-drowned. He had skin peeled from his back. That very piece of skin was discovered at the scene of one of Christian Radley's murders, which is why everyone thought Nathan's twin must have committed that crime too. But now… Why didn't Nathan mention the similarities? Why was this page removed? What was the real reason for his running away to Scotland? Was it the horror at what someone else had done? Or was it guilt at what *he* had finally done? I really don't want to be asking these questions, because I like Nathan and I've always trusted that he never gave in to his urges, but this blog is all about honesty, about confronting the truth, and now I'm even more anxious to hear what he has to say about this latest leak. Jesus, might this be from Nathan himself? Might he have sent me the page by way of a confession?

I need another drink.

CHAPTER FIVE

PRESENT DAY

Nathan is lying on the sofa trying to sleep off his hangover when the doorbell rings. It comes as such a shock that he convinces himself he's imagined the sound; he doesn't even know for sure that the cottage they're living in has a bell. Dr Richard Evans, their only visitor in almost four months, has always marked his arrival with a gentle knock. Nathan sits up on the edge of the sofa and reassures himself that he is still in Wales, that he is safe.

He doesn't need to look around him to fill in the details of the room; they are instantly imprinted on his mind, just as with every crime scene he's ever walked into. It's a gift that has helped him understand many killers and solve many cases, but sometimes he'd give anything to be able to forget.

The doorbell rings again and Nathan is up on his feet, twisting his head back towards the patio doors as he heads in the other direction. He spots that Katie is still a long way down the garden, carefully tending to the roses. At the end of the hallway Nathan tries to peer out from behind the curtain in the toilet to see who might be disturbing them. It's a long walk to reach the end of the dirt track leading down to the cottage, so it's unlikely anybody would have come here by accident. It's only when he sees a familiar flash of grey hair that he breathes a sigh of relief, heading for the door and opening it.

'Sorry,' says Richard, with a pained expression on his face.

'For this hangover?' says Nathan, with a laugh. 'I think I bear some of the responsibility for that.' When he sees the doctor isn't smiling back, he leans to one side to get a better view of the track behind, to make sure he has come alone. 'Is everything okay?'

Richard pauses and looks down at his shoes, the tip of a polished brogue twisting in the dirt. 'I need to talk to you, please. Both of you.'

Nathan leads the way back through the living room to the kitchen, opening the patio doors and calling for Katie to come in. Removing her gardening gloves, she spots the old doctor standing next to Nathan and beams broadly, but when the two men offer no smile in return her face changes.

'What's wrong?' she says, kicking off her muddy boots and dropping the gloves and secateurs on the side.

'Shall we have a seat?' asks Richard, moving back towards the living room.

'We can talk here,' says Nathan, nervously.

'It's about your friend, Mike Peters.'

Katie opens her mouth to speak, then closes it again. Then she breathes out slowly and lowers her shoulders. 'It's okay, doc,' she says. 'Tell Mike that if he needs the place for Ben, then of course he can have it back.'

'Who is Ben?' asks Nathan, trying to piece things together. 'Is this how you knew where Richard lived?' After she'd recovered, Katie had dodged his questions about how she knew about the doctor, and he's all but given up asking.

'It's not Ben,' says the doctor. 'It's—'

'Retirement?' says Katie, cutting him off. 'Of course, it must be time! And he wants to move out here, too? Well, why didn't he come and tell us himself?'

Nathan reaches out and places a hand lightly on her arm to settle her, but she pulls away, not wanting to accept the truth written in the sadness on Richard's face. She picks at the dirt under her fingernails until she finally finds the words. 'Mike's dead, isn't he?'

'I'm truly sorry,' is all Richard can say.

Nathan feels Katie's full weight against his arm, the words knocking her sideways like a physical blow.

'I told him he needed to take more care of himself,' says Katie. 'When did it happen?'

'Yesterday, I think.'

Katie nods, then lifts her head, her eyes searching, her detective's mind taking back control. 'How did you find out? Did Ben ring you?'

'I heard a headline on the radio. Just a headline, then I came straight here.'

'Mike's death made the news?' says Nathan, his concern suddenly peaking. DS Mike Peters had been one of the few people on the police force to engage with Nathan as if he were a true member of the team, and not some freak that brought them remarkable results; but the relationship he'd had with Katie had been far more like father and daughter. He was her mentor, especially when her real father's Alzheimer's had caused him to slip away. He'd offered his cottage to them when he knew they needed to disappear to survive. They owed him a lot. 'It wasn't natural causes?'

'I'm afraid not.'

'Oh, Jesus,' Katie says, reaching for the trainers she had worn on their run that morning. 'We need to go back.' Her hands are trembling, struggling to loosen the laces. 'Do they know who did it?' she asks, looking up at the doctor.

'I'm not sure.' He offers a look of concern. 'But the police want to speak to you.'

'How do you know that?' asks Katie, with a tilt of her head. 'You said you only heard a headline.'

'Because we are the headline,' says Nathan, with a grimace. 'And they think I'm somehow to blame.'

'I can quickly set them right about that,' says Richard, looking across at the empty bottles of wine on the side, evidence that they had all been together. 'I can also drive you back to London, whenever you're ready.'

'Let's go,' says Katie, already on her way to the door.

CHAPTER SIX

'We should never have left London,' says Katie, shaking her head as they race through the countryside.

'We needed time to recover,' says Nathan, from the back seat of the car. She can see he's holding on tight as they're thrown around bends by Richard's driving. She prefers to take the impact, her shoulder crashing into the door.

'We were innocent, and we ran away like cowards after we gave our testimony. We should have stayed, and fought for our lives back. We shouldn't have left the police department. It was the only place both of us knew what we needed to do, and how. It was the only environment where we could both cope with who we were.'

'You think I was coping?' asks Nathan.

'You were succeeding,' says Katie. 'Not just surviving. We had a purpose.'

'So the work is our only purpose?' asks Nathan, weakly.

They sit in silence for several minutes, Katie sensing that she is dangerously close to spilling her secret. Perhaps it is finally time.

'I should have been there for Mike,' she says.

'You can't blame yourself.'

'I don't.' She stares down at her stomach. 'That's the second time your weakness has cost me.'

'What's that supposed to mean?' asks Nathan, and she can hear the hurt in his voice.

'It means...' She draws in a deep breath to confess, but nothing comes. 'Let's just focus on the work.' She loosens her seat belt and reaches forward to fiddle with the radio, trying to find a station that might give her more information about Mike's death, but the car is old and the radio offers nothing but static. She asks Richard to repeat the headline he heard.

'*The police are looking for Nathan Radley and Katie Rhodes in connection with the death of Detective Sergeant Mike Peters, whose body was pulled from the Thames yesterday evening.*'

Katie thumps the door, making her fist throb. She focuses on the pain, thinking of the pain she's going to inflict on whoever is responsible.

'I don't understand why we can't stop at a payphone and ring the station,' says Nathan. 'They'll tell us what we need to know.'

'You know they won't,' says Katie. 'Weren't you listening? You're a suspect. You're the one they'll want to talk to.'

'Weren't *you* listening?' says Nathan, his voice hardening in a way she hasn't heard in all the time they've been away in Wales. 'We are *both* suspects.'

'There's no way they believe I killed my friend.'

'Whereas the brother of a serial killer…' A quick glimpse in the side mirror shows her that Nathan has sunk back into his seat, his head in his hands, muffling his final words. 'I thought you, of all people, believed in me.'

Katie feels her own frustration building. 'This has nothing to do with what I believe. This is police work, profiling. This is common bloody sense. Of course you're a suspect. And of course they want to speak to me too. We're connected – we disappeared together.'

'And yet now it seems we're going back apart,' mutters Nathan.

'Maybe we should,' says Katie, pressing her knuckles against the pain that's growing in her stomach and ignoring the sickening sense that she is destroying something precious with her words.

Richard has been uncharacteristically quiet since they left the cottage, driving fast, silent beside them as they've bickered, but now Katie can see him shifting uneasily in his seat.

'Can you drop me off as soon as we get to the outskirts of London,' she says to the doctor. 'I'll make my way from there.'

'But why not let me take you straight to the station?' he asks, eyes still fixed on the road ahead as he weaves to overtake an articulated lorry.

'Because I'm not going to the station.'

'Yes, you are,' says Nathan, leaning forward again, his fingers gripping the seat just behind her right shoulder. '*We* are going to the station. We have to trust in the law. And each other.'

Katie sees flashes of red behind her eyes that pulse in time with her racing heartbeat. In the last few months this anger has come frequently, and from nowhere, but there can be no doubt that it's justified now.

'Stop. I'm sick of you controlling me!'

'The problem is, I'm not sure you can control yourself,' says Nathan, softly. 'Richard and I have been concerned about you for a while. You've been trying to hide it from us. Maybe you've been more successful at hiding it from yourself, but this is not you, this is not—'

'Natural?' Before she knows it, she's turned in her seat and popped off her seat belt. The car is too old to have an alarm, but it's like she can hear it, screaming inside her skull. It's telling her to sit back and calm down, to save her energy for the investigation, but the hot rage is still drowning everything else out. 'My dad is dead, and I didn't even go to his funeral. Now my oldest friend is on a slab because I wasn't there for him. My face and my stomach have been sliced open because I grew too close to you. And you…' She pauses. This has been a long time coming, a pressure slowly building inside that she's finally about to release. She glances up at the mirror in front of her, seeing the scars and feeling the charge. 'You allowed your brother to take away my looks. But worse than that, so much worse, you allowed him to take away any chance of my ever being a mother.'

With the words spoken at last, she falls back into her seat. It's the first time she's said it out loud since the doctors broke the news to her in the hospital. She and Nathan had never discussed having kids, but the news that she no longer had a choice hurt her in a way she never imagined possible. Every time she and Nathan had enjoyed a moment together in Wales, when they'd laughed, when they'd shared a lingering look, when she'd accidentally allowed herself to imagine a future for them, she'd felt the pain of this truth twist inside her as keenly as the knife that had caused it.

She pushes out a long breath, wondering if she's ever going to draw one back in again. Her eyes are fixed on the window, fixedly avoiding the passenger side mirror in case she should see the damage she has done to Nathan with her revelation. She notices, through her tears, that the car has slowed considerably and that they're pulling in to the side of the road.

The doctor is the one to break the silence. 'You might not realise,' he says, tentatively, running one finger across a bushy eyebrow. 'You might not care… but this last month has been incredibly important for me. It's been more than ten years since I retired from my work,' he turns to look at Katie, blinking back tears, 'work that I stuck with at the expense of everything else. I've spent those years without any company, without any friends, trying to deal with what my job was doing to me, how it made me look so much to the welfare of others and yet seemingly not give a damn about my own.'

He coughs to clear his throat before continuing. 'Before I met you two, I'd given up. I had nothing to look forward to, other than…' He doesn't say the word. He doesn't need to.

Katie knows only too well what it's like to wait for death. She had sat for months with her dad in the care home, cursing herself whenever she found she was hoping that the end would come.

'Perhaps I was only welcomed into your home because you wanted to make sure I wasn't talking to anybody else, to check

I was keeping your secret. Whatever the reason, I've loved every minute we've spent together. And I've loved seeing the way you two are with each other. I haven't been with someone like that in such a long time.' He stops and swallows hard, turning towards the driver's side window, where vehicles flash by. 'I lost my partner in a car crash nearly forty years ago.'

He places a hand on the steering wheel and squeezes hard, meeting Kate's gaze again, tears on his cheeks. 'I dedicated my life to doing what they weren't able to do for my Maggie. But age,' he lifts fingers badly bent by arthritis, 'took that away from me. What fight I have left in me now will be used to help you two. I'll drive you to the station. I'll drive you wherever you want to go. I'll keep your secret. I'll keep quiet about whatever you want me to. But I will not sit here and watch in silence while you hurt each other like this.'

Through her own tears, Katie wants to reach out and touch the old man's hand, to reassure him that she's okay, that this is just a momentary blip and she will be herself again soon. But the fist in her lap will not budge. Nor will her conviction that she is right.

'All I care about,' she says, her mouth barely opening, 'is finding justice for Mike.'

'Then why are we sitting here?' says Nathan from the back. 'Let's go to the station. Find out the facts. Do what makes us *right*. Or, if it's too late for that, if we can't function anymore, even when working, then you go off and do your own thing. Hell, maybe you'll have to. Like you said, I'm the suspect. I'm the one they'll be locking up.'

She can hear Richard sigh, and feel her shoulders sink, but with the professional focus she'd always been famed for tingling beneath her skin, she nods at the road ahead and waits for them to start moving again.

CHAPTER SEVEN

Nathan and Katie are sitting in an interview suite at their old station. It's a room they're both very familiar with, although nothing really feels the same to Nathan anymore, not after what Katie has just told him. He's reliving every word over and over in his head, the pain and heartbreak more acute each time. He'd never dared to dream of having children before, the fear that they might turn out like him too strong.

But now he knows it will never happen; that although there are no two people more equipped to guide an innocent child away from darkness than he and Katie, two people who have seen it all and survived, they will never be parents. Nathan feels his body start to tremble as he considers what he would have done to protect his own, how much he would have sacrificed for a daughter or son. He finds himself starting to drift into a daydream, seeing himself in a parallel life, picturing the details and starting to believe, when the door to his left is flung open and he is startled back into the present.

'What the hell are they doing in the same room?' Nathan looks up to see a man with slicked-back black hair filling the doorway. DCI Ken Stocks, head of a different crime team to the one he and Katie were part of, is glaring at the low-ranking officer that has escorted them here following their arrival at the reception desk. Alongside Stocks and offering a similar glare is Katie and Nathan's former boss, Superintendent Taylor.

'Easy, Ken,' says Katie from a chair to one side of the table in the centre of the room. 'Nathan and I have been together for the past six months. Every single day. If we needed a story, we've had plenty of time to prepare one.'

'That's Detective Chief Inspector Stocks to you, Detective Inspector Rhodes. They haven't thrown you out of the force yet.'

'Glad to hear it, *sir*,' says Katie. 'Because if you're stupid enough to think that Nathan had anything to do with Mike's death, then you're definitely going to need my help.'

'This is the end of our conversation,' says the big man, his face flushing, 'until we've made this official.'

'You mean, you're going to charge him?' says Katie, failing to hide her disbelief.

'We have the evidence to do just that.'

'Like what?'

'Are you going to pretend you don't know?'

'I'm going to *reassure* you that we don't. Mike is dead, and you want to speak to us about it. That's everything we have.'

'Seriously?' Ken scoffs. 'The whole world has heard this story. Have you been living in a cave?'

'More like up a mountain. No television, no phone. No car to get back to London.'

Ken runs a hand across a stubbled chin. 'So how did you get back here?'

'The same way we heard what little we know. I got ill a while back and we needed a doctor. He became a friend, someone we could trust. He heard the headline on the radio and came to get us.'

'Where is he now?' asks the DCI, peering down the corridor.

'He was worn out by the journey, so I told him to go and find a hotel.'

Ken looks back into the room, eyes narrowing. 'Which hotel?'

She shrugs. 'Whichever one he's been able to find in the middle of the night.'

'Do you have a mobile number for him?'

'No mobile. But he'll be over in the morning to confirm he was with us when Mike was killed.'

'How do you know when Mike was killed?'

Nathan opens his mouth to answer, then realises, with a look across at Katie, who has just come to the same realisation, that they only know Mike was pulled out of the river yesterday evening. He could have been there for days.

'Whenever it was, we were in Wales,' Katie corrects herself.

Ken's eyes flick back to the corridor and he suddenly stiffens, instinctively lifting his hand to straighten his tie even though he isn't wearing one. He takes a step back and a woman enters the room. She's mid to late forties, with dark red hair styled into a bob so sharp and precise it could be made of plastic. Her face is unreadable, something that Nathan, with his eye for detail, finds instantly unnerving.

The woman points at Katie and gestures for her to leave the room, but Katie doesn't budge.

'I want to sit in on this,' she says, folding her arms.

The woman ignores her and moves over to an empty chair. Ken speaks next, his voice slightly pinched.

'You know how this works,' he says to Katie before clearing his throat.

Katie ignores him and bristles at the woman now sitting across from her, her fingertips pressed together, patiently waiting.

'It's okay,' Nathan says, reaching a hand tentatively towards Katie. When she turns to look at him, he can see that he was right to be concerned; the heat in her eyes has returned, the look of a caged tiger ready to attack.

'Fine,' Katie says, standing up quickly. 'There's no point wasting my time here, anyway. I've got a killer to find.'

'You're not leaving,' says the red-haired woman softly. 'You'll wait until we are done with Nathan and then you'll answer our questions.'

'Maybe after you answer one of mine,' says Katie, brushing off Nathan's hand as she leans in. 'Who are you, anyway?'

'All you need to know is that she is your superior,' says Stocks sharply, before looking over at the woman he's rushed to defend, as if seeking an apology from her for having interrupted. She nods, then waves her hand and Katie is shepherded towards the door.

'Wait,' the woman says, gently but effectively. 'I've changed my mind. She can stay. I don't doubt the two of you have had plenty of time to get your story straight. But the question is, have you told each other the whole story?'

'We tell each other everything,' says Nathan, hoping, after the revelation in the car, that that may finally be true.

'Domestic bliss, I'm sure,' she says, sarcastically. 'You could cut the tension in here with a knife.'

Katie takes her place back at the table as Stocks starts going through the motions of setting up the tape and registering who is in the room. He introduces the redhead in charge as Sam Stone from the National Crime Agency. Nathan studies her face, wondering why he's never heard of her before. She has deep, rich brown eyes like Katie's, but there's no life in them; no excitement, no anger, every emotion perfectly under control.

'We shouldn't have left without telling you all,' he hears himself saying. 'But we'd done everything asked of us, and we needed some time out of the limelight.'

'So where exactly have you been these past six months?' says Ken.

'The middle of nowhere,' says Nathan. 'I can point to it on a map if you want, but for now I guess you'll have to make do with Pembrokeshire.'

'And last night?'

'Enjoying a drink with Katie and the doctor.'

'You invited a friend for Valentine's Day?' says Ken, raising an eyebrow. 'Isn't three a crowd?'

The significance of the day hadn't even registered with Nathan until the doctor had suggested he leave them in peace for the evening, but Katie had insisted he join them. At the time it had seemed a typically caring act, but now he's wondering if it was another sign of Katie caring less than she used to.

'Let's just get to it,' says Nathan. 'What possible motive could I have for killing Mike? He gave us the house in Wales to use. He was the only one we trusted with the knowledge of where we were hiding.'

'Interesting choice of words,' says Ken. 'Why did you need to hide?'

'Because we needed time to recover without the world's media parked on our doorstep.' Nathan pushes his shoulders back and feels his temper rising. 'Perhaps if you'd managed not to leak my journal, I might have got a bit more peace.' The leak had happened during the inquest, when far too much of his life was already being shared with others. He'd walked out of court to a barrage of frenzied questions from journalists that told him the dark fantasies he'd written down in his youth, in a journal previously under lock and key at the police station, were now public knowledge. 'Have you arrested someone for that crime, by the way?'

Superintendent Taylor looks down and Ken Stocks shifts in his chair.

'Let's talk about the journal, shall we?' says Sam. 'Let's talk about the four pages that were missing.'

Nathan groans and looks towards the ceiling. 'I've been through this a hundred times. I've no idea why Christian took them out. And I can't remember what was on them.'

'Well, let me try and refresh your memory,' says Sam, reaching into her pocket and pulling out a sheet of A4. 'This appeared on the web page of a popular crime blogger yesterday morning.' Sam places the paper in the centre of the table and smooths it out.

As soon as he sees the tiny scrawl, filling every inch of the page, Nathan is back there, up in his bedroom in his family home, hoping against hope that by putting his increasingly dark and dangerous thoughts on paper they would become fiction, and not a reality that he couldn't resist acting out. Katie scrapes her chair in closer and starts scanning the words too.

'Let's just focus on this bit,' says Sam, lightly tapping the centre of the page.

Nathan starts to read.

'It's like art. Although not nearly as boring as the class at school…'

When he's finished, Nathan slumps back. 'I'd forgotten,' he says, looking across at Katie, who's wearing an expression of total shock. 'I mean, there were descriptions of thousands of murders in that journal, literally thousands. I can't remember them all. Even if I could, I must have found a way to blank that one out. It must be why that case had such an effect on me.'

'Just to be clear for the tape,' says Ken, raising his voice and leaning forward, 'the case you're talking about is the torture and murder of Steven Fish, the case that made you quit the police force the first time and go running for the hills. Wasn't it the case that pushed you to the edge of sanity?'

'I guess it makes sense,' says Nathan, rubbing his hands roughly across his face, realigning his features in an attempt to bring his thoughts to order. 'My brother must have taken inspiration from my teenage journal when he killed Steven Fish.'

'That would indeed make sense,' says Sam, lifting some of the papers on the table in front of her and tapping them straight, 'if Mike Peters hadn't just been killed in a far too similar way.'

It takes Nathan a moment to process what he's being told, but for Katie the response is instant, a hand shooting up to her mouth, failing to stifle a groan. 'Oh, Christ, tell me that's not true!'

'I'm afraid it is,' says Superintendent Taylor, finally joining the conversation. 'Nobody deserves to suffer like that, but Mike…'

The superintendent squeezes his eyes shut to block out the emotion. 'He was one of the best men we've ever had on the force.'

'This diary extract appeared on a popular true crime blog the morning before Mike was killed,' says Sam, coldly cutting in. 'I understand from Superintendent Taylor that it was being discussed in the office when Mike arrived for work. He read it and left the office without a word, and that was the last time he was seen alive.'

'We went to his flat early this morning,' says Stocks. 'And we found the kitchen table covered in notes and photos from old case files. Or rather,' Ken dips his head to one side, 'one specific case.'

'Your old colleague clearly didn't believe your twin Christian killed Steven Fish,' says Sam. 'And after last night, neither do we.'

Nathan closes his eyes and tries to find at least something that makes sense. It always used to be Katie, the way they felt about each other, the way they were able to work together in perfect harmony, but now even that has been left in doubt. He remembers the words his brother had said right at the end: *there's still plenty to reveal about that particular case.* Had Christian left them one last mystery? One more nightmare?

'We need to see his body,' says Katie, firmly. 'I want to see Mike Peters.'

Nathan opens his eyes and finds Ken Stocks shaking his head in disbelief. 'Have you not been listening to us? You're a lead suspect in his murder.'

'I've been listening very carefully,' says Katie. 'And what I'm hearing is that you absolutely need our help. Nobody knew Mike better than me. Nobody knows the Steven Fish case better than I do.' She jabs her forefinger on the table. 'Nobody knows this journal better than Nathan. I'm pretty sure the press are going crazy over this. In fact, knowing how leaky this place can be, I wouldn't be surprised if they haven't already heard about our return to London. This is super-high-profile. Career-defining.

Career-breaking. By tomorrow morning we will have an alibi for Mike's murder. If you still don't trust us, then by all means provide an escort. Hell, you can assign twenty officers to watch us if you want.'

Stocks is still shaking his head and opening his mouth, but before he can get a word out, Sam Stone cuts in. 'Fine,' she says, standing up and pulling her sharply pressed jacket around her shoulders. 'You can get started in the morning. And you will have an escort throughout this entire investigation. You will have me.'

CHAPTER EIGHT

Katie has never felt as alone as she does now, walking into the room where her friend and mentor, Mike Peters, is laid out in the cold of the mortuary. Her dad is gone, Mike is gone and Nathan is distant in a way she couldn't ever have imagined a couple of months ago. Having spent the last few hours of the night in a cell at the station, with Nathan in the cell next door, she doesn't feel rested. She feels on the point of collapse.

The sheet – brilliant white under the medical lights – is pulled up to just above Mike's chin. Katie leaves it there as she looks down at his face, still kind, untroubled, despite what she knows he's been through. She wants to say a few words, to make her usual promises about bringing him justice and to tell him how much she's always cared, but Sam Stone is close beside her. Worse still, the medical examiner, Dr Miles Parker, is lurking in the corner of the room. So far he's kept his distance, out of fear, she suspects, rather than respect for her feelings, but she knows it won't be long before they are at each other's throats.

Katie draws in a long breath, summons her hard-won professional strength, then carefully lifts the sheet. It feels strange and awkward to see an older man she'd always looked up to naked, but nothing is going to stop her getting to the truth. The line across his neck is smooth and unbroken, a confident sweep of the blade that ended fifty-four years of life.

'So the head wasn't removed completely?' she asks, not taking her eyes from the body.

'Not this time,' says Dr Parker, taking a step forward. 'But it's definitely the same killer. The removal of the skin from the back has a certain…' he lifts his hands and carves at the air, 'delicacy. On initial inspection, the blade used is likely the same. And perhaps the head remaining on is a refinement, an increased level of control. We certainly shouldn't consider it hesitation. Not many people could keep their hand that steady as they run a knife the entire length of a body.'

'Fortunately, not many people would want to,' says Nathan, who is standing well back in the opposite corner to Dr Parker.

'We know someone who's imagined it, though, don't we,' says Miles. 'In frightening detail.' Although she still can't bring herself to look at his face, Katie can hear the grin in his voice.

'Imagination and action are two very different things,' she says in Nathan's defence, glancing across at a series of blades on a nearby table, before finally looking Dr Parker right in the eyes, 'and you should be grateful for that.'

'Is that a threat?' he says, looking to Sam Stone for backup. 'Did you hear that, ma'am?'

'Stop it, you two, let's just get on with this,' says Sam, in a tone that suggests she's bored rather than bothered. She turns to Nathan. 'Are you ready?'

Nathan nods and steps tentatively forward. He's prepared in the way that he normally would be. For fear that the press would identify Nathan and Katie, Sam hadn't allowed them to travel to the river in Richmond where the body had been found, instead giving them access to photos and videos of the scene of discovery on her private laptop. Katie had to admit they were methodically compiled, as good as anything she might have taken herself, but Nathan has an amazing talent for spotting the details even the highest-resolution camera with a giant lens could miss. In the past, he's always worked from the crime scene, taking in the complete picture, the sights and sounds and smells.

On the journey over, in the back of a police van, Katie had tried to help by talking to Nathan about Steven Fish, the case Nathan had never dared to consider too carefully before, for fear it was so close to his darkest desires to kill that it might nudge him over the edge. Then she'd told him everything she knew about Mike, which only served to highlight how little she knew the man behind the uniform. The only real revelation she could offer was whispered in Nathan's ear above the roar of the engine as the van raced through the streets of London: that he had a younger brother. Sensitive, troubled, addicted to drugs, Ben Peters had been kept a secret from everyone other than her.

'That was who the house in Wales was intended for?' Nathan had whispered back. 'And who Richard had been looking after?'

She'd nodded.

'But he's not a suspect?'

This time Katie had shaken her head vigorously. 'No way. Which is why I'm not telling anybody about him yet. We'll get to him when we can, see how he's coping, but he won't cope at all if the whole world is on his doorstep.'

In the mortuary, Katie has retreated from Mike and is watching Nathan closely, waiting for his remarkable brain to kick into gear, producing all the familiar ticks and twitches, a sign that his imagination is taking over. But he remains perfectly still, with his head bowed. It looks as if he's praying, or paying his respects. His posture doesn't change, and his hands don't move, bunched into tight fists by his side. Finally, he lets out an exasperated groan and spins round to face her.

'I can't do it,' he says, and she can see that he's close to tears. 'It's – it's not there anymore.'

'Maybe you need some space,' says Katie, glaring at Miles and then Sam. 'A bit of privacy?'

Nathan steps away from the body and towards Katie, Sam just behind him.

'I think it's because I couldn't kill Christian,' he says. 'Not even for you. It proved to me that I wasn't a murderer, so now I can no longer think like one.'

Katie can see Miles scoff and shake his head in the background and again she has to fight the urge to march across and flatten his nose.

'I don't think that can be it,' she says, returning her attention to Nathan. 'It's more likely to be what this case reminds you of. You've always had trouble with the Fish case.'

Nathan places both hands on top of his head and slowly draws them down over his eyes, as if trying to wipe the tension from his face. 'Well, maybe now we know the real reason why. It wasn't just because of my brother's guilt – it was because I'd already been there in my mind, writing down a similar murder in my journal. I still can't believe I didn't remember that.'

'There are plenty of things we somehow shut out,' says Katie, thinking of all the happy memories of her dad that only seem to be returning now that he's gone. 'You just need time to adjust. And it's different because you know him.' She lowers her head and takes another fleeting look at the body. 'Because it's Mike.'

'Which is why I *have* to help.' Nathan's eyes are wide, his voice is trembling. 'If I can't even help you with this…'

'Let's go,' says Katie, firmly taking his arm and dragging him towards the door. 'You're still a good detective. You've still got a great mind. We can work this out a more traditional way. Together.'

Before they've even reached the end of the corridor leading out to the car park, they both know something is wrong. The muffled sound of a crowd travels towards them from behind a locked door at the end, which rattles like it's being shoved. A couple of flashes of a camera send Katie into retreat, hiding her face with her hand.

'How the hell did they find out we were here?' says Sam, following close behind.

'The same way Nathan's journal was leaked, I bet,' says Katie, kicking open the door back into the mortuary. Miles, standing at a sink in the corner, looks up as they enter, failing to put on a convincing look of surprise. She's about to charge when she feels Nathan grab her and pull her back.

'Think about Mike,' he whispers in her ear. 'Don't let anything stop us from finding the person that killed him.'

Katie looks across at the now covered but still familiar-shaped body on the table to her left, takes a couple of deep breaths and relents.

'Why?' she asks, staring straight at Miles. 'What possible reason could you have for getting in the way of an investigation into a colleague's death?'

'Not this madness again,' says Miles, turning off the tap. 'What am I supposed to have done now?'

'You told the press we were here,' says Nathan.

'I did no such thing,' says Miles, turning away to grab a towel. 'And that just about sums you two up, doesn't it? Accusation without evidence. Emotion over reason.'

'Let me apologise on Mr Radley and DI Rhodes' behalf for their unwarranted remarks,' says Sam calmly as she takes a couple of steps towards the doctor, who has his back up against the wall. 'Please rest assured that I will use my authority, which is considerable, to investigate who was really behind this breach of confidentiality, and that when I do find who was responsible, they will feel the full weight of the law.'

'That's good to know,' says Miles, swallowing hard.

'Now, I wonder if you could help us find an alternative way out of this building?'

Two minutes later, Katie is peering out from behind an emergency door. There's a courtyard to cross and a wall to scale, but she reckons if they time it right they can make it without being spotted.

'When did you say your man would be here?' Katie asks.

'We'll wait till he's texted,' says Sam, checking her phone. 'That way he'll definitely be waiting.'

Katie looks back up the corridor they've walked down and sees Miles's head pop out through a doorway, then disappear again.

'What's your problem with the doctor?' asks Sam.

'I dare to think beyond the science,' says Katie, with a sigh. 'That, and the fact that I've rejected his advances half a dozen times.' She touches her cheek. 'Not that he'll be making any more of those.'

'Well, whoever was responsible for leaking your whereabouts, they've really made things difficult for us. I was hoping we might at least have a day or two without the media on our tail.'

'So, you don't think we're to blame for Mike's death?' asks Nathan.

'Only in the sense that DS Peters was most likely killed to bring you two back.'

Katie gasps. It had always been a possibility, but hearing it from somebody else has made it so much harder to take.

'And not because he was getting somewhere with the Fish case, suspecting that Christian wasn't to blame?' asks Nathan.

'I don't know about that,' says Sam, checking her phone again. 'We still haven't been able to figure out what made him doubt Christian's guilt in the first place, but rest assured, Steven Fish is key to all this.'

'But he was a nobody,' says Katie. 'A petty criminal with a minor drugs charge, nothing else. Who would go to all this trouble?' She squeezes her eyes shut, desperately trying not to picture Mike's body.

'Minor or not, the drugs connection is a lead we should look into,' says Sam.

'Something tells me you already have,' says Katie, peering out, ready to make a dash for it. 'Perhaps it's the fact that a senior figure from the National Crime Agency is actively involved in this investigation, a figure who, I believe, now I come to remember your name, achieved her seniority thanks to high-profile successes in bringing down drugs gangs.'

Katie's not certain she has clearly remembered Sam Stone, or the link to drugs gangs, but she's willing to search for the answers she's not being given, and Sam's sigh suggests she's hit the mark. She decides to push a little further. 'Not so successful with Carl Watkins, though.' If saying the name brings the reaction from Sam Katie had hoped for, she doesn't notice it as Katie's too busy fighting to keep her own emotions under control. Carl Watkins is a criminal she's loathed like no other. She'd tried and failed to pin two murders on him, gangland killings that nobody else on her team seemed to care much about. Perhaps that's why Katie was so desperate to bring the victims justice. Or perhaps it was because she'd seen beyond the good looks and charm and *knew* that Watkins was responsible. Perhaps it was because she'd seen first-hand the damage his drug empire was doing to vulnerable people. She'd pushed herself to the point of exhaustion trying to uncover the evidence to put him away. Failing to find anything had brought disbelief and anger in equal measure, and with the merest mention of his name it's all come back.

'Can't win them all,' says Sam, with a shrug.

'We might be able to win this one, though,' says Katie, trying to refocus. 'If you start telling us what's going on. What is your interest in Steven Fish?'

'Just because I don't think you're to blame doesn't mean I trust you,' says Sam.

'And how exactly are we going to earn that trust?' asks Katie.

'By doing what you're good at. By helping me to find a killer.' Sam is looking back along the corridor they've just walked down, which remains empty. 'I like science. But science is telling me I cannot ignore the success rate your and Nathan's alternative methods have achieved over the last ten years.' She gestures towards the exit. 'So, when we're out of here, you take the lead.'

'Even if we're going over ground that you've already covered?'

Sam smiles. 'I've heard you were always relentlessly thorough. Besides, no harm in getting a different perspective on the same information.'

Katie stares hard at Sam, trying to get a sense of the woman, but she's closed to her in a way that both frustrates and intrigues Katie.

'I know where I need to go first,' she says.

'*I?*' says Sam, raising an eyebrow. 'You're not going alone.'

'I won't be. I'll be taking our doctor friend from Wales, Richard Evans.'

'Why?'

'Because the subject knows him. The man I'm going to visit will not talk if you're there,' she says to Sam, before turning to Nathan. 'Or you.'

'I understand,' says Nathan, and it's clear that he does. He recognises not only that she wants to speak to Mike's brother, but that this is nothing personal, no fallout from the argument they had the day before. Going their separate ways is strictly a professional need. He takes a couple of paces back along the corridor. 'I'm not coming with you, anyway.'

'What are you talking about?' says Sam, pointing to the car park. 'This way is the only option.'

'No, it's not,' says Nathan, pushing a hand through his thick black hair and tugging at the roots as if to test their strength. 'I'm going to do something I should have done after the inquest, rather than running away. I'm going to go and face up to the media.'

'And what do you think that will achieve?' asks Sam, still maintaining her calm despite the obvious frustration.

'First, it'll be a distraction for you lot. Secondly, I'll be able to get across my side of the story, at least try and answer some of those accusations. Thirdly, it's a way of speaking to the killer, letting them know I'm not hiding anymore.'

'It will royally piss off Taylor and Stocks,' says Sam.

'And there's another benefit I hadn't thought of,' says Nathan, with a half-smile.

'I can't let it happen,' says Sam, moving to block Nathan's path down the corridor.

'You can't stop it happening,' Nathan replies, turning to face in the other direction. 'If you want, I can open this door and call out for the press right now. That way you'll have to face up to the questions, too, and something tells me you don't want too much publicity on this occasion.'

Katie wonders if the change in Sam's expression is anger or amusement. She's seen so little emotion of any kind from the woman that it's hard to determine.

'Okay,' Sam says finally, releasing a long-held breath and reaching into her pocket to pull out a phone that's different to the one Katie has seen her using before. 'Here's what's going to happen...'

CHAPTER NINE

Nathan settles his breathing, sweeps his too-long fringe away from his eyes and then unlocks the door. At first he thinks he's going to be rushed by the crowd of maybe two dozen journalists, but as he steps out he finds they're keeping their distance, as if he might strike out, as if they believe all the terrible things they've written about him.

While he's given room to walk, there's little opportunity to speak, as each and every one of them shouts questions in his direction. He says nothing until he's made it to the middle of the car park, at which point he stops and slowly raises a hand. They eventually fall silent.

'I came here,' he says quietly, as the microphones move in, 'to see my friend Detective Sergeant Mike Peters. He was a good man, a remarkable detective, and was an essential part of all the successes our team has enjoyed over the years. He was thorough and honest and relentless and brave. We all owe him a debt of gratitude.' Nathan hears his voice thicken as the memories gather to support his words. 'Especially me. Because Mike didn't judge me the way most have…' He pauses and takes in the crowd, staring into television cameras and some, perhaps not journalists at all, who are holding up mobile phones. 'He was open-minded and fair, considerate and kind. He saw the good in people. He *believed* in people.'

'He believed you were guilty!' somebody shouts out from the back of the crowd. 'Peters found out that you killed Steven Fish, not your brother.'

'We don't know that,' Nathan calls back in reply, once again overwhelmed with how little he does know. 'What proof do you have?'

'Your *friend* Peters,' shouts out a different voice. 'He died the same way.'

'That's not what I meant,' says Nathan. 'I meant, how did Mike know? What made him suspect my brother wasn't to blame?'

'Why don't you tell us?' calls out another voice, a different voice, but in the same accusatory tone. 'Isn't that why you tortured DS Peters, to find out what mistakes you'd made, before killing him to shut him up?'

'Of course not,' says Nathan. 'I could never have hurt Mike. I could never hurt anyone.'

'Not even when you should have done,' says a third voice Nathan can't locate. 'Not even when you could have helped your partner. You could have saved Katie Rhodes all that pain.'

'I could have,' says Nathan, so quietly he doubts his words have carried as far as those standing just a metre or so in front of him. And it's from those very people that the next question comes.

'Where were you when DS Peters was killed?'

'A long way from here,' he says, lowering his head. 'And I shouldn't have been. I should have been here, for him.' He meets the gaze of a couple of the journalists directly in front, and again they retreat a few more inches. 'I guess we're all scared – scared of people knowing our thoughts, our desires, especially if those thoughts and desires aren't who we really are.'

'Your brother was a monster!' comes another shout from over to Nathan's left.

'He was,' says Nathan, nodding slowly. 'And while I'm glad I was able to help bring his horrific crimes to an end, I will never stop wishing I had seen the signs earlier. People died because of me, families have been torn apart because he wanted to play a game with me. It's a nightmare I had hoped was over. But I think…' Nathan pauses and considers the sky. 'I think whoever killed DS Peters is doing the same. They had no need to take his life the way they did,' he looks towards the back of the crowd, 'and it's clear that most of you already know the details of his death.'

'They wanted you accused of the crime?' asks a woman just a few feet away, her eyes wide, her phone stretched out in front of her.

'Initially. But they must have known I would soon be able to prove my alibi. And I do have an alibi.' He pauses, to let the crowd absorb that fact. 'No: what I think they wanted most was for me to return.' He turns to the nearest of the television cameras and leans in, his nose only inches from the lens. 'Well, here I am. And let me speak to you directly. If you want something from me, if you need to talk, then find a way to get in contact. If you blame me for something, if you want to kill me, then let that be your focus. But please do not hurt anybody else.'

Nathan hears an individual clapping of hands from over to his right, followed by a shout. 'Bravo! Still good enough for RADA.'

With nothing left to say, Nathan pushes his way forward and the crowd ahead of him slowly parts. He's bombarded by questions, and he ignores them all. As he reaches the far side of the car park, he feels a blow strike his shoulder and he stumbles slightly, but he keeps walking. Another blow, this time on his ear. He picks up his pace and very nearly collides with the side of a dark saloon car that appears out of nowhere. The windows are tinted, but he knows who must be inside, so he opens the rear door and jumps in, receiving a final, painful kick to his calf in the process. As the car pulls quickly away he can hear hands thumping against the sides and the roof, just as he's seen so many times as suspects he's helped to convict have been driven away from court.

CHAPTER TEN

'I'm afraid I don't know where we're going,' says Dr Evans, accelerating hard as Katie stares into the mirror to check they're not being followed. There are cars around, but she's confident they've given any pursuers the slip.

'You've never been to Ben Peters' house?'

The old doctor shakes his head. 'He's only ever come to me in Wales. And we didn't talk much. I wasn't his therapist, I was just trying to help him kick the drugs.'

'I've only been to his house once,' says Katie, thinking back with a thickening throat to the day she'd recognised the trust that had developed between her and Mike. When he'd parked the car outside his brother's house, she hadn't even known he had a brother. Nobody had known.

Ben's mental health issues had been diagnosed from a young age, as had the need for him to live a stress-free life. Time and again Mike had taken his brother away to the house in Wales, locking him up in an effort to help him shake his dependence. Time and again his brother would relapse. It was Ben who had insisted that Mike keep him a secret, to avoid damaging his brother's career, of which he was so proud; so that one of them at least could succeed in life.

Mike had mentioned Ben just before Katie had left for Wales, making her promise to come back and take care of his younger brother should anything happen to him. He'd been thinking of illness, of old age, she was sure of it; but there may have been another suspicion at work there. More now lingers. Part of her regrets that she didn't come here first; she knows that's what Mike would have wanted. But as usual she's thinking of the job, of justice, and, in this case, revenge.

'Take the next right,' she says, pointing at a sign ahead. 'I can't think of the exact address, but hopefully I'll remember the route as we go.'

Twenty minutes later, and they're parked outside a run-down terraced house on an equally run-down estate. Richard keeps quiet; it's one of the many things she's always liked about him, his ability to read a situation just right.

'There's a very good chance Ben doesn't even know what's happened to his brother,' she says, popping open the door. 'But it's important that he does know, and all the details. We both know he won't take the news well, but I'm afraid I will have to keep pushing to find out what I need.' It's an explanation Katie hasn't had to make in a while, Nathan always having understood what was necessary to get to the truth. She's often walked away from a witness hating herself for the emotional pain she's inflicted, but her justification has always been the result she knew would come.

Richard and Katie walk towards a red door, beside which a rusting car is jacked up on bricks. The front lawn is a mess of brambles and is surrounded by a crumbling wall. On the doorstep are three empty beer cans and a heavy peppering of cigarette butts, some hand-rolled, and some, she suspects, that contain more than just tobacco.

The first two knocks receive no response, but she's certain there's someone inside. This isn't based on any intuition she might have picked up over the years; it's the knowledge that Ben Peters hardly ever leaves his house. Of course, knowing he's in is one thing; whether he's capable of making it to the door is another. She smacks the door with even more force, wondering if perhaps Ben has heard the news and hasn't been able to cope.

No answer. She's about to move round to the back, which would most likely involve her circling the entire row of terraced houses and hurdling those back fences that are still standing, when the door finally opens and Mike Peters' younger brother Ben leans on the door frame in front of her, his face soaked with sweat and his pupils wide and black.

Katie almost gasps at how frail Ben looks. He'd always been smaller than his brother, a good five inches shorter and perhaps three stone lighter, but there's absolutely nothing of him now. She can't bear to think that he'd had another relapse in the time they were away and that Mike didn't feel he could use the house in Wales. Just as shocking as Ben's physique is the paleness of his skin. He looks like a ghost. He looks like his brother when she'd seen him just an hour before, laid out in the mortuary.

'I know you,' says Ben, although from the look on his face it's obvious the details haven't yet come to him.

'Detective Katie Rhodes. I worked with Mike for many years. He was a friend.'

'Katie Rhodes,' Ben repeats, pushing himself up from the door frame. 'Yeah.' He tries and fails to click his fingers. 'He talks about you.'

She waits for him to correct the tense. When he doesn't, she wonders if the drugs have taken him to a place where reality doesn't apply anymore, or if she was right about Ben not having heard the news.

'When did you last see Mike?' she asks tentatively.

'Same place I last saw you,' he says, and if his eyes could widen further she's sure that they would. 'You and that psycho's twin.'

'On the news?'

He nods enthusiastically, an action which threatens to send him toppling forward. 'I turned on the telly last night, hoping for some sport, when suddenly Mike's picture pops up on the screen, and then…' The weight of the discovery seems to hit him again. Ben expels a long breath and Katie throws out an arm, expecting to have to catch him.

'I'm so sorry,' she says, when he's found his balance. 'Can we come in?'

The word *we* suddenly registers with Ben, who looks over to where Richard is standing a little further back. He stumbles, lifting a hand as if to protect himself from imminent attack, but Richard offers a broad smile in return.

'You might not remember me, Ben,' Dr Evans says. 'You've been a little unwell whenever we've met.'

'I remember,' says Ben, before taking another step back. 'But we don't need a doctor. It's far too late for doctors now. Mike's dead, you know. Dead.' Ben staggers back into the house and Katie and Richard follow him inside, shutting the door behind them.

'I realise it's a very difficult time,' says Katie, 'and I'm very sorry for this disturbance. But I promised Mike I would drop in and check up on you if anything ever happened to him.'

'I don't need checking up on!' says Ben, kicking at an almost empty curry container and spraying the contents up the wall. 'God, even now he's gone he's still treating me like a kid, like I can't cope, not with my life. Or his death.' Ben had been making surprisingly good progress towards the back of the house, but now he slows, his shoulders sinking and his knees looking as if they're about to give way. Once more Katie reaches out, her fingers just a couple of inches from his back, ready to grab the foul-smelling, badly stained shirt that hangs loose on his frame.

'He was a good brother.'

Ben's got the tense right this time, and the pain in his voice reveals he's slipped out of the protective fog of booze and dope and whatever else is rushing round his veins. He sucks in a breath that causes him to cough, then stumbles into a tiny living room that looks like so many crime scenes Katie has visited.

'He *was* a good brother,' Katie says softly.

'And what was I?' says Ben, this time punting an empty beer can across the room so that it clatters against an oversized television screen. If the sight is bad, the smell is far worse; half-eaten takeaways, spilled booze and evidence that Ben didn't always make it to the toilet. Katie thinks about the cigarettes on the doorstep, and the absence, amid everything else, of the smell of smoke. Why had he gone outside to smoke? Was it simply habit? Katie thinks back to the last time she'd been here, how much tidier it, and Ben, had been; as if he was finally turning a corner. At the age of forty-nine, he'd left it late, but he still had years to enjoy with his brother, albeit within the confines of his house and his troubled mind.

'You were everything to him,' says Katie, perching herself on the edge of a sofa, ignoring the stains and the feeling that it might be about to give way beneath her. 'He was proud of every little victory you had.'

'And yet I imagine that you two,' he jabs a finger at them both in turn, 'are the only people in the world who know I exist.'

'That was your—'

He cuts her off with a raised hand and she allows him to. This is not the time for her to bully her way through a conversation.

'It's a good job I saw it on the telly,' he continues. 'Because nobody was coming to say, *please take a seat, Mr Peters... I'm afraid I have some bad news... Do you have anyone to be with you?* And all that other shit you see in cop shows.' Katie looks away, over at the telly, at the drops of beer trickling slowly down the screen. When she looks back she can see his accusatory stare turn to fear. 'Why are you here?' He tilts his head in contemplation, before his features freeze. 'Some people on the news were saying you and your partner might have killed Mike. Did you?'

'Jesus, no!' says Katie, reaching forward and clutching Ben's arm. Were he less under the influence, he might have drawn it back, but he barely seems aware of the contact. 'How could you possibly think that? He was my friend.'

'Then why did you leave him on his own?' says Ben.

As Katie considers the question she very nearly breaks, a tidal wave of repressed emotion threatening to come crashing down. It's only Richard resting his hand on her shoulder that keeps her upright. She hadn't noticed him moving close, but he seemed to have spotted where the conversation was heading.

'I needed to hide away for a while,' she says, taking in her surroundings and hoping that Ben will understand. She belatedly realises that all she has to do is point at the scars on her face, physical evidence of a very small part of what she's been through. 'I didn't think it would be forever.'

Silence follows, save for the sound of car tyres screaming in the distance and a dog she realises has been barking ever since they arrived.

'Katie Rhodes,' says Ben finally, with the faintest smile, as if another memory has risen to the surface and he's rediscovered the name. 'Yeah, you and Mike were real close.'

She nods and folds her hands in her lap. 'So were you. I know he told you things about his work. He did it because he wanted to involve you, to show you how smart you are.'

'If I'd been smart,' he says, before reaching for another can on the sofa next to him and draining the dregs, 'I might have spotted the danger he was in.' He tips his head back and squeezes his eyes shut. When they open he takes a step away from Katie. 'No, hang on. I remember,' he says. 'I remember I shouldn't be talking to you.'

'Why not?'

He seems to have lost the thread again, then he starts to wag a filthy finger. 'At the end, Mike started to have doubts, about everything, about everyone. He said not to trust the police. No, wait.' His words stop and so does the finger and the anger slips away as quickly as it had arrived. 'Other than you,' he says, slumping back onto the sofa before repeating his brother's words in a voice that sounds unbearably like him. '*Katie Rhodes is the only one you can trust. And if you ever need justice for me…*'

Katie crouches down next to Ben, but she can't bring herself to take the hand that is just a few inches away. It wouldn't be welcome, and fighting against the desire to comfort this man is that familiar hunger for knowledge, to drive the case forward. She stands back up, needing to move and allow her body to mirror the activity of her mind.

'I'm so sorry,' says Katie, words that she had never said as a police officer because she knew they would never help. It would never bring those people back. 'I will find who did this.' When Ben looks up at her, eyes wide and childlike, she can tell that he believes her.

'He was happy,' says Ben, looking happy himself for a fleeting second as he realises the can he's reached for on the floor next to the sofa is a full one. He pops open the top and takes a large swig. 'For the first time since you'd gone. He was doing something on his own, making progress in a case.'

'The Steven Fish case?' says Katie.

'I don't know names. I've never been able to deal with names. But there was a murder, they lost their head.' Ben draws a finger across his neck. The naive fascination with something so gruesome is suddenly replaced by a very adult fear. 'Is it true what they're saying on the telly? Did Mike die like that?'

'It was similar,' says Katie, wanting to lie, but again feeling that it might impact on what they're getting out of this witness.

Ben screws his face up and thumps his forehead with such ill-judged force Katie's frightened for a moment that he's knocked himself out. But when he sits back up there's a clarity in his eyes.

'He was being followed, you know.'

'I didn't know. Do you know who it was?'

'He wasn't sure. A woman, maybe. Cut-off hair.' He holds a level but shaking hand just above his shoulder.

Katie feels her stomach twist. 'Sam Stone?'

He looks at her, and for a moment she's certain he's about to nod, but then his shoulders slump. 'I told you I don't do names.'

'You saw her yourself?'

He tilts his head. 'Maybe. Everything's so blurred. I feel like I did. And I feel like I might have recognised…' Now his head is shaking. 'No. I can't have done. It must have been Mike who told me.'

'When was the last time you spoke to Mike?'

'On the day he was killed.' Ben looks around the room, an act which causes him to lose his balance. Eventually he stops and points at a phone half tucked under a filthy blanket. 'He called me. Told me to lock the doors and not let anybody in, said he was coming straight over.' Ben thumps his forehead again. 'He was worried about me, like I was the one in danger.'

Katie can feel her excitement growing, the thrill of the chase, a rush she has to admit she's missed despite the events that have led her here. 'Can you remember his exact words?'

Ben shakes his head. 'I'm not really one for "exact". But it was definitely something like that. *You're in danger, Ben*, he said. *Stay inside*. As if I ever do anything else.'

'And you've not shared this with anyone?'

'Like…?' He holds his hands up and gestures at the room, as if it represents the whole of his life. Besides, '*No police. Only Katie Rhodes*. Those are words from Mike. I'm a hundred per cent sure.'

Katie pushes herself up and gives Ben's arm a gentle squeeze. 'You've been a great help. Is there anything you need?'

'Just to be left alone,' says Ben, reaching for the television remote and turning it on. 'That's all I've ever wanted. Just my programmes and other distractions.' Kate follows his eyes to a little packet of white powder on a DVD case on the floor. Quickly determining that it's not enough to kill him, she's happy to grant him his wish and go.

Standing on the doorstep with the doctor, Katie starts to scan the street. She'd like to get a team in for door-to-door to follow up on a theory, but she'll give Ben a little longer. There's also Mike Peters' warning to consider, about not trusting the police. And the question of why they're not already here.

'What are you thinking?' asks Richard, stepping out on to the badly cracked front path.

'Mike's last calls,' says Katie. 'The team will already have had a chance to trace them. And yet they haven't visited.'

'I'm far from an expert on technology, but if Ben's right about his brother not trusting some of your colleagues, then might he have had another phone they couldn't trace?'

'In which case, where is it now?' says Katie, pulling out a mobile given to her by Sam. She stares at the device and considers what else she's just been told: Mike believed he'd been followed by a woman with cropped hair. Unless it was Ben who saw her and recognised her. Either way, it can't be a coincidence. She doesn't believe in those.

'Can you be followed with that phone?' asks Richard, recognising Katie's concern.

'Undoubtedly,' she replies with a sigh. She considers doing what she can to prevent that: turning off the GPS tracking unit, or even dropping it in a bin, but as she looks back at Ben's house, she realises it's already too late. She decides instead to head for the place that started all of this: the internet.

Searching *Nathan Radley* in her phone's browser, she sees there are already headlines about his visit to the mortuary and statement to the press. It seems strange to see his face in the photos, for almost the whole decade they'd worked together he'd successfully avoided being photographed at all. She scans a couple of hastily written articles. His denial is there. So are the accusations. And then, with a quick search of social media, she finds some of the anger. Plenty of people still believe him to be guilty. Plenty of people want him dead. She feels a sudden protectiveness, a desire to be with him, to tell him she believes in him, so she searches through the phone's address book to try and find a way to get in contact with Sam, but there's only one name on there, and not even a name, just a single letter: C.

She calls the number and doesn't get through. When she checks the call history, she finds it's the only number Sam has ever called from this phone. The calls go back more than three years, regular and very short, but just under two years ago the calls from this end stopped getting through. Although that doesn't prevent Sam, if that's who was making the calls, from trying. In fact, Katie can see she's tried hundreds of times. Then, a year and a half ago, the calls stop completely.

'I don't like this,' says Katie, staring over at a concerned-looking Richard. Although if she's being honest with herself, this is what she's been missing – the doubt, the excitement, the unpredictability, and, perhaps most of all, the danger. As a colleague once far too accurately suggested, she's only ever happy when she's chasing shadows in the dark.

CHAPTER ELEVEN

'Still no response from your partner,' says Sam, lowering the mobile phone from her ear and peering at the screen. She's sitting next to Nathan in the back seat of the car. The driver in the front is a young man with very short blond hair, who hasn't said a word in the half hour it has taken them to reach the edge of the city.

'I think some of those people wanted to kill me,' says Nathan.

'I think you're probably right,' says Sam, running her finger across the screen of her phone then lifting it towards Nathan. She presses a button and a video starts to play. 'The question is, have any of them killed already?'

He watches the crowd of people, which seems much smaller on the screen, perhaps only a dozen people.

'Could the killer have heard about my being there in time to rush across?'

Sam glances over her shoulder. 'It wouldn't surprise me if they've followed you from the very beginning. I think I heard you suggesting yourself that Mike Peters was killed to bring about your return. That being the case, they will have been waiting in the most obvious places.'

'The police station,' says Nathan, nodding his head. He tries to think back to anyone he might have seen outside, but he'd been so distracted when they arrived they could have been sitting in a bloodstained shirt on the steps out the front and he's not sure he'd have noticed. He searches the faces on the screen, playing the video several times, but there's nobody he recognises and nobody that stands out.

'We have to be even more careful,' says Sam. 'Your face was pretty well known before, but now…' Again, she lifts the phone towards him, an enlarged image of him in the centre of the screen. He looks a little lost, but no way near as lost as he feels right now.

'I could shave my hair off,' he says, pulling at the long strands at the back of his neck.

'It'll make little difference. Especially once we've caught up with your partner.' Sam touches her cheek, indicating the scars that Katie has no way to hide. 'Any idea where she is, by the way?'

'No, none,' says Nathan, holding Sam's gaze.

'Hmm,' says Sam. 'I could have sworn you said in the interview yesterday that she told you everything. Although I did also sense a little bit of tension between you. Quite understandable, I suppose.' Sam stares out of the window as they pass a school, kids racing around the playground. 'I couldn't have smacked somebody over the head with a metal bar. Especially if they were my twin brother.'

'I should have done it,' says Nathan, gripping the handle of the door. 'He deserved to die.'

'He did die.'

'Too late,' says Nathan, quietly. 'Too late.'

Sam leans forward and whispers something to the driver, who nods and pulls over to the side of the road. He then climbs out of the car and walks away while Sam switches to the driver's seat.

'What's going on?' asks Nathan, twisting to watch the driver disappear round the corner.

'He's got work to do,' says Sam, indicating to pull away. 'And so have we.'

They continue driving in silence for another five minutes, before the car pulls up at a locked metal gate. A board on the gate says something about the site awaiting planning permission for construction of a business estate, but Nathan isn't looking at that: his attention is drawn to the sign behind. It's badly scratched and covered in graffiti, but even with half the letters missing he still recognises the name of the school.

'You know where this is?' Sam asks, turning to face him.

'You think I could forget?'

Sam pops open her seatbelt and reaches into the centre console for a key. 'Come on,' she says, climbing out of the car.

'What if I don't want to?' he calls after her.

'I'm not asking you to try and enter Steven Fish's killer's mind,' she says. 'You've already proved back at the mortuary that it would be a waste of time. We're just going to look at the scene. There might be something you missed the first time around, seeing as you were so distracted.'

Distracted was the very last thing Nathan was the day he came to see Steven Fish's body. His focus was such that he couldn't step back, couldn't withdraw from the horror of it all. Not until Katie had physically dragged him away. But by then it was too late. There was a smile on his face that told his partner, and him, that he could no longer be trusted to perform his duties.

'I'd like Katie to be here with me.'

'As would I,' says Sam, shaking her phone and giving a look of frustration. 'But she's obviously tied up elsewhere. So for now you'll just have to make do with me.'

The school is exactly as he remembers it from two years earlier, apart from the few remaining windows, which have now been smashed. Despite the damage, he can picture kids running around in the playground. Worse still, he can picture his and Katie's child running around, until, like the fantasy child that he or she will always be, they disappear.

'I hated school,' says Sam. 'Too many rules.' It's an unexpected admission for many reasons, and to Nathan it doesn't ring true, but he decides to go with it to break the silence and to try and find out more about the person he's with.

'Public?'

'State. My parents couldn't stretch to the kind of place you went to.'

So many of the details of Nathan's life were shared with the world after his brother's death. Old school friends gave interviews in which they claimed to have seen the darkness in the twins long before. There was even a girl Nathan had once dated who claimed she 'had felt uncomfortable around him'. He could hardly blame her for that. If she'd had an inkling of what was going on in his mind during those adolescent years, the constant battle between fantasy and reality, then she would have felt a lot more than uncomfortable.

'What did your parents do?' asks Nathan.

'They argued,' says Sam.

'I meant for work.'

'Pretty much the same thing. They were human rights lawyers. On the side of righteousness, but not of wealth.'

'Did they want you to join the police?'

'They wanted me to be quiet most of the time. Human rights were not always observed at home, you see.'

Nathan does see, and he feels a little sympathy as well as understanding. His dad had been strict. His dad had also worked in law.

'They must be very proud of you now.'

'Both dead. Heart attack and a stroke. They worked too hard. Didn't know when to stop. Until they *were* stopped, one within a year of the other.'

'Goodness, I'm sorry,' says Nathan.

'Could have been worse,' says Sam, flashing Nathan a look that makes him certain she's well aware of the fate of his parents: death by cancer and suicide, and on the very same day. And then, of course, there's his brother.

'Siblings?' he asks.

'Just me,' says Sam. 'Which is just the way I like it.'

Nathan's already spotted the absence of a wedding ring on Sam's finger. Although far more evident is the absence of any kind of warmth. He can't imagine what sort of man or woman could ever share a life with someone who gives so little of themselves away. That said, she's talking to him now, and he's enjoyed the brief distraction from what lies ahead.

Steven Fish was murdered in the school assembly hall, his body tied to the gym bars on the wall, the skin peeled from his back, a knife drawn up the length of his body and his head cleft from his shoulders and carefully placed beside his body on the floor. When Nathan steps into the building he sees it all as he had on the day that he and Katie had arrived. It's like he's slipped into one of his fantasies, only he's not reliving a murder, he's standing on the outside watching his own descent to the edge of insanity. He sees himself standing in front of the body, absorbing all the information. Then he sees himself smile, and Katie drag him towards the door. Nathan wants to do the same now, to run for the door and put as much distance as he can between himself and this place, and these memories. But when he does so, he realises something he hadn't noticed before.

He is alone.

'Sam?' he calls out. It feels strange to use her name like that, as if they're friends, but not as strange as it feels to get no response. With the exception of the confrontation with the press, she's barely been more than a metre away from him all day, and now she's disappeared. He calls out again, and hears nothing beyond the echo of his own voice in the empty hall. Is she playing a trick on him? Is she giving him space to think? If so, it isn't working. All he can think is that something isn't right.

He starts to move towards the door, entering the long, unlit corridor he came in by. It seems so much darker now that he's on his own. His shoulder bumps into the frame of the door. He continues forward, heading for the daylight at the end, trying to keep his nerves and his imagination under control. He calls out again one more time, the way he might have done as a child when he was having one of his many nightmares. Then, suddenly, a light at the end of the corridor explodes in front of him as pain registers from behind. He knows he's been hit by something hard, but that's all he has time to think as the floor rises up rapidly towards him.

When Nathan comes to, it takes him a moment to figure out where he is. His face is pressed up against something hard and his hands and arms are bound. The truth comes in waves, each one more horrifying than the last. He is in a school. He is in the assembly hall. He is tied to the bars on the wall in the same way that Steven Fish had been. He tries to locate specifically where the pain he is feeling is coming from. His head, obviously, although that's still attached. And his back, which feels like it might be on fire.

He hears a sound and tries to turn towards it, but can only twist his neck a short distance. In the process of doing this, causing himself more pain, he realises the sound is his own. He quietens himself and steadies his breathing, only to realise there's someone else, breathing slowly, rhythmically, just inches from his ear. He can't hear them over the sound of blood thumping at his temples and in his throat, but they're so close he can feel their breath on the back of his neck.

'What do you want?' he asks in a fragile voice.

'The truth,' comes the reply, so soft he can't tell if it's male or female, or even if it's real. Might all this be his imagination? Might this be the madness he had feared the Steven Fish case would ignite? If he could so vividly imagine a stranger's murder, couldn't he do the same for his own?

Nevertheless, he decides to play along. 'The truth about what?'

'Fishhh…' The last two letters of the name are drawn out and accompanied by an agonising pressure on the wound on his back.

'That was my brother. My brother killed him.'

The force on his wound grows stronger and again he hears himself cry out.

'What do you want?' he asks again, this time close to screaming the words.

'The truth.'

'I can't… I don't…' Sweat, or perhaps blood, is dripping from his brow as he considers where this is heading. He knows what Fish went through. He knows what Mike went through. The murders were slightly different, but the end was the same. And before that, there was torture. He hasn't had his head stuffed down the toilet bowl like Fish, perhaps because those toilets aren't there anymore, but that's hardly a relief, knowing what comes next. He strains to look across at one of his hands, sees the fingers still following a natural curl. Some of them won't be like that for long. But he might get a glimpse of his killer as they attach the pliers and twist. He won't be able to tell anyone else, but at least he'll know. A hand presses hard against the side of his head, preventing him from moving, and he feels cold metal grip the tip of his little finger.

Nathan knows what pain will follow; he imagined it the day he stood over Steven Fish's body. Instinctively, he falls back on his only defence: he closes his eyes and he can see her, every inch of her, every scar that he's traced with his fingers, every perfect curve. He knows what's coming; can taste a pain more agonisingly and beautifully perfect than his wildest dreams. He digs deep within himself, looking for a light in the darkness. That name, those curves, those scars, that smile. He sees Katie so clearly he almost believes he can reach out and touch her with hands that are no longer tied to bars in front of him, with fingers that are not being twisted and broken.

He has no idea how long he remains in that place within, where he sees nothing but Katie, and feels nothing but his love for her. When he retreats it's because some part of him knows that he can, and that the worst is over.

CHAPTER TWELVE

Katie pushes past a police officer and enters the hospital room where Nathan is being kept. He's hooked up to a couple of machines that instantly reassure her he is still alive.

He's on his side, a thick bandage across his shoulder, and when she walks to the other side of the bed she can see that the fingers of one hand are wrapped up as well. She goes cold at the thought of what he must have been through. She'd first heard about the attack when she'd checked the headlines again on her phone, but there had been no details.

Now those terrible details are all too clear. Steven Fish had been the case that had sent Nathan running for Scotland. It had also been the unsolved case that had nearly ended her career. She'd done everything she could to try and find the real killer, but her motivation back then is nothing compared to what she feels right now. She leans on a bar at the end of the bed, looking down on a still partially drugged Nathan, gripping so hard she feels certain the metal will bend.

'He's going to be okay?' she asks, turning to Richard.

'Physically, yes,' he mouths, out of view of Nathan, and she knows exactly what he means. Nathan had been struggling enough before, but now Katie doesn't know how he'll ever recover. She touches his good hand gently to stop the room from spinning around her, and he wakes, offering a smile of such purity that it gives her hope.

'I guess they'll believe I'm innocent now,' he says, slurring his words. He tries to lift his hand towards his shoulder, but the grimace suggests it's a movement that is costing him dearly. 'Unless they think I somehow carved the skin from my own back.'

'Where's Sam?' asks Katie, feeling her anger rise again. 'And where was she when this happened?'

'From what I overheard, she was found lying face down in a pool of her own blood in the playground.'

'Found by whom?'

'Her driver.'

'What was she hit with?'

'Same thing that hit me, I'd imagine,' says Nathan, with another grimace as he connects some of his pain to the side of his head. 'Why?'

Katie looks towards the window, drawing in a long breath and trying to control her growing suspicion. 'It just seems *coincidental* that she took you there and then you were attacked.'

'I don't think it was coincidental at all,' says a voice behind Katie. She spins round to see Sam standing in the doorway, a hand on the back of her head and blood on her previously immaculate white shirt. She looks a state, but the focus in her stare is as hard as ever. 'It's exactly what Nathan was asking for during his little press conference earlier.'

Katie had watched the video on the journey over, and she can see the truth in the other woman's words. 'Why isn't he dead then?' she asks. A question that sounds a little harsher than she'd intended. But then comes another question that's exactly as planned: 'Why aren't *you* dead?'

Sam pulls her phone from her pocket. 'Because I was able to make a call.'

'Something you weren't you able to do with me,' says Katie. 'I wondered where you and Nathan were earlier. There was no answer when I tried to ring you.'

'Well, we're talking now,' says Sam, calmly. 'And what do you have to tell me? Did you find out anything during your *private* meeting?'

'Oh, I found out plenty,' says Katie, remembering the warning that Ben had given her about this woman. 'But I'll keep it to myself for now.'

'As you wish,' says Sam, moving to sit on a chair on the far side of the room. 'But I don't think we're going to solve this case by keeping secrets.'

'Nor do I,' says Katie. 'So perhaps you should start by telling me who C is.'

Sam Stone's face had already been pale, but now it's the colour of the wall behind her. The change is so dramatic and alarming that Richard moves quickly across to her.

'I'm all right,' she says, shaking off his attentiveness. 'Just a wave of dizziness.' She collects herself and looks up at Katie again. 'Sorry, you were saying?'

'C,' says Katie, pulling out the mobile phone Sam had given her. 'Who is it?'

'Nobody of interest to you. An old friend. We're not in contact anymore.'

'Despite your best efforts,' says Katie, thinking back to the call history, dozens of attempts that hadn't got through.

'Am I not allowed a private life?' asks Sam.

'You're suggesting it was a boyfriend?' asks Katie, still pushing hard, despite the awkwardness she can sense in the room.

'A failed relationship,' says Sam. 'Do you not think me capable of those?'

'The failed bit, most definitely,' says Katie, before turning away and walking to the window. She knows she's gone too far, and is on the verge of offering an apology when Sam stands up.

'I'm signing myself out of here,' she says. 'But I will be back tomorrow. I'm guessing both of you are more motivated than ever to help bring this monster down, so I hope you'll be ready to be part of a team.'

'Tomorrow?' says Katie, looking over at Nathan. 'I don't think he'll—'

'I'll be fine,' says Nathan. 'They've patched me up pretty well. Besides,' he twists painfully to look over at Richard, 'I'll have my own personal doctor in tow.'

When Sam has gone, Katie moves over to the bed and carefully sits on the edge of the mattress, reaching out to stroke Nathan's fringe away from his eyes. She hasn't touched him that tenderly in so long, he does little to hide his surprise.

'You're sure you're going to be okay?' she asks.

'As long as I'm working,' he says. 'That's what we need to concentrate on. Nothing else.'

CHAPTER THIRTEEN

Nathan's exit from the hospital does not go unnoticed. A much bigger crowd of journalists than the one he'd addressed outside the mortuary has gathered, and it takes two policemen to escort him through. He'd agreed with Katie to meet her at the police station, and he hopes that she's managed to get there without all this drama.

He's helped into the back of a police car, and he has to lean forward for the whole journey so the wound on his back isn't pressing against the seat. He's on enough drugs to dull most of the pain, but he's refused the amount the doctors prescribed, wanting to keep his mind focused on the job, and the pain helps to keep everything sharp.

No questions are asked on the way to the station, but the two police officers in the front can't help but glance at him in the rear-view mirror. He wonders what these officers see him as now – a victim? A suspect? A threat? There have always been doubts from those he's worked with, those who didn't understand or accept his ability; not that he's ever fully understood it himself.

When he's finally at the police station, Nathan is pleased to be escorted past the interview suites and up to the offices where he's played the lead in so many investigations in the past. Katie, Sam and Richard are waiting for him there, as are Superintendent Taylor and DCI Ken Stocks. The walls and whiteboards of the room they're in are covered with material – photos, timelines, financial records, phone records – most, he assumes, relating to the Mike Peters murder, though some perhaps are tied to his own more recent experience.

'How are you doing?' asks Katie, moving quickly over to him. They don't touch or hold eye contact for long, but Nathan's glad to have her nearby.

'I'm ready to go,' he says, moving straight across to a wall where various photos of Mike Peters are pinned to a board. Katie has followed him over, but seems reluctant to get too close to the images. Nathan's surprised at this, then he sees his mistake; she's not scared for herself, she's scared for him, purposely blocking him off from another wall of photos and another victim she doesn't want him to see.

In all the time he'd spent in court, talking about his brother's crimes and hearing testimony, Nathan had always managed to turn a blind eye to the visual evidence of his brother's death. He'd been there at the end, and even watched Christian lift the knife to his own throat, but had collapsed in shock at the exact moment the blade made contact. Here, in vivid colour, is the aftermath. Here is the body that for so many years – before Christian used a plastic surgeon to change his appearance – had been identical to his own. And here he can see it lying lifeless on the floor of an abandoned warehouse.

'Is this relevant?' he asks, turning to Taylor.

'I'm sorry you're having to see that,' says the superintendent, 'but yes, of course it is. For a long time we've believed your brother killed Steven Fish. Now, in Mike Peters' identical wounds, we have evidence he might not have.'

'Identical according to Dr Parker.'

'Whereas yours are not,' Ken Stocks interrupts. 'Possible differences, according to his initial examination.'

'We know Miles's motivation,' says Sam. 'He doesn't want to accept Nathan's innocence.'

'I can't say I was ready to myself,' Nathan hears Ken Stocks say under his breath.

'So, what do we have?' asks Nathan, glancing at Katie. When he looks closely he can see how tired she is. He doubts she'll have slept at all, most likely coming straight here to work her way through the evidence. 'Have Forensics got anything from the school, or my clothes?' He looks down at the brand-new outfit delivered to the hospital. It's not at all the casual look he'd adopted in Wales; rather the formal jacket, shirt and tie and the kind of brogues he'd worn right back at the start of his career. Given the sizes are exactly right, he's sure Katie has had some input.

'Just you and Sam have been identified at the school so far,' Katie says, shaking her head and shooting a quick look over at the other woman. 'But it's a difficult scene to process. Kids have been through there in recent days – drinking, smoking and smashing windows.'

'What about a weapon?' he asks, lifting a hand to the back of his head. 'Any idea what Sam and I were hit with?'

'Something hard and flat,' says Stocks. 'Given the traces of dust, possibly a brick.'

'Not found?'

'We've found hundreds of bricks – the place is crumbling away.'

'So we don't really have anything,' says Nathan, unable to hide his frustration.

Katie moves in front of him, giving him the same look of encouragement she has many times over the years. 'We have the statement you gave at the hospital. We have a voice you might recognise again.'

Nathan falls into the nearest chair, the sudden movement registering in his shoulder and in his broken fingers.

'So, we just sit and wait,' he says, with a sigh.

'For what?' asks Taylor.

Nathan nods at the wall on the far side of the room, where he's recognised the sheets of photocopied paper, all bearing his tiny handwritten descriptions of murders. 'There were four pages torn out of my journal,' he says. 'That means we've got three more to go.'

CHAPTER FOURTEEN

BLOG: Seeing Red
The anonymous, unfiltered truth about crime and the criminal justice system

So much has happened, I can't keep up. So, they're back! You'll all have seen the videos and heard Nathan's words, and we know from the shots of Katie visiting the hospital that she's there, too. Initially, when I saw the headlines that Nathan had been attacked at the same place Steven Fish was killed, I feared the worst, but my sources are telling me he's doing okay. I know the cynical among you are wondering if he staged this to try and prove his innocence, but come on – there's no way you'd put yourself through that.

I'm biased. To be honest, I've always liked what I've seen of Nathan Radley. First, I like that I've seen very little of him. He's solved a hell of a lot of crimes, and never once stepped into the limelight to take the praise. When he came out and spoke the other day it was because he had no choice. I suspect he did it to help Katie get away from the press. He may also have been trying to encourage Steven Fish and DS Peters' killer to attack him, and not someone else.

Secondly, I love the way his mind works. I've been to some pretty dark places myself, and there's an honesty in his words that is so refreshing. So many people won't go to the darkest corners of their own minds, but Nathan has spent the last ten years hunting shadows in the dark to keep us safe.

I guess that's one of the many reasons I work so hard to keep this blog anonymous. The internet is full of sanctimonious, superficial bullshit, people offering opinions because they think it makes them look cool or it'll gain them a couple more followers. And those that do try to be honest are attacked for it.

Here's some honesty for you: I do drugs. I'm not saying that to encourage others, because it's dangerous – it's certainly taken me close to the edge a couple of times. I do drugs because it settles the whirring in my head. It makes me calm when I'm not. It makes me happy when I'm not. It also helps me to dream. I'm not saying I can do what Nathan does, but there have been times when I'm really high that I've felt like I understand other people, like I've got a proper sense of what they're thinking. Of course, most of the time they're thinking, *Christ, who is this druggie staring at me?* But the point is…

Guys, an email just arrived. I know exactly who it's from, because nobody else sends me emails. And it's real. I've checked it, verified it, given my face a dunk in cold water and a couple of slaps. There's absolutely no doubt that I've just received another one of the missing pages from Nathan's journal. What does it mean? Does it mean there's going to be another murder?

I'm writing this as I'm thinking it, and I'm thinking as fast as I can. It feels like I'm involved somehow, if you see what I mean, like I'm a little bit responsible. I don't know what to do with it. Should I go to the police? But then, what more can I tell them? I don't know who's sending it. All I have to give them is the page. This page:

I'm looking forward to this one. I look forward to all of them, but this one is going to be special, because it'll be more intimate than most. I've already got the victim lined up. They're looking a little dazed and confused, but I'll wait till they've figured out who I am and what's going to happen to them before I deliver the final blow. I've chosen the heaviest hammer I could find. I haven't been to a shop, I'm not that stupid. I found it in my dad's old toolkit. He won't miss it.

The nail is a little rusty, but it's definitely long enough to do the trick. I just hope I don't miss. It's not the end of the world if I do – not my world, at any rate – but it would be nice if I could look competent when the police arrive to inspect the crime scene. I wonder what they'll think of it. Will they think it's my job (not if I miss the nail they won't)? Will they think I'm trying to make some kind of point? Ha, ha! I just hope they find it interesting, something worth investing their time and effort in.

As for the victim, I'm pretty sure it will be over quickly, and if I manage to smash the nail right down to the skull in a single blow (a big ask, but I'm quietly confident) then there shouldn't be much blood. Not that they'll care that much about that, but if their family *scrub that, no family for my victim. And no words when they recognise me. Just a realisation that they're getting what they deserve*

I've read that five times now. I can't stop reading it and can't stop imagining it. The drugs aren't helping, not anymore, and there's nothing I can do before they start to wear off, but I keep picturing the murder and wondering who it might be. Not someone I know, I barely know anyone, but maybe someone Nathan and Katie know. Shit! Poor Nathan, how much suffering does one man have to go through? No, no, it might be all right, he'll fix, he'll solve it. We just have to have faith in his abilities.

CHAPTER FIFTEEN

'Do you remember this one?' asks Katie, tapping the computer screen in front of her. On the scan of the page from the journal posted on the blogger's site, the central area has been highlighted by several strokes of a fluorescent marker.

'I do,' says Nathan, looking away. 'My dad was always really precious about that toolkit.'

'Do you remember who the victim was supposed to be?' asks Sam.

'Nobody specific. I tried not to think of anyone in particular, for fear that would make it more likely to happen. I was just trying to exorcise my thoughts.'

'So do we think that somebody is going to die like this, or that it's already happened?' asks Katie. She's moved over to the office window and is staring down at the street below. There are hundreds of people out there, walking, cycling, driving, running – living.

'Does it make any difference?' says Nathan, sadly. 'We have no idea who the victim might be, or who is responsible for the killings.'

'We do know the likely weapon, though.'

'A hammer,' says Sam. 'Are you suggesting we should interview anyone who has access to a hammer?'

'Well, it depends how accurately the killer wants to re-enact this,' says Katie, struggling to keep calm. 'Do you know where your dad's hammer is now?' she asks Nathan, watching as his face slowly comes alive.

'I'm pretty sure Christian took it before he moved to Cornwall.'

'Again, how does this help us?' asks Sam, with a frustrated sigh. 'We already know that the killer has a connection to Christian, because they have pages that had been removed from the journal when he was in possession of it.'

'It most likely means they've found his home,' says Nathan, wide-eyed again. 'Not Cornwall, his real home. The place he stayed while he was hiding here in London that the police could never find. They've found the pages that Christian had torn out.'

'But why would he have torn them out?' asks Sam. 'How are they any different to the others?'

'That's not for me to judge,' says Nathan. 'All those thoughts…' He looks up towards the ceiling. 'It's all the same to me. I thought it, I wrote it, I tried my best to forget it. And towards the end I wasn't even really there.'

'What do you mean?' asks Katie.

'It was the start of the daydreams, the fantasies, whatever you want to call them. I was drifting off into other places – not other people's minds, but not really my mind, either. And as I did so, I somehow managed to write it down. When it first started happening I was fascinated. I read every word. But once I'd read a few, I didn't want to read any more.'

'Comes back to the question of whether you could have committed a crime you didn't know about,' says Stocks.

'Not if you're looking to solve this case, it doesn't,' Katie cuts in, ignoring the glare from the senior officer. 'The question is, how did the killer find Christian's home? It's unlikely they simply stumbled across it.' She moves across to a map pinned to the wall. On it are marked all of the locations where Christian was known to be over the course of the Cartoonist killings, painstakingly mapped by Mike Peters and his team using CCTV, often tracking him from the care home where he worked. 'That would be far too much of a coincidence. They must have known each other.'

'I don't think Christian would have trusted anyone enough to let them into his life. He couldn't even do that with me, his own brother.'

'Because you're not a murderer,' says Katie. 'Perhaps he would have trusted someone else if he knew they wanted to kill with the same hunger he did.'

'So is that what Mike's death was? Was it someone else feeding their hunger?' Nathan lifts his broken hand. 'And what about me? Was I left alive because I couldn't kill Christian? Because I didn't know who killed Fish?'

'You think they were just checking you hadn't uncovered what Mike knew?' asks Taylor.

'What did Mike know?' says Nathan. 'Have we even figured that out yet?'

'We've been through his papers, his house, everything,' says Taylor. 'There's nothing that jumps out.'

'So what next?' asks Nathan.

'You mean *who* next,' says Sam, pointing back at the latest page on the blog. 'I suppose we just wait and see.'

*

The call comes in an hour later, and within twenty minutes Sam, Katie, Nathan and Richard are pushing their way past a police cordon to find the body, propped up against a wheelie bin, the head an indistinguishable mess of blood and brain. Katie points out the long rusty nail sticking out from a patch of sticky hair.

'It looks like he missed a few times before he hit the nail,' says Sam.

'A *few* times?' says Katie, trying to find a face in the confusion of broken skull and bone. She turns to look at Nathan, who has stayed back a little and is slowly scanning their surroundings like she's seen him do at so many crime scenes before. She hopes he finds something, but she's doubtful.

'Do we know who he is?' asks Richard, who's kept at an even greater distance than Nathan.

'No way of telling from that,' says Sam, gesturing towards the pulped head and face. 'Perhaps they were trying to disguise the identity.'

'Perhaps,' says Katie, slipping on a pair of forensic gloves that she's found in Sam's car and reaching carefully forward and tapping at the breast of the victim's worn brown blazer, before slipping her hand in and slowly pulling out a wallet. 'Nigel Hartham,' she says, before adding, 'Dr Nigel Hartham.'

Katie hears a sound from behind and turns to see that Richard has stumbled backwards and fallen against the side of the alleyway. His face is pale and his mouth open, registering the shock where words aren't coming.

'You know him?' says Sam, reaching out to grab the old man before he falls.

Richard manages to nod, but his breathing is short and wheezy. Katie and Nathan both rush to help support the doctor, while gently guiding him away from the body and onto a step nearby. Given a little time and a sip from a bottle of water commandeered from a nearby PC, Richard is finally able to talk.

'Is this about me?' he says, blinking back the tears. 'Are people dying because of me?'

'Who was he to you?' asks Nathan. 'An old colleague?'

'And a good friend,' says Richard. 'He helped me when I started getting unwell.'

'With the PTSD?' asks Katie, before wondering if she should have shared this in front of Sam.

'I couldn't cope,' says Richard. 'I wasn't thinking straight. I wasn't doing the right things.'

'Like what?' asks Sam.

'Not here,' says Katie, lifting the elderly doctor to his feet. Looking over her shoulder, she can see that a crowd of onlookers have started to gather at the end of the alleyway. Some might be media, some just members of the public, but with mobile phones and instant uploads there doesn't seem to be much difference anymore.

Ten minutes later, and they're parked down a backstreet, having given any potential pursuers the slip. Katie and Sam are sitting in the front of the car, Richard and Nathan in the back.

'How might this be connected to you?' Sam asks the doctor, as sharp and seemingly uncaring as ever.

Richard lowers his head and runs a hand across the thinning hair on top. He draws in a long breath and for a moment Katie doesn't believe he's going to speak. When he finally manages, his voice is so weak she finds herself gripping his arm and giving it a squeeze.

'Nigel Hartham is the only one I've ever told. He protected me.'

'Protected you from what?' asks Nathan.

'From everything,' says Richard. 'For forty years I'd worked hard to save patients, to keep them alive. It didn't matter who they were – and I've worked with everybody, rapists, paedophiles, you name it – I did what I could for them, equal effort every time.

'The problem is, when you've been on the other side, when you've tried and failed to save their victims, mopped up the blood they've spilled, watched good hearts stop beating in your hands,' he lifts his hand as if reliving a specific moment, 'and you know there are black hearts out there still beating because of you, well…'

Katie can tell that Sam wants to jump in, but she flashes the superior officer a look that warns her to give him space to tell his story. He swallows hard and reaches out to squeeze Katie's hand. 'I told you about losing my wife, didn't I?'

'You did,' she says, softly.

'What I didn't tell you was that the man who drove into her on that day was drunk. Of course, forty years ago the law was very different, but he still shouldn't have been behind the wheel of that car. And the worst thing is, I saved his life. I didn't know who he was when they brought him into the hospital. I didn't know what had happened to my Maggie because of him. If I had known...'

The doctor lifts his crooked old fingers to the bridge of his nose and squeezes hard. 'Then, at the very end of my career, when my illness had already taken hold, when I couldn't sleep, could barely eat, and when the shake in my hands was getting harder and harder to hide, the past came back to haunt me, to challenge me. And I failed.'

He pauses and takes a slow, wheezy breath, as if to summon up the strength to explain. 'I wasn't front line anymore, I was helping with mental health assessments and addictions, people like—' He cuts himself off before mentioning Ben by name. 'Anyway, they were short-staffed and there'd been a big road traffic accident, multiple fatalities, and I found myself helping out.

'I was working on one of the drivers, and I could smell the alcohol on his breath. He was young, maybe twenty-five, about the same age as the guy I'd saved all those years ago, and I couldn't stop thinking about...' Richard hesitates as if struggling to find the right word, but Katie is sure that he's had it all along. 'Revenge.'

'You killed him?' asks Sam.

'I didn't save him,' says Richard. 'And there was a chance I could have done. I wasn't working alone, but I was the only one who realised he had internal bleeding. By the time the others caught up, it was too late. All I did was keep my mouth shut, and yet it's haunted me ever since.'

'I'm sorry, but I'm still not sure how this could connect to the recent crimes,' says Nathan, looking down at his taped-up fingers. 'Are you suggesting it could have been a relative of the victim?'

'There was an inquest,' says Richard, nodding. 'Its conclusion was what everybody else was thinking – that I was too old and shouldn't have been there. But I told my friend the truth. I told the man who's now lying dead in an alley because of me.' Richard starts to cry and Katie pulls him in close.

'I don't think it's related,' says Nathan. 'These crimes are related to my brother and to Mike and to Steven Fish.'

'We can't dismiss the possibility, though,' says Sam. 'Can you remember the name of the man who died?'

Richard snorts, not looking up from Katie's shoulder. 'You think I'll ever forget? His name was Thomas Shaw. He has a family, too, a son who must be twenty-five years old by now. I used to look him up sometimes – he'd often post about how hard life was without a dad, and after a while it became too much to take. That's when I got rid of all my devices and moved back to Wales.'

'We'll investigate it,' says Katie. 'But I think Nathan's right, this is unlikely to be connected. And I think you should focus on all those people you helped to save, rather than the ones that slipped away.' As she says this, Katie places a hand on her stomach and thinks of the efforts the doctors must have made with her. Were they giving their all? Could they have done more, acted faster, and saved not only her life but the chance of giving life to another?

'I'm going back to the police station to see what I can find,' says Sam.

'You can drop us off at the hotel, then,' says Katie. 'Nathan and Richard both need a rest.' Katie pulls out the mobile that Sam had given her earlier, waving it towards her. 'You know where we are if you need us.'

CHAPTER SIXTEEN

Nathan is back in the run-down hotel room, staring out of the window at the downpour that's started. He finds it hard to believe that less than two days earlier he was sitting in their picturesque cottage with a glass of wine in his hand, staring out across the Pembrokeshire hills, shielding his eyes from the sun. That seems a world away now. That seems like a different life.

Katie is sitting on the edge of the bed with the doctor, who seems to have aged another ten years since the discovery of his friend's body. She is talking to him in a hushed voice, consoling him and, Nathan suspects, gently pressing for any extra tiny detail that might help them with the case. Nathan feels so useless now, suddenly longing for the return of the gift that he had for so long considered a curse.

'You should be resting,' Katie calls across to him.

He smiles back, touched and in some ways relieved by her concern. He needs to find a way to prove to her that he can still be helpful to the investigation, so he nods and returns his attention to the world outside, a world in which a serial killer is preparing for their next move.

He yawns, and lets his thoughts start to drift back more than twenty years, to when he was teenager writing his journal. Those had been difficult times, struggling to cope with changes in both his body and his mind. The journal had been a form of release, a way of making his terrible dreams – which came both day and night – seem less real. He can picture himself as a skinny younger man scratching his tiny handwriting onto the page, sometimes, as he'd recently revealed for the first time, in a kind of trance, purging himself of awful thoughts. There had been hundreds of pages, maybe thousands of crimes. When he'd been asked at the inquest about the missing pages, he'd been unable to say why they might have been removed, because he had no way of knowing what was on them. But now he has two of those pages. If he looks at them, if he reads them carefully, might he spot the connection?

'Can I borrow your phone?' he asks Katie.

She hands it to him without asking why, but he can tell she wants to know. He has nobody to call, no friends in the world other than her, and now even their relationship is being tested.

The extract is all over the news and the various social media platforms he checks: jokes, comments, articles, comparisons. It's clear that everyone has an opinion on what's happened before, and what might happen next. He quickly finds the website of the blogger who's been receiving the pages first-hand and, moving to a chair in a corner of the room, he starts to read his own words again.

Something's not right, he can feel it, but it takes him a while to pinpoint exactly what – and then he remembers: he and his twin had once agreed on a shared handwriting style, to infuriate their mother, seamlessly do each other's homework and generally cause mayhem as the identical little rascals they were. It had taken weeks of practice, but eventually they had it down to an art form. Only the brothers could identify the minute details that differentiated their handwriting.

Nathan stares at the text at the bottom of the first extract, the page which had described the murders of Steven Fish and Mike Peters. Then he checks the second page, that predicted the way Dr Nigel Hartham would meet his end. He waits until he's absolutely certain before sharing his discovery with the room.

'I didn't write all this,' he says, passing the phone back to Katie with a shaking hand. 'Christian has changed some of my words.

Look here…' He points at the screen, but the writing is tiny and he takes the phone back to enlarge the text. With his broken fingers it isn't easy, but eventually she can see where he means.

'The tail of that "s" and the curl on that "e", that's definitely Christian's handwriting. And if you look really closely, you can see there's one more line that's just a little more squeezed in than the others.'

'*I've walked down here before…*' Katie starts to read, '*but back then I never imagined this might be a place where I would kill. It had always been Mother's dream, a place of tranquillity, and I know it will be the same for me once my own dream has become a reality.*'

'And on the next page,' says Nathan, impatiently waiting for Katie to scroll down to it. 'Towards the top there's something about a twisted oak that's grown around a barbed wire fence, with a single letter carved above it in the bark.'

'Do you remember that place?' asks Katie, excited now.

Nathan shakes his head, searching his mind again and finding the same answer. 'I'm pretty sure I've never seen that tree, but if the first bit is about my mother, mine and Christian's mother, then perhaps…'

Katie jumps to her feet, before turning back towards Richard. 'You should stay here.'

'You're forgetting who has the car,' he says, holding out a hand for her to pull him up.

'We should tell Sam,' says Nathan.

'Not yet,' says Katie, deftly flicking off the back of the mobile and unhousing the battery, before slipping all the parts into her pocket. 'We'll give her a call if we find anything important.'

CHAPTER SEVENTEEN

Despite all that's happened, Katie is struggling to keep a smile from her face when she looks over at Nathan from her place in the speeding car. She's remembering what it was that she loved so much about him: he was troubled but brilliant; dark, but capable of bringing so much light. She remembers the early days, before Nathan had arrived on her team, and how she would carefully study old cases and read book after book on the workings of a killer's mind. It was her fascination. It was her obsession. With Nathan, it was like having a killer as a partner. He could tell her things no book or crime scene ever could. And for a long time she believed he could be trusted, so much so that she had grown closer to him than to any other person she had ever known. Things are different now: complicated, damaged, and yet still there's nobody else she would rather have alongside her.

'Any idea what we're going to find?' she asks, as Richard drives them over Kingston Bridge.

'I can think of some things,' says Nathan. 'I'm just hoping I'm wrong.'

'But your brother must have been expecting you, and only you could recognise the things he added to the journal.'

'Unless he was the one that tore the pages out. We've never found out where he was living. Maybe we were never supposed to find his additions. Maybe they're nothing more than evidence of Christian trying to be like me, reading through my journal and adding a few of his own dark thoughts, reconnecting with our childhood. And of course, the killer might not know what they found in these pages. They might simply have seen them as a source of inspiration, or instructions Christian had left behind. Work to be done, perhaps.'

Katie nods as she checks the side mirror for the hundredth time, reassuring herself that they're not being followed. She might have taken the battery out of the phone Sam gave her, but Katie doesn't doubt the woman could find another way to track their movements. Her instincts have told her not to trust the new-found freedom Sam was allowing them. Was this as a result of Nathan's attack? Had that been proof enough of their innocence? It's a nice thought, but she's far from convinced.

Nathan directs Richard to a road that runs alongside the river in Isleworth, and Katie recognises it as being just two streets away from where Nathan had lived when they were working together. She'd visited there plenty of times, but only gone in on a couple of occasions, mostly arriving very early or very late to pick him up and follow a lead. On the opposite side of the river Katie can see a group of young mothers keeping a close eye on their children as they play. She tries to ignore the lurch in her stomach and looks away.

'Follow me,' says Nathan, climbing slowly out of the car once they've parked up. Katie can see that some blood has soaked through the bandage and through his shirt. Even with the baseball cap and sunglasses that they've purchased, this would be enough to draw attention. She's pulled her long hair forward to part-cover the scars on her face as they head back along a riverside path towards Richmond, passing under the Teddington Bridge and then the railway bridge. Immediately on the other side of the bridge, Nathan turns and points towards a huge white three-storey Victorian property set well back from the river.

'That's what he was talking about,' he says. 'That's where my mum was born and raised. Whenever she walked us along here she would tell us it was her dream to return one day.'

'I know the feeling,' says Richard. 'That's why I went back to Wales, to the place of my birth. You can never really go back, though,' says the old man, sadly. 'What's done is done. What's seen cannot be unseen.'

'That's probably why my mum never tried to buy the place,' says Nathan, still staring up at the house. 'Even after she'd made her millions writing novels. It had to remain a dream, nothing more. And then, well, we all know what happened next…'

'Well, let's go and see who does own the place,' says Katie, striding down a bank of grass, over a fence and onto a long gravel drive.

It doesn't take her long to realise that it's a care home, as she approaches the back of the building and sees a line of elderly folk seated around the edge of a large room with a television on in the corner.

'Oh,' she says, as they approach. 'I don't think this is going to be much help.'

'Damn it,' says Nathan. 'I was probably wrong about what my brother was referring to.' He squeezes his eyes shut and looks up to the sky. 'Perhaps Christian knew our mum better than I did.'

They make their way slowly back to the riverbank, and Katie takes Richard's arm as they struggle up the muddy bank to find that Nathan has stopped on the pathway ahead of them. She can see the blood on his shirt has spread, and she's about to ask him if he's okay when he spins towards her, his eyes wide and burning bright.

'Napoleon!' he says.

'What about him?' asks Richard. Katie knows better than to speak. She's seen Nathan like this many times before, at a moment of connection, of revelation.

He turns back towards the river and points at a wooden fence with a gate in the middle. Just over the fence Katie can see the top of one of the houseboats. To the right of the gate is a nameplate: *Napoleon*.

'It was the name of our first pet,' says Nathan. 'It was a cat, a beautiful tabby cat, and it used to spend most of the time sleeping on my bed.' He lowers his voice and Katie isn't sure he's speaking to them at all. '*Never on Christian's bed. Could Napoleon have sensed what he was really like? Was that the start?*'

'Was what the start?' asks Katie, letting go of Richard's arm and walking towards the gate through to the houseboat.

'Napoleon disappeared. Ran off, my mum said. But the cat would never have done that. He loved us too much. Loved me too much.'

Before the gate is a small set of wooden steps, and Katie climbs to the top and stretches up on tiptoe to try and look over, but it's just too high. She tries the gate and finds it's locked.

'Can you give me a hand?' she calls to Nathan, and it's literally only one hand that he's able to offer – the broken fingers of the other remaining down by his side – along with a knee for additional support. The balance is precarious, but she gets there in the end, peering over at a tiny, single-storey houseboat. The curtains are drawn, the paint is peeling and the patch of grass leading down to the water's edge is overgrown.

'I don't think anybody has been here in a while,' she calls back to Nathan.

'I imagine for nearly a year,' he says, nodding slowly, and Katie is reminded that it has been almost that long since Nathan's twin brother ended his life.

CHAPTER EIGHTEEN

Nathan is surprised that Katie has made them wait for the rest of the team. In the old days, she would always have played by the rules, for fear that her carefully gathered evidence would become inadmissible, but the last time they'd worked together she'd been more reckless.

'Strength in numbers,' she says by way of explanation as the cars and vans arrive. Nathan knows the press will follow, and their location is almost impossible to keep from their view, with vantage points on the bridge on the other side of the river and on the river itself, if they can find a boat to use.

'I need to get in there,' he says, rattling the gate again.

'You need to wait for the warrant. We don't know for sure that it's anything to do with your brother.'

'Do you see this lock?' he says, pointing at the thick Chubb. 'It's the very same lock I used to have on the shed where I kept my bike, next to the flat where I lived, which is not more than half a mile from here at most.' He points back over her shoulder, in line with his mother's house. 'And then there's the weathervane on the roof. Quite distinctive, the cat chasing the mouse. We had exactly the same one on the roof of our family home up there.' This time he points up the hill to Richmond. 'I remember Dad risking his life to fix it. Back then I used to think he was invincible.'

'You don't have to convince me this is the place,' says Katie. 'And I'm as keen to get in there as you are, but we have to do this right. For Mike's sake.' As she says this she stares out at the river, which is flowing fast and high.

'A coincidence that he was pulled out a mile or so downriver from here?' asks Nathan, following her gaze.

Katie looks at him, eyes burning. 'You know I don't believe in those.'

When the paperwork finally arrives, the lock is broken off the gate and two armed officers are the first to go through. They call out that it's clear, although Katie could have told them the same from her brief look over the fence.

As Nathan walks up to the only door, he wonders how long his brother lived here. Wrapped up in his work most days and nights, and not wanting to bring back memories of his childhood, Nathan didn't spend long walking around the area where he lived, but there had been occasions he'd followed this path, or sat on a bench on the other side of the river. Had his brother known he was there? Had he been watching him? Given the proximity, Nathan knows there's a good chance his brother was watching a lot of the time, a suspicion that is strengthened considerably the moment Nathan walks through the door.

It's identical. Not in shape and size – Nathan's flat had been far larger – but the pictures and the decor and the television, even the bottles of wine are the same as those that he had bought. To see this leaves Nathan horribly dizzy, and he just manages to stop himself falling heavily on the arm of the sofa, the same sofa he had picked up from a charity shop. How much effort had his brother gone to, to match these items? And why?

'He wanted to be like you,' says Katie, as if reading his thoughts.

'I'd always wanted to be like him,' Nathan replies. 'Until I found out what he was really like.' He continues to move around the small space, wearing the paper shoes provided for him and trying not to touch any more than he has to. For more than half an hour he and Katie consider every item, and watch as the Forensics team work round them.

It's only when they're finally back outside that Nathan feels like he can properly breathe. It had seemed not only as if he had been in his brother's home, but also in his brother's mind, the darkness gripping him from the inside.

'I don't know what that's told us,' he says, managing to smile across at Richard, who has remained outside.

'You're losing your touch,' says Katie. She looks suddenly uncomfortable at this choice of words, perhaps worried he'll be sensitive about his other failings.

'Tell me,' he says, offering a smile.

'You must have noticed the dust?'

'Hardly remarkable. Christian's been gone for almost a year.'

'Did you notice the areas where there *wasn't* any dust?'

Nathan has always had a remarkable memory for places, and every inch of his brother's home is available to him, helped by the fact that it had been so similar to his own. He considers what he's seen, and only now realises that there had been places where the dust hadn't settled.

'On the side in the bathroom,' he says. 'On a shelf in the bedroom as well, I believe.'

'Which means?'

'That someone else has been inside in the last year?'

Katie nods.

'Looking for something? The missing pages of the journal?'

'Perhaps. Perhaps also looking to remove any evidence of their having been there.'

'Long-term, you mean?' says Nathan. 'No chance of that. There'll be DNA.'

'Well, maybe something specific that could help us identify them if they're not on the system. A photo, obviously, or clothes…'

Now Nathan's thinking of the gap in the wardrobe, where shirts and trousers identical to his own had been pushed along the rail on their hangers. 'You're suggesting my brother had someone living here with him?'

'Is that so impossible?'

'Given what he was doing, yes. And not just to other people. Look at what he did to himself. You're telling me somebody living with him would have accepted him changing his appearance like that, ruining his looks?'

'Somebody equally troubled might,' says Katie, her attention suddenly drawn elsewhere. Nathan follows her gaze and sees that Sam Stone has arrived. Most of those on the scene would consider her as calm and controlled as ever, wearing a pair of dark glasses despite it being overcast, but Nathan is starting to read her a little better and can see as she approaches that she is angry.

'Of course, if there was some mystery girlfriend,' says Katie, with Sam still out of earshot, 'another troubled soul, able to hide their true selves from society, perhaps even able to rise to a position of authority... I mean, it makes you wonder who the "C" was Ms Stone was calling on her mobile until about a year and a half ago.'

Nathan turns away to try and cover his gasp. Perhaps it was the tiredness, perhaps the smack to the head, or perhaps he could only ever think of his brother being alone; whatever the reason, he hadn't made the connection until Katie asked the question. Now that she has, the possibilities seem endless.

'I doubt she made a mistake giving me the phone,' says Katie, as Sam strides closer. 'She knows exactly what she's doing.'

'Did you forget to call?' asks the senior policewoman, her lips barely moving.

'Issues with the mobile you gave me,' says Katie, patting her pocket. 'Same trouble I had earlier when I tried to call you and I couldn't get an answer.'

Sam sighs loudly. 'So, what do we have here?' she asks, nodding over at the houseboat.

'The place where Christian lived,' says Nathan, staring hard at Sam to try and determine what she might be hiding. He's also trying to figure out if his brother might have had an attraction to this woman, although it wouldn't have been to how she looks, he realises that. It would most likely have been the same things that he finds intriguing: the fierce intelligence and the sense of unpredictability. 'The contents of this floating home are almost identical to those in my old flat,' he continues. 'But beyond that, we've had no startling discoveries.' He tries to keep his voice steady as he considers what they might just have uncovered.

'Well, let's leave it to Forensics then,' says Sam. 'See what they can turn up.'

'You don't want to go in?' asks Katie, surprised. 'This could be key.'

'I trust in my colleagues to fill me in on anything significant,' says Sam, starting to walk away. Nathan might have expected Sam to go inside if she'd wanted another defence against her DNA being found in there. Despite the suit, contamination could in theory (and in desperation) occur. But then they're still quite a way off demanding that a senior officer be tested against their discoveries.

Nathan can see the blond-haired man who had driven him and Sam to the school where Steven Fish was found deep in conversation with one of the PCs who had been first on the scene.

'Where have you been?' Katie calls after Sam.

Sam turns back and slips off her glasses. 'You know, I'd heard there might be some insubordination issues, but I could never have imagined it would be quite this bad.'

'Where have you been, ma'am?' Katie asks again.

'If you must know, reading up on Steven Fish. I still believe he's central to this case. Not only was he the first victim, but as far as I'm aware he's not directly connected to any of us. DS Peters was your friend. The victim at the hospital was a friend of Dr Evans.' She stops and looks up at Nathan. 'And obviously there's Christian Radley.'

'You never had a run-in with Fish, then,' asks Katie, 'in your work bringing down drugs gangs?'

'Fish had one charge of possession. A small amount, possibly for personal use. I don't bother with the petty stuff. I look at the big players, guys like Carl Watkins, that you were so keen to mention earlier.'

Nathan can see Katie's fists bunch at her sides. He knows how much it had hurt her to fail to pin two murders on Carl Watkins. The man was a scumbag, no question about it, but he had also proven himself a master at avoiding the law. It was an open secret that he'd made his huge fortune from hurting people and selling drugs, primarily heroin, but he'd never served a day behind bars, always seeming one step ahead of the police. 'Has he resurfaced, then?' asks Katie. 'Last I heard he'd performed a disappearing act a couple of years back.'

'Still a no-show,' says Sam, putting her glasses back on. 'And I can assure you I'm in no rush to see him again. Now, I'm going to visit Steven Fish's mother. You can join me or not, I really don't care.'

'If you want to get anything out of Wendy Fish then you're going to need us with you,' says Katie.

'What about the doctor?' asks Sam, nodding over at Richard, who's staring out at the river watching a group of swans float by.

'He's coming too,' says Nathan. 'I'm not leaving him on his own.'

'Fine,' says Sam. 'I'll organise a police escort to get you through the crowd.' She nods towards a group of people in the distance, some of who are clearly press, some just passers-by wondering what's going on. 'Put the phone on,' she says to Katie, nodding down at her pocket. 'And I'll call you when we're ready to go.'

As Nathan watches Sam walk away, Katie turns to him and answers the question he'd been about to ask.

'We need to keep her close.'

CHAPTER NINETEEN

The journey to Steven Fish's flat takes less than twenty minutes, thanks to Sam's aggressive attempts to shake off any unwanted press attention. Katie had feared there might also be a gathering at their destination, but as they pull into an empty street, she assumes the reporters have been drawn down to the discovery of Christian's houseboat. Indeed, a quick look at the mobile phone that she's reconnected tells Katie that the internet is alive with theories about what they've found down by the river, including one suggestion that Christian had been discovered alive in there, his death another elaborate hoax set up by corrupt police. Along with the craziness, there's also a lot of fact – photos of her and Nathan just minutes old, a timeline she might have drawn herself and a map showing the locations of the recent crimes.

'What do we know about the blogger who's getting the original pages?' she asks Sam. While Katie might have her suspicions about this woman, she's been in the game long enough to know she needs to consider all possibilities.

'Nothing yet,' says Sam. 'They've been clever, not registered or paid for the domain, and using a free blogging platform. But I'm sure we'll track him down soon enough.'

'Do we know the blogger's a guy?' asks Nathan.

'Fair point,' says Sam. 'He, or she, does seem to have a bit of a crush on our friend Nathan here.'

'That'll be symptomatic of the drugs they're taking,' says Nathan, with an embarrassed smile.

'You're a handsome man,' says Sam, looking up at the rear-view mirror. 'From what I've seen, you have plenty of admirers online. I've heard talk in the office, as well…'

'This isn't pertinent to the case,' says Katie, feeling her face flush, as she stares at the side of Sam's face. She doesn't know what's annoying her more. The way the senior policewoman looked at her partner, or Sam's smooth, scar-free cheeks. And then there's the crazy thought that if Sam had been with Christian, if there'd been an attraction there, then mightn't Christian's twin feel the same way? The case is her focus, the desire for revenge for Mike's death as great as ever, but Katie can't seem to suppress these thoughts.

'Everything is pertinent,' says Sam, without bothering to look across, 'until we know what's going on. Sex, lust, desire – they're all powerful motives. And you only have to read Nathan's journal to understand how those emotions can intensify into the desire to kill.'

Katie twists to look at Nathan in the back and she can see his unease. 'As I told you in the interview at the beginning, I haven't read the journal,' she says. And it's true. Even at the inquest she'd tried to block out the readings from pages of it as much as she could, for fear of knowing too much about the man she thought she loved. It was against her usual practice, against who she's always been as a person, desperate to know more, no matter the cost, but with Nathan it was different. With Nathan, she was willing to restrict her normal behaviours to protect whatever it was they had.

'What else do we know about this blogger?' asks Nathan, trying to steer the conversation back to more comfortable ground. 'Why might they have been chosen to receive the pages of the journal?'

'I understand he, or she, has previously posted stuff alleging police corruption,' says Sam, 'pointing the finger at some fairly senior figures.'

'At you?' asks Katie.

'Are we at the right place?' asks Sam, ignoring the question. Katie looks up and sees that they have arrived at Steven Fish's family home. At the age of twenty-five Steven had still been living with his mum, and Katie assures them as they climb the steps to the third floor of a ten-storey block that although it's been almost two years since her son's death, Wendy Fish will not have allowed a single thing to change.

They knock, and the front door is thrown open by Wendy. When she sees Katie and then Nathan she takes a step back, her face visibly paling.

'I suppose you think I should take that as evidence you weren't to blame?' she says to Nathan, nodding down at his broken hand.

'I did not kill your son,' says Nathan softly. 'For a long time I believed, as you must have believed, that it was my brother, but now—'

'Now it's all fucked up again,' says Wendy, shaking her head. She peers past Katie's shoulder and down at the street below. 'I hope you haven't brought the world's media with you.'

Katie wonders if Wendy might not feel disappointed that they haven't. She'd always been very quick to ignore police advice and go to the press to try and find justice for her son. Not that Katie had ever blamed her for doing so, knowing that she would have done exactly the same.

'Can we come in, please?' Katie asks.

'If you think it'll help Steven get what he deserves, you can do whatever the hell you want.' Wendy spins round and walks back into the flat, leaving the door wide open.

Down the corridor, and they enter the living room, although the room appears to be no such thing. It's become more of a shrine to the son Wendy has lost, with photos of him everywhere. Katie recognises some of them from copies in his case file.

They're offered a cup of tea and all but Sam say yes, with Richard offering to go and help in the kitchen. When they've both returned and placed the full tray on a table in the centre of the room, Wendy can't wait any longer.

'I saw you on the news,' she says, jabbing a finger at Nathan. 'Getting all emotional over the death of your friend the police-man. That never happened with Steven, did it? You ran away to Scotland without a word.'

'I'm sorry,' says Nathan, lowering his head. 'But I couldn't cope.'

'You think I could?'

'You heard my testimony,' he says. 'Your son's death was so horrific I thought it might send me over the edge.'

'And you think it didn't take me there?' says Wendy, standing up and moving to one of the photos of her son. The one she picks up shows him in his school uniform, with a mass of unkempt hair and a broad smile. Katie can't help but wonder what her and Nathan's child might have looked like at that age; at any age.

'So if your brother didn't kill Steven, then who did?'

'We don't know,' says Sam, cutting in.

'And who are *we*?' asks Wendy. 'I've had visits from half the police force telling me how sorry they are for failing to find the man that killed my son, but while you're obviously police, I have no idea who you are.'

'My name is Samantha Stone. I work for a police agency, primarily looking at organised crime.'

'Then what are you doing here?' Wendy brushes a hand carefully across the top of the photo she's still holding as if there might be dust on it. Katie is almost certain that there's none. 'My son was not part of any gang.'

'And you're absolutely sure about that?' asks Sam.

'Are you absolutely sure you want to ask that question?' says Wendy, carefully placing the photo back on the mantelpiece, as if she might need both of her hands free.

'I'm not trying to upset you,' says Sam, maintaining her usual calm. 'I just think if we're going to find the man that killed Steven then we need to stop being polite. We also need to stop tiptoeing around people's feelings.'

'You've clearly already stopped doing that,' says Wendy, looking across at Katie for support.

'How heavily was your son involved in drugs?'

Wendy's face twists in anger and confusion. 'What the hell has that got to do with anything?' She turns to Katie. 'His death had nothing to do with his past. And that wasn't even his past. It was a one-off. He told me he was helping somebody out.'

'Who?' says Sam, still not holding back.

'A friend,' says Wendy, now starting to look a little scared of Sam, who rather than taking a seat has squatted in front of her.

'A girlfriend?' asks Katie.

'I don't think so,' says Wendy. 'I'm not even sure he was interested in women in that way.'

'You never told me that!' Katie snaps in frustration.

'Because I didn't know for definite,' says Wendy, lowering her head. 'He never told me. Never trusted me.' She looks up at the largest of the photos of Steven, framed extravagantly in gold. 'A month or so back, I heard somebody talking. It's that sort of area – we're close, but people like to gossip.' She looks up briefly. 'Not to the police. They didn't know I was around, and I heard him saying Steven had been seen arm in arm with a man. I asked him if he thought Steven was gay and he said he didn't know, said he'd always thought my boy was putting on some kind of a performance.' She shakes her head. 'There was certainly truth in that.'

'Did they say what the man looked like?' asks Katie. 'The guy your son was with?'

'No. They weren't talking at all after I asked that.' It appears that Wendy isn't either, because she's shrunk back in her chair, arms wrapped around her.

'Might we have a look at your son's bedroom, Mrs Fish?' says Richard, eventually. For a moment Katie had forgotten the doctor was there, and is relieved by his presence and his calming voice.

'If you tell me who you are,' says Wendy. 'I know you're far too old to be police.'

'I'm far too old to be anything anymore,' says Richard with a disarming smile. 'But I used to be a doctor. I'm here to check Nathan's okay with his injuries.'

Then Wendy looks down at the tape around Nathan's fingers.

'Why do you think you're still alive?' she asks Nathan, making it sound like an accusation.

'I don't know,' he says. 'I think someone is playing a very cruel game.' He flicks the briefest of glances at Sam, which thankfully she doesn't seem to notice.

'Whatever they're playing, we're going to win,' says Katie.

'There's no winning with this,' says Wendy, staring at the scars on Katie's cheeks. 'You should know that.'

Steven Fish's bedroom is immaculate, in a way Katie doubts it was in the time he was alive. There's an expensive-looking laptop and some smart-looking clothes in the wardrobe, but nothing to suggest he was living a secret life. He had worked in restaurants and bars for most of the years since leaving school at sixteen, and had always aspired to being an actor. There's a photo of him standing with his arm around two friends. He'd been a good-looking guy, but not in the conventional, leading man way, with a nose that was a little too large and rather small eyes. In the photos his hair was always very carefully styled and Katie remembers standing over his body in the morgue, the pathologist holding the head back in place and trying to straighten a few tufts of hair to neaten him up. He'd looked so different then, so helpless, so young, and she'd had to turn away so as not to share her emotions with Dr Miles Parker, a man she never wanted to share anything with.

Evidence. That's what Katie has to find, and that's what she's looking for as she slowly searches the room. She spots nothing of interest, other than Nathan, who is standing in the centre of a pale green circular rug, absorbing the detail. However complicated the emotions between them, it's very simple professionally: she needs him. She takes a step across, aware that Wendy Fish has remained in the doorway, making sure that no objects are taken. She's watching Sam closest of all, who has opened all the drawers and even got down on her knees to look under the bed. She must know that the room has been thoroughly searched before. She must know that it's been searched by Katie.

Katie is looking for something new. There's no change that she can identify since the last time, but Wendy's speculation about her son's sexuality has changed her focus. His mobile phone had been found with the body, and there were no unusual photos and no record of calls made that were in any way suspicious. What was suspicious was how little that number had been used, which had led Katie to believe that he was living another life, fooling the police, even fooling his mother.

Lost in thought, Katie doesn't notice that Wendy Fish has moved alongside her until she speaks.

'Do you have any children?' she asks.

'No,' says Katie.

'Then you don't understand what it's like to lose one,' says Wendy, lowering her head.

You have no idea what I've lost. Katie bites her lip and nods in sympathy.

'He was such a proud boy,' says Wendy, stepping forward to a wall on which there are several photos of people Katie recognises from interview. There's also an acceptance letter to a drama school.

'He didn't go?' Katie asks, already knowing the answer, part of her thoroughness with the investigation.

'He got distracted,' says Wendy, lifting the framed letter from the wall. 'But he hadn't given up. In fact, after the drugs thing I think he found new focus, because more than once I caught him with this.' She lifts the frame. 'Dreaming, I bet, about all those amazing roles he was going to play. And how much money he was going to make. Money to take us out of here.'

Katie starts to think about Steven's sexuality again, about a role he was already playing for his mum and his friends. Then, as Wendy is about to replace the picture, she catches a glimpse of something on the back.

'Might I have a look?' she asks.

Wendy reluctantly hands the frame over.

Katie turns it over and sees that something has been scratched into the back. It's a large C above a twisted line with 'x's along it.

Katie suddenly feels a hand reaching past her and grabbing the frame. She thinks it's Wendy, but when she turns she can see that it's Sam. She can also see the shock on her face.

'What is it?' asks Katie.

Sam looks at her, eyes wide and unblinking. Then she breathes out slowly and transforms back into the controlled Sam. 'I must have been mistaken.'

'C,' says Katie, pulling out the phone that Sam had given her. 'You're not mistaken.'

'It's not Christian,' Sam says, quickly.

'Are you sure about that?' says Katie, moving in close and standing face-to-face with Sam. 'Because there was something on one of the torn-out pages of Nathan's journal, a description of an oak twisted around barbed wire with a C carved in the bark.'

Sam spins to stare at Nathan, her mask of control slipping again.

'The words were written by Christian,' says Katie.

'Then we need to go,' says Sam.

'Why?' asks Wendy. 'What's this about? What have you found?'

'We will call you as soon as we have anything,' says Sam, already moving towards the door.

'I promise,' says Katie, reaching out and squeezing Wendy's arm before rushing after Sam with Nathan and Richard, not wanting to fall too far behind.

CHAPTER TWENTY

'I shouldn't be taking you with me,' says Sam, as they sit in the outside lane, passing traffic as if they've got the blue lights going. There is no light, and no siren, and something is telling Nathan this is not strictly police business. 'But I need your help.' Her voice breaks, the first time Nathan has heard it do so. 'And I'm not sure I can go through with this alone.'

'Are you going to tell us what's going on?' asks Katie.

Sam is gripping the steering wheel tightly, her chest rapidly rising and falling. 'I know... I think I've always known, but then there's always a chance I'm wrong.' Nathan's never seen her like this before, and the fear in her voice is starting to scare him. 'Let's just wait till we get there. It will be easier to explain.'

There takes them another thirty minutes, and it's well out of London. In fact, the location they arrive at feels so remote, Nathan finds it hard to believe they're within thirty minutes of anywhere. Despite the excitement and the doubt and the fear he can sense in the car, he's enjoying being out in the countryside again. The return to London has been far too intense, for any number of reasons, and he feels like he's breathing a little more easily now.

'This is it,' says Sam, turning off the engine of the car. She nods towards a field on their right. Nathan stares up at a huge twisted oak tree on top of a hill, then follows a heavily rutted track down to a farmhouse, the broken-down walls of which are overgrown. They are not overlooked in any direction, and there's no evidence of anyone else having come here recently.

Sam takes a deep breath and turns towards them. 'I think there's a body here,' she says. 'And I need you to help me find it.'

'Whose body?' asks Katie.

'I'm not sure. There are several possibilities.'

'You still don't trust us enough to share?' asks Katie, not hiding her frustration. 'Because I'm happy to start sharing the doubts I have about you.'

'You're right to have them,' says Sam, pushing her door open. 'But I think things will become clear if we find what we're looking for.' She climbs out and starts walking up the hill towards the twisted oak. It takes a while for Katie, Nathan and Richard to catch up, the old doctor in particular struggling on the heavily rutted ground. He's holding onto Katie, no doubt to avoid hurting Nathan's back. He's most likely also noticed the way that Nathan has started to slip into something approaching a trance, absorbing as much detail as he can of his surroundings. In some ways, this is unlike any murder scene Nathan's ever been to – far too picturesque – but he's certainly been to places like this in his mind and committed some terrible imaginary crimes in among the trees.

Sam has stopped by the twisted oak and is leaning awkwardly over the barbed wire fence that is digging into the tree. Nathan can't make out what she's looking at and knows there's no chance of him doing the same in his current condition, but Katie reaches over from the other side and takes a photo on her mobile for Nathan to look at. A small 'C' has been carved into the bark. On the other side of the fence it's thick woodland and bramble and there's no chance you'd find this mark unless you'd been shown it, or put it there yourself.

'Christian?' asks Nathan.

Sam shakes her head. 'Carl.'

'Carl *Watkins*?' says Katie, with the aggression that always seems to flood her when she uses that name. 'Is that the same "C" that was on your phone?'

This time Sam nods. 'This goes no further,' she says, looking to her left and right, as if there's a chance she might be overheard. 'Carl was helping me, feeding me information. He was a brilliant source. He was one of the reasons I was able to climb so high, so quickly. We tried to avoid using phones, and so we decided on places where it was safe to meet. This was one of them. We were supposed to meet here two years ago, but he didn't show up. No word. No explanation. I tried to phone him, but there was nothing. Nobody seemed to know anything about his whereabouts. And then they found Steven Fish's body.'

'What was the link between him and Steven Fish?' asks Nathan, pointing at the tree and the hidden mark. 'There clearly was one.'

Katie nods. 'And despite what you've told us, I think you've known there was one all along.'

'He'd mentioned him,' says Sam, running a hand through her hair, which for the first time is starting to look a little tangled. 'Just once, in passing. I couldn't remember the context, but once Fish's body was found I remembered the name.'

Nathan can see that Katie has her eyes closed, the way she always used to when she was thinking hard, pulling things together. 'Was Carl Watkins the friend that Wendy Fish talked about, the man that Steven was keeping the drugs for?'

'I doubt it,' says Sam. 'Carl didn't deal in quantities like that.'

'Was he the man who was seen arm in arm with Steven?' asks Nathan. 'That would certainly explain why nobody was talking, if they'd recognised him and were scared of retribution.'

'Carl wasn't gay,' says Sam.

'You knew him that well?' asks Katie.

'I had to know if I could trust him,' says Sam, with a level gaze. 'That meant I needed to know all aspects of his life.'

'You've told us what Carl did for you,' says Katie, her eyes now wide open. 'What was it you did for him?'

Sam takes a tiny step backwards, and at the same time Nathan shuffles forward. He thinks he knows what's coming, and he wants to be there to stop Katie doing anything stupid. 'I gave him a little information,' says Sam. 'Helped to keep him out of prison.'

'For fucking murder!' says Katie as Nathan reaches out to grab her sleeve and pull her back, sending a sudden bolt of pain through his shoulder that makes him cry out. Katie stops in her tracks to check he's okay.

'Is this what we're looking for here?' asks Nathan, taking the chance to distract Katie further from her hostile intentions. 'Is it Carl Watkins' body, or one of his victims, that we're going to find?'

'Like I already said to you, I knew his business,' says Sam, forcefully. 'He wasn't a murderer.' Sam lifts a hand to cut off Katie's attempt to jump in. 'But he would have done what was necessary if his life was in danger.' She stops and considers the landscape around them, breathing in deep through her nose. 'And maybe that's what happened here. If somebody had found out about our planned meeting, then Carl might have killed them and then gone to ground.'

'You make it sound like that's what you desperately hope happened,' says Katie. She hasn't backed up, and is now just a few inches from Sam's face.

'Of course I do,' says Sam. 'I broke at least three drugs rings with his help.'

'While helping *him* grow his own empire.'

'Judge me all you like,' says Sam, 'but you don't know the reality of that world.'

'I don't know the reality?' says Katie, and again Nathan is moving forward, ready to put up with the pain in his shoulder if he can hold Katie back. 'The doctor and I here know the fucking reality! Only yesterday we—' She cuts herself off, and Nathan can see her face flush. She hadn't mentioned Ben Peters by name, and Nathan knows there's every chance Sam will be able to trace the address they'd been to through the phone, but Katie's embarrassed by her mistake. It's something she would never have done when he'd worked with her before, more evidence perhaps of how she's losing control of her emotions.

'My point,' says Sam, continuing as if she has no interest in what Katie had been saying, 'is that there are no winners in the war against drugs. If you take somebody down, there's always somebody else to take their place. All you can do is make them work hard to maintain the status quo, and to make them doubt themselves and each other.'

'That's certainly what's happening here,' says Katie, with a frown which highlights the scars on her cheeks. 'I still don't think you're telling us everything.'

'That's because I don't know everything,' says Sam. 'I don't know, for example, how this connects to Nathan's journal and to Christian and to whoever killed DS Peters and Dr Nigel Hartham. Perhaps it is the Thomas Shaw that Richard talked about earlier.' She gestures over at the doctor, who had been digging the toe of his brogue into a puddle, seemingly wanting to be anywhere but part of this conversation, but is now looking up. 'Although that's not a name Carl Watkins ever mentioned, or that came up in my research.'

'We need evidence,' says Nathan. 'We need to call in the team and see if there is a body here.'

'No,' says Sam, quickly. 'Nobody else. I can't have anyone else knowing about my link to Carl.'

'I bet you can't,' says Katie. 'That's the sort of connection that would ruin the career it had made.'

'This isn't just about me. If it becomes public knowledge, how I gathered my intelligence, then plenty of good policemen are going down, and even more criminals are going to have their convictions quashed. Is that what you want?'

'I'm not talking about public knowledge. I'm talking about our team.'

'The same team who leaked Nathan's journal?' Sam asks.

'Let's just see what we can find,' says Katie, turning and striding off down the hill. She's angry, but she's not reaching for her phone. Instead, she has her head held high, just as Nathan had on the way up, looking for signs, looking for answers.

CHAPTER TWENTY-ONE

While Nathan remains at the top of the hill, Katie begins her search at the bottom. It's been raining so heavily that by the time she's back at the road they arrived on, her shoes are covered by two inches of mud, and she's almost slipped over several times. She stands, hands on hips, surveying the area. In reality, there's little chance of them finding a body like this. They need to call in a team, some cadaver dogs, maybe even a helicopter with a camera to reveal disturbed earth, but Sam has insisted they do it alone. Katie's not sure she believes Sam's story. At the very best, she doesn't think she's being given all of that story.

Sam is standing somewhere between Katie and Nathan, halfway up the hill, as if she's trying to watch them both. Her attention is not, it seems to Katie, on finding Carl Watkins, and again Katie wonders if she knows more than she's telling, that perhaps they're wasting their time. Katie has been outsmarted by Watkins before, and she wonders if the same thing has happened to Sam. Or perhaps Sam is hoping to distract them from the truth. But then she'd had no reason to mention Watkins' name at all, other than to stop them thinking that the 'C' was for Christian.

On the two or three occasions they had met, Carl Watkins had been a charming man. This had been in spite of the contempt and anger Katie was showing for him, glaring across the table in an interview room. He had always seemed to be in control, as if he fully anticipated that he was going to be walking out of the police station without being charged. Katie had never had a doubt in the world that Watkins was guilty, but there had never been enough evidence to charge him. Now she's looking for evidence of his death, something she had dreamt about plenty of times. Not perhaps at her hands, but at the hands of one of his rivals. Might that be who they're looking for here? But then what's the connection to Mike? Mike had put a few drug dealers away over the years. Could that be motivation enough for them to take his life in such a terrible way?

As she works through the possibilities, Katie is fully aware of her surroundings, looking for the kind of details that she would have fed to Nathan, back when his gift for vividly imagining himself committing the crimes was still intact. Part of her is pleased he can't do it anymore. It might give him a chance to get away from the work that had obsessed both of them for almost a decade, and put his brilliant mind to another use. But there's also part of her that can't help but be frustrated. Nathan had helped her to solve so many crimes. She had played her own part, built her own reputation for gathering evidence, for logical deduction, but at the end of it all they were a team. Her climbing the ranks was as closely tied to Nathan as Sam's was to Carl Watkins.

Carl Watkins. Repeating that name in her mind, she grimaces as memories flash up of the man and of the damage he had done to so many people – people like Ben Peters. It doesn't matter that he might have assisted Sam in bringing down a few of his rivals, Katie seems to be able to summon up only one emotion for Carl Watkins, and if he's somewhere near here, his body rotting away, then she for one will not be shedding a tear.

'I have it!' When she hears the cry, Katie starts running, ignoring the brambles tearing at her legs and arms, and the mud, which threatens to send her crashing down with every stride. By the time she's out of the abandoned farmhouse and staring back at the hill, she can see that Nathan and Sam are running too, and Katie realises the voice she had heard calling out was Richard's.

He's standing about ten metres from the car, pointing down into the ditch. Katie arrives before the others, and following the old man's shaking arm she sees what she at first mistakes for the bright white cap of an enormous mushroom. It's only when she's caught her breath and found her focus that she's able to figure out what it really is. The top of a human skull.

'Is it him?' says Sam, slipping as she arrives besides them and crashing onto her knees. After she's looked into the ditch she doesn't get up.

'How did you know?' Sam asks Richard with an accusatory glare. 'I've been here, lots of times, and I've never…'

'Calm down,' says Katie. 'You can see that recent rainfall has washed away the bank. You probably wouldn't have seen anything two days ago.'

'Unless it wasn't the rain,' says Nathan.

'What are you talking about?' asks Sam.

'The pages of the journal. The clue that brought us here. There was no need to share that, unless they wanted us to come here. And if they wanted us to come here, then they probably wanted us to find the body.'

'We're calling this in,' says Katie, pulling out her mobile.

'But we don't know who it is,' says Sam, panic in her eyes. 'It might not be Carl. If he's not dead, just in hiding, then sharing this discovery will be putting his life at even greater risk.'

'Your *crime*,' Katie emphasises the word, 'can be kept secret for now. But as Nathan just pointed out, we can easily explain how we ended up here. We can say you followed Carl here one day on surveillance and later saw the markings on the tree. You've proved very adept so far at telling stories to cover up what you've been doing, so I'm sure you'll be able to come up with something convincing.'

'Crime?' says Richard, looking down at the skull.

'Not that crime,' says Katie, before looking back at Sam. 'At least, I don't think so.'

CHAPTER TWENTY-TWO

BLOG: Seeing Red

The anonymous, unfiltered truth about crime and the criminal justice system.

If you're reading this, please stop now. I can't take it anymore. I know I've always talked about wanting to be involved and how cool it would be to play a part in a murder investigation, but this is different. It's like I'm to blame in some way. I mean, I know what people will say, that all I have to do is stop posting the material, but surely that wouldn't help, or *save*, anybody.

Whoever this killer is knows who I am, or rather, knows how to reach me. Nobody is supposed to know that. I've worked hard for my anonymity. I don't mind admitting I'm scared. If I've offended you in any way, then I'm really sorry. If I'm just a random choice, then please, I'm begging you, pick on someone else.

Jesus, look at what you've got me writing. I should stop. I should also quit with the drugs. I reckon they're making me paranoid. I've already got up three times to check my front door is locked. And there's no way I'm going out anywhere tonight.

Something new has just dropped into my inbox. It's a video. Fuck, how do you know? How do you know to get in contact when I'm in the middle of writing something new? Are you watching me? Have I been hacked?

No, no, no. I have to stop. I really am getting paranoid. I'm no threat to you. I have no idea who you are and I very much doubt you know who I am. All I need to do is shut up and share the video you sent me. For the rest of you out there, in case it doesn't download, or you crash the site, which, given the phenomenal interest in this case is increasingly likely, here's the briefest description. It shows Nathan and Katie standing at the bottom of a hill with the senior policewoman who was with Nathan when he was attacked at the school the other day, and the doctor, who I believe lived with them in Wales. They're all staring down into a ditch. I don't know where they are. But I have a horrible feeling I know what they've just found.

CHAPTER TWENTY-THREE

'Someone was watching us,' says Katie, staring down at a series of footprints leading away along the side of a field to woodland in the distance. A team with dogs has already been out, but they've come back with nothing, the trail seeming to end just a few hundred yards away.

'Do we know for sure it was the killer?' asks Sam.

'You read the blogger's latest post,' says Nathan. 'Who else could have sent the video to them of us standing down there?' He gestures down the hill, back towards the car, which has now been surrounded by several others and a couple of Forensics vehicles. 'And would an innocent passer-by, not that this is the sort of place anyone just passes through, have bothered covering their tracks by doing this?' He holds up an evidence bag containing the remains of a mobile phone, crushed into the tiniest pieces.

'We might still be able to identify where that came from,' says Katie.

'I doubt it,' says Sam. 'I'd put money on it being pay as you go and print-free.'

'Or maybe it'll just have the same prints as the person who was living on Christian's houseboat with him,' says Katie. Nathan can see she's staring at Sam. 'Someone who knows they're not on our systems.'

'You think Christian wasn't living alone?' says Sam. 'Why haven't you told me this before?'

Katie glances back at the place where they'd found the body. 'We're not really the ones who've been holding back until now, are we?'

'You think it was a woman?' asks Sam.

'We had wondered if it was you,' says Nathan, 'what with all the calls to "C" on your phone.'

'I worked with Carl Watkins to further my career. How on earth could being with Christian have achieved the same outcome?'

'I believe that, in addition to breaking a few drugs rings, you were also involved in the solving of at least two murder cases,' says Katie. 'Perhaps Christian was able to help you in the way that Nathan has helped me.'

Sam scoffs. 'And you think I just overlooked the murders Christian had committed?'

'You did for Carl,' says Katie.

'That's not the same,' Sam protests. 'They weren't to fulfil some sick urge, they were business. I had to let his crimes go to keep him onside.'

'And that makes it acceptable?' asks Nathan.

'He didn't commit them himself.'

'Just gave the order,' says Katie. 'Just like his heroin has indirectly killed hundreds. You're right, it's so much more acceptable.'

An uncomfortable silence settles over the group and they return to looking around the area. They've already taken photos with Sam's phone, the same phone they'd watched the blogger's video on, of the point of discovery, and they've also taken their own video of the rest of the expanse of dense woodland surrounding them.

'The helicopter will be here soon,' says Sam. 'If they're hiding out there, we'll get them.'

Nathan carefully hovers one of his boots next to the nearest footprint they'd found. About a size eight had been the initial assessment, although there's something about the downward pressure within the print that's making Nathan wonder if they're not being misled again.

'At least the footprint and the video make you look innocent,' says Katie, scowling at Sam.

'That's because I *am* innocent.' Her shoulders seem to sag a little as she looks back down the hill where they found the skull. 'I had nothing to gain from killing Carl.'

'If that is Carl. If it wasn't somebody who found out about the two of you, somebody you needed to keep quiet.'

Sam shakes her head. 'We were very careful. Nobody knew about us.'

'Christian's addition to Nathan's journal suggests otherwise,' says Katie.

'Nobody ever followed me here. I took all the precautions.'

'What, about Watkins?' asks Katie. 'Might he have known Christian? Might he have used him, the way he so evidently used you, maybe got him to do a bit of his dirty work?'

'No way he kept that from me.'

'And if there was someone living with Christian, a woman perhaps, could they have got behind his defences?' asks Katie. '*Like you did with Watkins?*'

Sam closes her eyes and remains still for a moment. Nathan wonders if she's searching through her memories for something to say, or already has all the information and is double-checking what she's willing to reveal. He, like Katie, doesn't believe they've had the full story from Sam. 'He was distracted,' she says, finally. 'At the end. There was something troubling him. In fact, he was scared. Scared like I'd never seen him before.'

'He didn't trust you enough to tell you what it was?' asks Katie.

'We had no secrets,' says Sam, quickly.

'Might it have been the murder of Steven Fish?' asks Nathan. 'You said yourself that there was a connection. And if he'd heard about the brutal killing of Fish...'

'He'd heard,' says Sam. 'I asked him about it, and he didn't seem that bothered.'

'People can feign disinterest,' says Nathan, watching the policewoman closely.

Sam seems aware that she's being watched, and a broad smile spreads across her face. 'Ah, yes, I'd forgotten about your acting skills, Mr Radley. RADA, no less. Although your greatest performance was convincing your partner that your criminal urges weren't taking hold.'

'Let's stick with this case for now,' says Nathan, not rising to the bait. 'I'm interested in the relationship between Carl Watkins and Steven Fish.'

'There was no relationship,' Sam snaps back.

'I see,' says Nathan, believing that there was. 'And yet Carl did mention him a couple of times.'

'He mentioned you two more than a couple of times,' says Sam. 'And never favourably.'

'Criminals are never fans of the police,' says Katie. 'Unless the police are working with the criminals.'

Sam sighs and casts her attention upwards, drops of rain striking her face. 'You just don't understand it, do you?'

'You're right,' says Katie. 'I don't. I don't see how helping a man like Carl Watkins helps anybody. Other than Carl Watkins.'

'Three drugs rings broken,' says Sam, holding up the appropriate number of fingers.

'Two murders unsolved,' says Katie, doing the same.

'They were not good people.'

'Whatever helps you sleep at night,' says Katie. 'I think you fell for that charm. I mean, Nathan's performances were nothing on Carl's.'

'You didn't know him. He wasn't what you think.'

'Oh, I imagine he was far worse. I only got a glimpse of his criminality when he slipped up. Or rather, when both of you slipped up.'

'I wasn't working with the devil.'

'That's exactly what you were doing. The problem is you're blind to it, even now.'

Nathan is watching the toing and froing between Sam and Katie. Katie is worryingly close to the edge again. But more worrying still is Sam. She's like a different person to the one Nathan had watched calmly walk into the interview room and hold command with Ken Stocks and Superintendent Taylor. He's sure that Katie is about to push Sam some more, to take advantage of this weakness, when the same two senior detectives come into view, having toiled up the hill.

'It looks like we've finally solved the mystery of Carl Watkins' disappearance,' says a panting Ken Stocks. He pushes up his lip on the left side and taps some bright white molars. 'Two gold teeth, just like Carl had. I'll never forget that bastard's smile as he walked away grinning from whatever we threw at him.'

Nathan glances across at Sam and, as expected, sees her pain at hearing confirmation of the victim's identity.

'No way of knowing if it's the same killer,' says Superintendent Taylor. 'Very different MO.'

'But the location was referenced in the latest page of Nathan's journal,' says Sam, pulling herself together rapidly.

'Written by Nathan?' asks Ken Stocks.

'Added later by Christian,' says Katie.

'Really?' says Stocks, looking unconvinced. 'So might Watkins be one of Christian's?'

'I don't think so,' says Nathan. 'Although I wonder how he knew about this place.'

'I was wondering how you lot did.' says Taylor, looking around.

'Surveillance,' says Sam, jumping in before any of the others have a chance. 'Carl Watkins was clearly a person of interest to my organisation, and to me in particular. I've been to this place before. I remembered the twisted oak and the barbed wire.'

'Still a bit of a stretch,' says Ken, sounding unconvinced.

'Not when you consider when Watkins was last seen,' says Sam. 'It was just before Steven Fish's death.'

'So was there a connection between them?' asks Taylor. 'I remember Fish had a minor for possession.'

'Maybe there was a link,' says Katie, glancing across at Sam. 'I'm sure it'll all come out in the end.'

'But when is that end coming?' says Stocks. 'I mean, don't get me wrong. If it's the Carl Watkinses of the world that we're digging up, then I'm in no rush, but Dr Hartham, and of course, Mike, are needing justice to be done.'

'What did Mike know?' asks Taylor. 'If there was a connection between Fish and Watkins, and Mike had doubts about Fish's death, then had he found a link? And if so, why wasn't he telling us?'

'Maybe he didn't trust you,' says Katie. 'Maybe he had doubts about people senior to him. You never know who's making deals with who.' This time Kate doesn't look across at Sam, but Nathan has no doubt where this comment was aimed.

'Do *you* trust us?' asks Ken, staring hard at Katie. 'Or have you been reading too much of that blogger's anti-police bullshit?'

'It would be interesting to know where Mike was heading on his final day,' Sam cuts in. 'After he'd seen that page from the journal.' This time it's Sam who glances across at Katie. 'Yes, I'm sure it'll all come out in the end.'

Taylor has his hat tucked in its familiar position under his arm. He's also wearing the usual worn-out look he always gets during the bigger cases. This one in particular seems to be taking its toll, more than most.

'Interesting that the blogger admitted to being on drugs,' he says. 'Because I think that drugs are right at the heart of this case. I know that Dr Hartham spent a long time working with drug addicts during his career. And your friend Dr Evans, the same.' Taylor nods down the hill and Nathan can just make out Richard, leaning against the side of a police car. Alongside him is the colleague of Sam's with the short blond hair. The two appear to be engaged in conversation. 'I understand he was the one that spotted the body, by the way.'

'He stayed back at the car, while the rest of us came up to the tree that had been referenced in the journal,' says Katie.

'Still, quite a spot for a man of his age. For a man of *any* age,' says Ken.

'You surely don't think…?'

'I don't exclude,' says Ken, looking at each of their faces in turn, 'anybody.'

'Nor do I,' says Sam. 'Interesting that you mentioned the blogger's claims of covering up crimes. Any skeletons in your closet?'

'Amazing,' says Stocks, with a shake of his head. 'You had such a reputation for self-control. Also for barely saying a word. And yet now… It's like this case is personal to you, somehow.'

'I won't go into your reputation,' says Sam, her icy stare returning. 'Although you are most certainly living up to it. But yes, this case is important to me. A young man was tortured. A good policeman is dead. A good doctor is dead.' She leans to one side to get a view of the ditch at the bottom of the hill, where a tent is being erected over the body. 'And now someone who I have invested an awful lot of time in is dead. Fuck the politics, and fuck the stats – this is where we put it all on the line.'

Ken Stocks doesn't appear to know how to counter this, and in the end he doesn't need to, because a young policeman hurries across. 'We've found some letters carved into the tree,' he reports breathlessly to the DCI.

'We know about that,' says Sam. 'I found the "C" before. Along with the twisted oak, it was what convinced me this was the place in the journal, it was why it wasn't such a *stretch*.'

'Hang on,' says Katie, stepping in front of the young police-man. 'Did you say letters?'

'That's right,' he replies, looking back to where he'd run from. 'And it wasn't on the twisted oak. We found them on the back of the next tree along.'

Nathan, Katie and Sam are instantly on the move. Sam is the first to reach the tree and she leans around, ignoring the barbed wire fence threatening to tear a hole in her shirt. 'Fresh,' she says. 'Two letters. BP.'

In all the time that Nathan has known Katie, he's never failed to be amazed by her speed of thinking in the most stressful and difficult of situations. The answer comes to him rapidly, but by the time he opens his mouth to share, Katie has already turned and is heading off down the hill at a sprint.

CHAPTER TWENTY-FOUR

Katie has never wanted to be as wrong in her life about anything as she does now, but from the moment they throw the car onto the kerb outside Ben Peters' house, she's certain this particular nightmare is about to come true. The front door is wide open, not something Ben would ever have done. He was scared of the outside world and scared of the people in it.

Sam has been asking questions all the way, but neither Katie, nor Nathan, nor Richard in the back have been answering them. She is first through the door to find out for herself, wearing latex gloves and being careful not to disturb anything, in spite of her speed. Katie wonders what Sam's thinking when she sees the state of Ben's place. There's food and possibly worse on the walls, scorch marks on the curtains and stains that might or might not be blood on the carpet. What there isn't is a body. Again, Katie feels the faintest hope that despite the initials carved into the bark and the open front door and what her gut is telling her, Ben is going to come staggering back from one of his rare trips out to buy food and drink, or to visit his dealer.

They all stand in silence for several minutes, hearing nothing more than dogs barking, cars over-revving and occasional indistinct shouting in the distance.

'Can you at least tell me what we're waiting for?' says Sam, finally.

'To be proved wrong,' says Nathan.

'But who lives here?'

'Somebody who could, in theory, connect all the crimes.' As he says this Nathan looks across at Katie, and she realises that he's seeking her permission to continue. She nods, hoping to hear confirmation that her own theories have been based on a semblance of logic. 'Richard, here, cared for Ben. Ben was troubled.' He stops and corrects himself. 'Ben *is* troubled. And in his troubles, he's turned to drugs.'

'I first saw him maybe five or six years ago,' says Dr Evans. 'Sadly I couldn't help with the psychology of his addiction. I don't think anybody had ever been able to help with that. But I was able to check on his health and provide some kind of support when he needed it.'

'Drugs have ruined his life,' says Katie, spreading her arms. 'I'm not sure if you got a chance to see their impact as part of your arrangement with Mr Watkins.'

'My sister died of a heroin overdose when I was sixteen,' says Sam. 'So I'm well aware of the damage drugs can do.'

'But I thought you told me you didn't have any siblings?' asks Nathan.

'I don't,' says Sam. 'Just like I don't have any parents. Not anymore. See how much we have in common?'

Katie stares at Sam. She wouldn't put it past her to have made the story up about her sister. She wouldn't put anything past her. But for now she's going to take it as true.

'I'm sorry,' Katie says, unable to think of anything else to say.

Sam shrugs. 'It's why I got into what I do. Why I've always needed to feel like I'm getting somewhere, doing whatever is necessary to make some progress. It's also why I felt the need to understand the *human* side of the business.' Sam's head falls forward a couple of inches, but she's soon back up straight, and has settled her gaze on Katie again. 'But enough about me. I want to know what connects this place to Carl, or to Steven Fish, or to—'

She's cut off by Katie pointing behind her shoulder. They're standing in the middle of the living room, surrounded by dirty clothes, empty bottles, even a few books that look well thumbed. Nothing is in order, nothing is in the place you would expect it to be. Other, that is, than the thing Katie is pointing at. Sam turns and sees the photo, sitting in the centre of the mantelpiece above a rusty-looking three-bar fire. Moving across and carefully lifting it with a gloved hand, Sam sees what Katie doesn't need to see. Ben and his brother looking straight at the camera. The two brothers look very different, but Katie expects Sam will still spot the truth, perhaps see it in their eyes or in their smiles.

'Why didn't I know about this?' asks Sam. 'Why didn't anyone know?'

'That's how Ben wanted it. No attention. No fuss. And no embarrassment for Mike.'

Sam nods. 'So this is where you came the other day?'

'I'm sure your phone would have told you where we'd gone.'

'I don't have time to follow everybody,' says Sam. 'There has to be an element of trust.'

Katie recalls what Ben had told her, that Mike hadn't trusted this woman at all. And she wonders if the real reason Sam hadn't bothered finding out who lived here was because she already knew.

'Did he tell you anything valuable?' asks Sam.

'No,' says Katie, looking across at Richard, who has as always remained in the background. 'He was obviously devastated by his brother's death.'

'And could that explain this?' asks Sam, gesturing towards the empty room. 'Might he have gone off? Might he have done something stupid?'

'What about the initials carved into the tree?' says Nathan.

'A coincidence?' says Sam.

'No such thing,' says Katie. 'The killer wants us to know what's going on. They've been feeding us clues. It's all been so carefully choreographed, like they know where we are at any time, like they know exactly when to—' She stops suddenly as a horrible thought rises to the surface. With a shaking hand, she reaches into her pocket and pulls out her mobile phone.

CHAPTER TWENTY-FIVE

BLOG: Seeing Red
The anonymous, unfiltered truth about crime
and the criminal justice system

Don't do drugs. That's my advice. I got a bit paranoid last time, started hearing things around the house. But there's zero chance that anyone's here. There's certainly no chance that *they* are here. I've been careful. I've been careful my whole life. Nobody knows who I am. The nutjob – *and yeah, I'm happy to call you that* – might have found a way to get in touch through the internet, but that's as far as it goes. Absolutely zero chance of me getting my neck slit, or whatever sick technique he steals from Nathan next.

And to be honest, this killer isn't worth my time, because he doesn't even have original ideas. He's not even a copycat killer, because he's copying murders that haven't even taken place, not outside of Nathan's mind. In fact, he's more like an actor, like Nathan once aspired to be, because he's being fed the lines and all he's got to do is act them out. I suppose there's a bit of casting in there, too, because he's got to choose the victims, but I'm starting to wonder if they're chosen at random, because I can't see a connection between Detective Sergeant Mike Peters and Steven Fish and Dr Nigel Hartham. Rumour is, the latest victim is Carl Watkins. Can't say I'm sad about that one. About time that bastard's past caught up with him.

My concern is for Nathan. How must he be feeling, seeing his darkest and most dangerous fantasies being carried out by someone else? Does he feel guilty? Does he think those murders wouldn't have happened if he hadn't written his journal? From what I understand, he wrote that journal to stop his own urges from taking over, getting them down on the page and out of his system.

I've been flicking through my copy of his journal – and yes, I've had a copy printed – and I've been wondering which of his fantasies I would use on the killer. *The Plagiarist!* That's what I'm going to call him, because he acts like he's some kind of proper artist, but there's nothing original about his performance. He's not even a nutjob. He's a *con*job.

I know what you're thinking: you're thinking he's going to come and get me. I've already told you, nobody knows where I am. I've also had time to think about how The Plagiarist was able to send me stuff while I was writing my blog. It wasn't because he was watching me. It's because I'm utterly predictable. I write this shit at pretty much the same time every day. It fits in well with my job – ooh, I've got you wondering what it is, haven't I? I've also got you wondering if there's anything about to come in right now. Well, as it happens… I've read a thousand of Nathan's dark dreams. But this one is different. This one has broken my heart:

I can't bear to see Dad suffering any longer. He wouldn't need to be if that doctor had done his job and spotted the cancer when he first had a chance. But this isn't about that useless bastard. There are plenty of other pages in this journal where he's getting what he deserves. No, this is about Dad, about bringing his suffering to an end.

I want it to be quick. And I don't want him to know it's me. I definitely don't want Mum or Christian to know what I've done. I think the best way is drugs. He's on so many at the moment that he might not even notice. He's also asleep for a lot of the day. If I could get past Mum, if she wasn't watching him every waking moment, holding his hand, weeping… At least she won't be looking out for me. She'll think I'm still at RADA, but I can put on an act for my academy friends and for her, pretending I'm out drinking, then driving back in the early hours. I've done it before, ignoring Dad's order to stay away. He wasn't pleased to see me. He's never been pleased when I've ignored his orders. Or maybe it was because I saw him cry.

It would have to happen in the middle of the night, anyway. That's when Mum's so worn out she can't keep awake, and when Dad's lost in his dreams or nightmares, or wherever it is that he goes when his eyes are shut and the pain seems to leave him for a short while. I want to give him too much of something, but if I do, I know Mum will only blame herself. I think what I need to do is sneak into the room and prop his body up, as if he's woken, and as if he's managed to reach for his pills. I'll drape one arm across to the other and make it look like he's injected himself, a way to bring the pain to an end. It'll look like his choice. I'm pretty sure if he had the strength it would be his choice. If he wakes when it's happening, then maybe he'll look me in the eyes and I'll know that he's trying to thank me. I'll also get a chance to tell him what I was always too scared to tell him when he was okay. That I love him.

Last words. That's what I'm worried about. What was the last thing Dad said to Mum? Have they been able to say all they wanted to? They didn't talk that much when he wasn't ill, at least not that I ever saw. But they definitely cared for each other. And needed each other. I don't reckon Dad could have coped without Mum. She was the one that got him to forget about the rules sometimes, to put down his work and have a laugh. But how's Mum going to cope? What if she can't cope?

'Watch out for your mum.' If he went now, those would be Dad's last words to me. An instruction. An order. Typical, in that

sense. But there was something in his eyes as he said it that really scared me, like he knew something I didn't. This family has secrets, I don't doubt that, but Mum and Christian are the untroubled ones, the ones I've never worried about, and so I can't think what he might have meant. Probably he just meant take care of her, which, obviously, we will. I'll do whatever I can to ease her pain. The same way I'm planning to ease his.

Enough. It's time to be honest with myself, end this relentless fantasy. There are so many murders described in this journal, and I've genuinely believed I could commit every single one of them. I may still, if my own sickness takes me over the edge, if I lose control. But this one is the exception. I can write the words, I can picture it in my mind, but I know I'm never going to be able to go through with it. Dad will die, there can be no doubt about that anymore, but I will play no part. My sickness cannot help with his.

CHAPTER TWENTY-SIX

'You must remember that?' says Katie, holding the phone up towards Nathan. He nods slowly, the emptiness he'd felt inside back then returning. He'd only needed to see a couple of words for it all to come back. It was from towards the end of the journal, perhaps only a week or so before both of his parents were dead and he stopped writing it. He'd still managed to fill maybe a dozen pages in that final week, the dark thoughts pouring out of him along with the tears. The writing had been catharsis; the writing had been a desperate attempt to cope.

'Is that how we're going to find Ben?' asks Katie, her eyes wide with fear.

'I think so,' says Nathan. 'The question is, where?'

'What about the rest of the page?' says Katie, pressing the phone up to his face and trying to scroll down. 'Is there a location on there? There must be something.' She stops suddenly and her eyes go even wider as her face pales, revealing the lines of scars down her cheeks.

'Oh, God,' she says, turning and running for the stairs. Nathan tries to keep close behind her, but such sudden movement pulls at his shoulder injury, leaving him momentarily frozen and breathless. When he has caught up with Katie and with Sam, he finds her wrenching open a door off the passage upstairs. He'd looked there before, finding an airing cupboard full of bags of rubbish, but Katie is pulling them out of the way. And then she steps back, a hand rising to her mouth.

When he stretches painfully across to get a view inside, Nathan can only make out Ben's face. It's enough to know that Ben is dead.

'I should have known,' says Katie, falling towards Nathan. He catches her, at some expense to him, but he's not about to let go. 'This is where he would hide. When it was all too hard. When the world outside his house and the voices inside his head got too much.' She pushes back, her focus returning. 'But how did the killer know? How could they *possibly* have known what only Mike and I were aware of?'

'They tortured Mike,' says Sam. 'They could have found out that way.'

'But what's the point?' says Katie, her anger rising. 'Why Ben? He hasn't hurt anybody. He couldn't have hurt anybody.'

'Maybe he knew something,' says Sam, finally looking across at Katie. 'Maybe he told you something?'

Nathan is remembering Ben's words. He'd been uncertain, so much so that they'd dismissed the possibility, but he'd suggested that it might have been him, not his brother Mike, who had seen the woman with bobbed hair. As Nathan stares at just such a haircut on Sam, he sees movement out of the corner of his eye and, instantly recognising the danger, he's able to get across and block Katie off before she can get to Sam. He doesn't have the strength to hold her for long, but after a short struggle she steps back and looks at her fingers. Nathan can see the blood on the tips and he knows that it is his own blood, coming from the wound on his shoulder.

'Richard will help me with that,' he says, glancing down at the doctor, who is halfway up the stairs with a look of concern on his face. 'If you two want to fight, then do it away from the crime scene. There might be answers here, answers you're never going to find smacking lumps out of each other.'

'If I find you had anything to do with this…!' says Katie, jabbing a finger at Sam.

Sam looks untroubled by the threat, but Nathan senses she's having to fight to keep things under control. 'I told you what happened to my sister. I found her. I found her like…' Sam isn't looking into the airing cupboard. In fact, she doesn't seem to be looking at anything at all, her expression telling them she's drifting back to the moment of discovering her younger sister.

'Your stories seem far too convenient to me,' says Katie.

'Convenient?' says Sam, and Nathan can see that she's starting to break. There's a rage in her eyes that scares him, that reminds him of some of the psychopaths he's come up against in the past, but again he makes sure he's blocking the space between the two women.

Richard is alongside him now and peering into the cupboard.

'Oh, Ben,' he says softly. 'We fought so hard.' The misery in the old man's voice seems suddenly to calm the situation. 'Do we know for sure that he didn't do this himself?' asks the doctor. 'We know he wasn't coping well with his brother's death. He was vulnerable.' Richard glances across at Katie. 'Maybe we shouldn't have left him alone.'

'This was murder,' says Katie, looking horrified by the sugges- tion. 'Or are you suggesting they came here, found him hidden away in a cupboard and just happened to have a page describing that exact death to release to the world?'

'I'm sorry,' says Richard, lowering his head. 'I was being foolish. I just prefer to think it was Ben's choice. And that he didn't suffer too much.'

'We all wish that were the case,' says Nathan. 'And I'm sure Katie values your input as much as I do.' He gives Katie a sharp look, which she matches in return. 'There's just a little too much emotion at the moment.'

'I'm not going to offer any apology for that,' says Katie, moving towards the stairs. 'It's fuel. And it's going to fuel me finding out who did this and making them pay.' Her eyes quickly flick to

Sam. 'I may have been away for a while, but I haven't forgotten how to hunt down the truth.' As she passes Richard, she leans in. 'I'm sorry if I upset you,' she says quietly. 'And you were right.' She casts one last look back at the airing cupboard, dipping her head and perhaps offering the promise of justice that Nathan's seen her offer at so many other crime scenes. 'We shouldn't have left him alone.'

*

Nathan and Katie sit on the back doorstep of Ben's house. They can hear the press and members of the public gathered outside at the front, and all around them people are getting on with their jobs – taking photos, collecting samples, picking through the evidence of Ben's tragic life. They'd like to be working themselves, at least to feel actively involved in finding justice for the Peters brothers, but the fatigue is such for both of them that they know they'd only go stumbling into something, perhaps losing a valuable forensic clue. Richard has patched up Nathan's shoulder and Katie, too, is doing her bit to make him feel better by sitting close to him on the step and allowing him to rest his hand on hers. He can feel the tension in her body, and there's obvious anger when she glares across at Sam, who's fielding calls on the other side of the tiny, rubbish-filled garden.

'You think I was being irrational, don't you?' she says through gritted teeth. 'You think I completely lost control. But I think, given all that's happened, I'm doing pretty fucking well in keeping things together.'

'Undoubtedly,' says Nathan, giving her hand a squeeze. 'I think the only reason I'm coping is because I've managed to convince myself this isn't real, that it's just another one of my far too vivid nightmares. I keep thinking I'm going to snap out of it, wake up in a sweat back in Wales.' He wants to add *with you by my side*, but there's still an awkwardness between them.

'Why Ben?' Katie asks. 'You think he saw Sam, maybe when she was following Mike?'

'I think it's more likely Mike told his brother about a woman with bobbed hair. Either way, we don't know for sure it was Sam. And perhaps Ben's death wasn't to shut him up, but to ease his pain, an act of compassion.'

'You think that was compassionate?' asks Katie, pulling her hand away.

'If they were following my words, if they understood why I wrote them,' says Nathan, wanting to grab the hand back again, to feel that warmth. 'Maybe Ben didn't just happen to see the killer. Maybe he knew them.'

'I told you before, nobody knew Ben. Just Mike and me.'

'And Richard,' says Nathan, smiling across at the doctor, who's leaning against an old fridge. The doctor smiles back, but the smile looks as fragile as the rest of him.

'Yes, Richard,' says Katie, and Nathan can feel the tension grow.

'What?' he asks. 'What's worrying you?'

'He seemed a little too keen to have us think it was suicide.'

'He just wasn't thinking clearly,' says Nathan, convinced that Katie is doing the same. 'He couldn't see that it would have been too great a coincidence.'

'Yes, coincidence,' says Katie. 'That's my other issue. Don't you think it's strange that I became suddenly and violently sick in Wales, and had to go and fetch a doctor, the very same doctor that now seems to be involved in this case? After all, he's known three of the victims – Mike and Ben Peters and Nigel Hartham. And don't forget, Nigel Hartham had shared one of Richard's secrets.' She turns to look at Nathan, covering her mouth with her hand by pretending to be scratching her nose. 'What if there were more secrets? What if he didn't stop at letting people die on his operating table?'

'You can't seriously suspect him,' says Nathan quietly, keeping his head down. 'Besides, he was with us when Mike was killed. He was our alibi!'

'They don't know for sure when Mike was killed. Richard could have driven back from Wales…'

'And Ben?' says Nathan, looking over his shoulder and once again vividly picturing the body curled up in the corner of the cupboard.

'Richard came here,' says Katie, 'with me. He heard what Ben had to say. Heard that there might have been more he wanted to say, but couldn't remember it at the time. Maybe Mike had found out something about the doctor. Maybe that the doctor had killed Carl Watkins.'

'For what possible reason?'

'Revenge, for the damage his drugs have done. Richard worked with addicts. He was working with them at the end, when his PTSD was taking hold.'

'Steven Fish?' says Nathan. 'You honestly think a seventy-five-year-old man is going to torture and behead a young man who happened to have been caught with a small amount of drugs on him?'

'That young man was in some kind of relationship with Carl Watkins. Emotional or professional, I don't know which, but maybe he ran into Fish while hunting Watkins down.'

'And how did he do that?'

'God knows,' says Katie. 'Maybe one of his former patients, a former client of Watkins, gave him some inside knowledge. Do I have to have it all figured out?'

Nathan resists the urge to tell her he doesn't think she has any of it figured out, moving on, instead, to his next question.

'And what is Richard's connection to my brother? Do you think they were living together?'

'Is it so ridiculous? Your brother didn't have a dad. Maybe he needed a father figure. Maybe your brother sought psychiatric help and they ran into each other that way.'

Nathan tries to keep his voice calm and to remember all that Katie has been through. She can be excused a little madness herself.

'And the video taken from the top of the hill where Carl Watkins was buried? How exactly did Richard do that, when he was down at the bottom of the hill?'

'For the very same reason it doesn't clear Sam. If they were with your brother then they're not your typical loners. They might have found someone else to help them out.'

Nathan shrugs. 'I can't say I agree, but it's good to be able to talk this through.'

'Yeah,' says Katie, kicking at a tiny stone and sending it flying across the small patch of practically grass-free lawn. 'Just like old times.'

'Yeah,' says Nathan, picking at the tape on his broken fingers. He looks across at Sam. 'I do agree that we're not getting everything out of her.'

'And you saw her reaction when I questioned the story about her sister,' says Katie. 'There's anger in that woman.'

Justifiable is the word that pops into Nathan's mind, but he doesn't share it with Katie for fear of bringing her own anger back. 'Maybe this isn't like old times,' he says. 'I mean, I've lost my ability to read people's minds, and you've…' Nathan fears he's led himself into an argument, and so he's relieved to see Katie smile.

'I've clearly lost the plot.' She stares across at the elderly doctor, bending awkwardly to sniff the flower of whatever unidentified weed is growing in the corner of the garden. Katie's smile quickly vanishes. 'Maybe my instinct has gone.'

'In which case,' says Nathan, glancing over his shoulder at some white-suited forensic officers moving methodically through the house, 'we're going to have to rely on science.'

*

It's another few hours before science helps them. Nathan is slumped awkwardly in a chair in the hotel room, unable to sleep because of the pain in his shoulder. Katie is lying flat on the bed staring up at the ceiling. Richard is in the room next door, and Nathan believes he can hear the old man snoring. It's not a quiet room by any stretch, but the two of them still jolt when Katie's phone starts ringing.

'Hello?' Katie answers, putting the mobile on speaker.

'This is Miles.'

'Hello, Dr Parker,' says Katie, cautiously. Nathan knows that their relationship has become so strained over the years that he rarely calls her directly.

'I've been instructed to ask you if you know a man called Thomas Shaw.'

Katie's eyes meet Nathan's, and she gives him a look that sends a surge of excitement running through his tired, broken body.

'Why?' asks Katie.

'Because we've found a couple of DNA traces at the scene of Ben Peters' death. He's come up on the system as having previous – plenty of it, in fact. Including attempted murder.'

'That's very interesting,' says Katie. 'Does the system happen to have an address?'

As soon as Dr Parker has given it to her, she hangs up and is heading for the door, Nathan hot on her heels.

'Should we wake the doctor?' he whispers, as they step out into the corridor.

'No,' says Katie.

'What about the team?' asks Nathan, now starting to worry about the flush that's rising to Katie's face and the whites of her knuckles around the car keys she's taken from Richard in case they were called away urgently. Nathan knows her well enough to sense that she still has her suspicions about the doctor and doesn't want him going anywhere.

'You heard the call,' says Katie. 'Parker was instructed to tell me. The rest of the team must already know.'

'But did you tell them about Shaw, about the connection to Richard?'

'I must have forgotten,' says Katie, her annoyance seeming to shift instantly to horror. 'Or maybe I dismissed what Richard told us. Jeez, if I hadn't, if we'd gone straight to Shaw's place, then might we have saved Ben?' Without waiting for an answer, she barges open the door to the stairs. 'Let's not waste another second.'

CHAPTER TWENTY-SEVEN

It's getting late in the day now, approaching half past eight and already dark. The lights and the engine of the car are off and Katie and Richard are parked in front of the house they've come to see. It's a large detached property with a white Range Rover in the drive. Katie can't help but notice how different it is to Ben Peters' tiny, run-down house. During the journey over Nathan has been asking plenty of questions, but Katie has barely heard them. All she can think about is getting to this man.

She's across the road, through the gates and up the drive in a matter of seconds, not caring that Nathan is still struggling to get out of the car. After she's pressed the doorbell, she realises she should probably have taken a more cautious approach and that Shaw could easily be heading straight out the back, if he hasn't disappeared already. She's still considering this when the door is flung open.

'Who the fuck are you?' asks the man she takes to be Thomas Shaw. He's crossed a pair of heavily tattooed arms and is planted in a broad, threatening stance. His hair is cropped short and he's wearing jeans and a white T-shirt that fits tight to his gym-honed body.

Katie opens her mouth to answer, but nothing comes out. The image from the photo on the mantelpiece of Mike and Ben has suddenly formed at the front of her mind and it's all she can think about, those two brothers smiling, those two brothers dead.

'Hang on a second,' says Shaw, unfolding his big arms and jabbing a finger at the air in front of him, just inches from her face. 'I know who you are.' He's seen her scars, and she's feeling her scars, reminding her of what had happened the last time there had been any hesitation, the last time someone hadn't done what badly needed doing to a violent psychopath.

Shaw's looking down to his left. She follows his gaze and sees a gun on the table just inside the door. She gives the big man a shove in the chest and he stumbles backwards. She moves in after him. Her arms feel as light as air, ready to swing, to make contact, to inflict pain. But he's readied himself, too, and he grabs her by the hair and swings her down the corridor, sending her tumbling further into the house.

As she slams into a doorway and slips to the floor, she catches a glimpse of a large glass table in the living room. On the table are several bags of white powder and more than one syringe. When she looks back up at Shaw he's looming over her, a look in his eye that speaks not only of drug use, but also of an intense and uncontrolled rage. She knows she can match that, surpass it. She kicks out at his ankle, but it has little effect and she soon feels hands around her throat. She pulls at his fingers, but they're locked in place and she can feel the air leaving her as he lifts her up off her back and onto her knees in front of him. What hasn't left her is her desire to do this man harm, to bring an end to his life. She claws at his eyes and he lets out a high-pitched scream, but he doesn't let go. She tries to dig her thumb into the corner of his eye, but he's able to lean back from her and is out of reach, while maintaining the grip that she's now certain will kill her. She moves to raise a knee to strike him, and manages to get a fingernail to his cheek, tearing at the flesh in the same way Christian's knife tore at her cheek. Still he's not letting go.

This isn't how she pictured it. She's come close to death plenty of times before, but she'd always imagined she'd make it through to a natural end, quietly slipping away in a care home like her dad, or drifting off into a final sleep. Ever since she started to look with adult eyes at the world around her, she's had a burning desire to make things right, to find justice and reason and to fight against anything that might get in the way of that, but the fight is finally leaving her and all she can think is that she's leaving nothing behind – no child, no victory and no words of love.

Everything slows. Her final few moments. There's a calmness and a silence, despite all that's going on outside of her mind. She's drifting, drifting into nothingness, no heaven, no hell, just an end to thought, to pain, to feeling.

And then a bang. Her senses have been fading fast, but there can be no doubt about that explosion of noise. Nor can there be any doubt about the change in the expression on Thomas Shaw's face. Suddenly his eyes widen, then a moment later his fingers loosen and he falls forward. Katie falls under him, desperately trying to draw breath. He's blocked her view of everything, and it's only after she's finally managed to refill her lungs that she can inch herself partly out from beneath his massive form.

Nathan is standing a few feet in front of her at the entrance to the hall. He has a gun lying flat in the palm of his hand and he's staring down at that gun with an expression of total disbelief.

'It's okay,' she says with a rasp as she struggles to push Thomas Shaw off her. Shaw is gasping for breath in the same way that she is, but there's a gurgling sound, too, and she can feel the blood dripping from his mouth onto her neck. Her strength is gradually returning and she finally manages to release herself from under him. She's barely had time to rip open Shaw's T-shirt and place her hand on his wound, before the big man's breathing stops. Almost at the very same time she sees a shadow fall across them, something in the doorway blocking the security light. Katie thinks it must be Nathan, but when she looks up she sees that it is Sam.

'We have to do something,' Katie pleads, not having the time or energy to wonder what she's doing here.

'The ambulance is on its way,' says Sam.

'It's too late,' says Nathan blankly, as he continues to stare down at the gun in his hand. 'Too late.'

CHAPTER TWENTY-EIGHT

'What have I done?' says Nathan, as he rocks back and forth uncontrollably. He's slumped in the back seat of a police car, tucked around the corner from Thomas Shaw's house. *Thomas Shaw*, the name that he will carry with him for the rest of his life, along with the moment he held up the gun and pulled the trigger, which is currently playing on a loop in his mind. Nathan is in a paper suit, having had his clothes taken for forensics. He presses the injuries on his back into the seat behind and the pain is extraordinary, and yet still he pushes harder, certain it's the very least that he deserves.

'You've saved your partner's life,' says Sam. 'You've most likely also avenged the death of your friend, Mike Peters.'

'I could have stopped him another way. I could have talked to him.'

'Not with DI Rhodes as she was. She wasn't talking to anyone.'

'You heard her,' says Nathan. 'She knocked on the door, he recognised her as police and he went for the gun, so she shoved him back.'

'I wasn't there for the first bit,' says Sam. 'But that's certainly the story you should stick to. Of course, in reality I think she would have gone for Shaw anyway. It was guaranteed from the moment she received the call from Dr Parker. And that, by the way, is why I believe Dr Parker called her directly. He hasn't admitted as much, he claims he thought it was the right thing to do given the personal nature of the case, but I think he knew she would go charging over there. I reckon he hoped she might do something reckless.'

'No way,' says Nathan. 'The two of them don't like each other, but he's not going to put her life at risk.'

'I think it might have been her career he was hoping to put at risk. He had no way of knowing that Shaw would have a gun and be doped up to the eyeballs, willing to do anything to protect the pile of drugs he had in his living room. But we could all have predicted Katie would step outside of professional lines.'

Nathan draws in a long breath and tries to regain his focus, or rather to redirect it to something other than the crime he's committed. 'Is there any connection between Shaw and Carl Watkins?'

'Not that I was ever aware of,' says Sam, losing his gaze and staring out of the window. 'But I'm starting to doubt I knew Carl as well as I thought I did.'

'So Shaw could have killed Watkins?'

'He looks to be the most obvious candidate. But then it's not clear how Carl died. There's not an awful lot of him left.'

'You went to see the body?'

'That's where I was when you were at the hotel.'

He's trying to piece things together again, build a timeline, find some sense, but everything seems to be spiralling around him. 'But then how did you get here? How did you even know to come here if Dr Parker only called us?'

Sam hesitates, her eyes narrowing, as if trying to decide whether she should tell the truth. 'I followed you,' she says eventually. 'I tracked the phone I gave to Katie. I'd just got back into town and I could see you were on the move. I hoped you might have a lead, one that you were once again not sharing with me. I came straight here.'

'And arrived just too late,' says Nathan, falling back against the seat again and losing himself in the pain.

'Do you trust your partner?' asks Sam. She asks it in such a casual way that the significance of the question doesn't hit home for Nathan at first. When it does finally register, he can do little to hide the anger in his voice.

'Of course I do. Why?'

'Because she's not in a good place at the moment. You saw that for yourself back at Ben Peters' house, when she tried to attack me. From what I understand she's not been herself since Steven Fish died and you ran off to Scotland.'

'She had a lot to think about,' says Nathan, sounding as defensive as he feels. 'Her dad was ill.'

'I know about her dad,' says Sam, in a way that makes Nathan wonder if she really does. And not just the story reported by the press, but the whole story. His suspicion is strengthened by what she says next. 'We know she's capable of unrestrained rage. But do you think she's capable of murder?'

'No,' says Nathan quickly, before realising that just half an hour ago he would have said the same of himself.

'What if she believed they were guilty of murder, maybe several murders, and yet they'd managed to get away?'

'You're talking about Carl Watkins?' Nathan makes the connection instantly. 'You think Katie killed Carl Watkins?'

'I think she wanted to. I imagine you think that, too.'

'Desire and reality are two very different things. Nobody knows that better than me.' The image of Thomas Shaw's body flashes up again in Nathan's mind, the blood spreading across his white T-shirt. 'God, this is the rubbish we had to put up with at the start of this nightmare. Now we've got to the end, have we come full circle?' He presses the heel of his palm into the centre of his forehead, then suddenly looks up. 'Unless you don't believe it's the end?' He's searching for answers in Sam's face, but she's lowered her mask again, keeping him out. 'Do you not think Shaw was guilty, after all?'

'I'm sure he killed your friend Mike Peters and his brother Ben. Scientific evidence certainly seems to support the latter.' Sam rubs her temple with the knuckle of her thumb. 'But I can't help thinking that the murder of Carl Watkins *felt* different, somehow.'

Nathan considers her words and, despite himself, is willing to accept there's truth in what Sam's saying. There had been something different about the Watkins murder, a different intensity of emotion on the part of the killer, perhaps. But what about Katie? He had been away in Scotland. Katie had been back in London, and by all accounts had been losing control, drinking and sleeping around. He knows only too well how much she had hated Carl Watkins for escaping justice time and again and how much she wanted to see him punished for his crimes. Might she have taken that next step, the one he had considered himself on many occasions?

'Have you ever killed anyone?' he asks Sam.

She faces him, taking her time before answering. 'I've thought about it. I've dreamt about it. Perhaps not as vividly as you, but there was plenty of intent. And I've done things that I'm not proud of to get to the truth, things that some would consider morally questionable. But no – no, I have never taken a life.'

Nathan looks at his hands again, rubbing at the palm with his thumb as if it might be dirty. He wants to go back to the hotel and scrub his whole body, to rid himself of several layers of skin on the outside, in the hope that it might help the churning mess on the inside.

'That's not to say I never will,' Sam continues, turning away. 'In fact, in the right circumstances I would definitely kill.'

'Protecting someone you love?' asks Nathan, thinking of the sight of Katie having the life squeezed out of her by Thomas Shaw.

'Or avenging them,' says Sam, quietly, wrapping her hands around the steering wheel.

*

It's the following day before interviews have been completed and Katie and Nathan have a chance to talk. And yet when it comes down to it, Nathan feels like he can't talk, not about the man that he has killed and not about Carl Watkins, the man he so desperately hopes Katie hasn't killed.

'But you're doing all right?' she asks him, placing a hand on his arm. They're sitting in a borrowed, unmarked police car, parked up down a dead-end street where they can't be seen.

'I don't think it's sunk in yet,' he says. 'It's something I'd always imagined doing. Then it was an impossibility. And now...'

'He deserved it,' says Katie sharply. 'That's what you have to remember.'

'Still,' says Nathan, 'it would have been good to have a chance to talk to him, to find out why.'

'That'll come out soon enough, when they've been over his house and through his past.' Katie tips her head to one side and adds hesitantly, 'Could your brother have been gay?'

'My brother could have been anything,' answers Nathan, truthfully. 'And he absolutely could have kept it hidden from me.'

'Well, if he was gay, then perhaps that's a link to Steven Fish.'

'And Carl Watkins?'

'I know Sam said she didn't know of a link between Shaw and Watkins, but there were a lot of drugs at Shaw's house. And he was clearly making a good living somehow. I'm sure if we dig around...'

Now it's Nathan's turn to hesitate. 'But the Carl Watkins murder felt different to me. Did it to you?'

Katie looks at him, clearly trying to figure out where he's hoping to take this conversation.

'I haven't had a chance to consider the evidence,' she says. 'All I've seen is the top of his skull. Have we even had it confirmed a hundred per cent that it's him? I mean, I know Stocks talked about the gold teeth, but Watkins was always the most slippery of characters. I'm sure he's capable of faking his own death.'

Nathan stares back at Katie, considering Sam's earlier words about his partner. It feels like a betrayal to even consider the accusation that she might have taken Carl's life, but there's comfort there, too, he can't deny it. Nor can he deny the reason for that comfort. His brother, his twin, had said it himself, had talked about the desire to feel less alone. He and Katie could be killers together. The very thing that Christian had wished for himself.

'Sam has gone to see what's left of the body. She seems happy to accept it's Watkins.'

'And yet I'm still not happy to accept that woman's view on anything,' says Katie. 'Certainly not on Carl Watkins.'

'Well, even if it is him, we don't have anything to link it to the murders of Mike and Dr Hartham. I mean, we have no reference in the journal, not that we know of. We do have the link to the murder of Steven Fish, who, coincidentally or not, was killed just before Watkins disappeared.' Nathan swallows hard and measures his words. 'Maybe Watkins was killed as revenge for Fish. Maybe whoever took Watkins' life mistakenly believed he was responsible. After all, he had got away with two murders before.'

Nathan considers the timeline. Fish had died, Nathan had run, Katie had started to go off the rails. He'd always believed it was purely down to his leaving and her dad's illness, but might it also have been guilt?

He shakes his head and hears himself saying *no*.

'No what?' asks Katie. 'What are you thinking?'

'It's nonsense,' he says. 'I'm overcomplicating this. There's only one killer for Watkins, Hartham, Mark and Ben. It's Thomas Shaw.'

Katie lifts a hand to her neck where the bruises are starting to show. 'I bear the evidence of how crazy he was.'

'But why do you think he attacked me?' asks Nathan, lifting his broken hand. 'And yet didn't kill me?'

'Now that *does* feel different,' says Katie. 'And according to Dr Parker, your wound doesn't quite match those on the backs of Mike and Steven Fish.'

'I'm not sure I trust anything he says anymore.' Nathan hesitates, wondering if it's wise to share another of Sam Stone's accusations. 'Sam thinks Parker phoned you because he knew you'd rush over to the Shaw property, and he hoped you'd do something stupid.'

'And Sam might be right on this occasion. Parker's loathing for me is getting beyond a joke. We need to watch him.'

Nathan nods and runs his good hand through his hair, wondering if there's anyone he trusts anymore. He looks hard at Katie and finds his answer. He will not doubt her. She could not hide her guilt from him.

'We need to watch everybody,' he says. 'And everybody will be watching me. Can you imagine the press coverage this is going to get?' He can; he can picture the headlines very clearly. For so long they've painted him as a killer, and now he's proved them right.

'Forget the press. We just need to focus on the job.'

'I doubt I'm going to be able to do any investigating for a while. There'll be another inquest. At the very best I'll be suspended.'

'Taylor and Stocks will pull a few strings. Maybe Sam Stone will, too. You'll be back on the team soon enough.'

'Yeah, maybe.' He's not convinced. He's not convinced he wants to be back looking for killers, not now that he only needs to look in the mirror. He knows there's a difference, can rationalise the intent and the need to act, but still…

'I don't suppose I could drop you off at the hotel?' he asks, realising he needs time and space to think things through. 'Richard can drive you if you need to go anywhere.'

'Where are you going?'

'Somewhere to try and get my head straight.'

'Fine,' says Katie, starting up the engine. 'I've got plenty to try and get my head around, too.'

CHAPTER TWENTY-NINE

BLOG: Seeing Red
The anonymous, unfiltered truth about crime
and the criminal justice system

The relief is overwhelming. The moment I heard they'd got the guy and that he was dead, I don't mind admitting I had a little cry. It's not that I felt in any kind of danger – once the paranoia of the drugs had worn off – but it's been a lot of pressure being a spokesman for The Plagiarist. I see the papers have started to use my nickname for Thomas Shaw. I guess that means I'm having the last laugh.

There are still questions, though, connections that haven't yet been made. Why, for example, was Nathan attacked but left alive? Was it purely because he taunted Shaw when he spoke to the press? Was it because he then went back to the place where Steven Fish was killed? Was it because Shaw had some kind of connection with Nathan's brother, Christian? I mean, obviously there was a connection, because Shaw had the torn-out pages from the journal, the very pages he's been sending to me, but I don't know if he just found them somewhere – perhaps at the houseboat that people are saying belonged to Christian – or whether there was some kind of relationship between them. Maybe he just hurt Nathan because Nathan is friends with Dr Evans.

I didn't know who Richard Evans was until the journos dragged out that old court case. I knew he'd been in Wales with Katie and

Nathan, and I guessed he might have had a link to Mike Peters'
brother Ben, but I had no idea he'd been charged with negligence.
Sounds like he got away with it, too, or rather the hospital did,
putting an old guy in the front line who clearly wasn't up to it.
That's not to say Thomas Shaw should have sought his own justice
for the death of his dad, but I lost my dad coming up for two
years ago, and I know how much it hurts.

Ben Peters. There's someone else I didn't know about. There's
somebody that no one in the world knew about, from what I'm
hearing. He only ever left his house for food and drugs. Not
that I'm criticising. I don't exactly get out much, other than to
go to work.

Speaking of work, I have to admit it's been good being there
during the day and hearing all my colleagues talking about The
Plagiarist – they've been using that name, too! – and even about
my blog, never knowing that it was written by me. I'm pretty
good at pretending, you see. It's what's kept me out of trouble
over the years, writing things that the authorities don't want to
hear. Knowing things that I probably shouldn't.

I guess I was the perfect choice for Thomas Shaw. He knew
I'd give you the unedited truth, unlike the police, who I bet are
already trying to work out the best version of that truth to give
you. Central to that will be how they deal with Sam Stone. I've
done my research, I know about the drugs rings she broke to rise
within the National Crime Agency. I also know she, like Katie
Rhodes, like all the police, never managed to get Carl Watkins.
There's plenty more to her story, I bet you. But I also bet you're
never going to hear it.

I'm worried about Nathan. I was worried for him before, when
I heard his testimony in court, when I heard about his attempts
to take his own life so that he would never take anybody else's.
And now that's happened. He's done what he's always feared he
would. He has killed somebody. From the speculation in the

press, I understand it was totally justified. He was protecting Katie, and that's good, that's great, that's hopefully a sign that things are defrosting between the two of them, because there's also been speculation that things have been strained. But I can only imagine how Nathan's suffering at the moment, coming to terms with being a killer.

I just hope that Nathan doesn't do anything stupid. I feel like I've been through so much with him, watching him suffer, watching him struggle against himself, and I really couldn't bear it if he gave up now. So if you're reading this, Nathan, stay strong. And if you're a colleague of his and you get a chance, do please keep an eye on him.

CHAPTER THIRTY

Nathan has his feet pressed together, as if standing to attention, and there's certainly that kind of stress in his body. He has his hands behind his back, the good hand playing with the tape on the bad hand, pulling at the fingers, teasing the pain. He's cold, although he knows it's not the only reason that he's started to shiver.

He can picture the body under the ground in front of him. A skeleton by now, stripped of everything that had made his father look real: the eyes, the mouth, the muscles, the hair; although he knows that the hair had gone before death, a sign of the fight against the illness that had taken his life away. He thinks of the page from his journal so recently shared with the world. Would it have been better if he had been able to help his dad slip away? It wouldn't, as it turned out, have made more than a couple of weeks' difference to his dad, but it could have taught Nathan an important lesson, about how it feels to take a life, and how he never wants to do it again.

He turns to his mother's grave just a few feet away. Her headstone is covered in flowers and kind words, left by those who loved her books. But there are also things left by those who blame her for what Christian did, those unable to believe she was blind to the monster that her son was becoming, accusing her of being complicit in some way. The only comfort he takes from her suicide is that she didn't have to see where her son's darkness would lead. Unless she'd somehow known all along. Unless that had been the real reason she couldn't continue.

Nathan is alone in the churchyard among the graves. Most of these poor souls will have died of natural causes, some in accidents, and some will have ended things themselves. There's even a chance that one or two will have lost their lives as the result of a crime. How many people are still suffering from his brother's actions? And how many will now suffer as a result of what *he* has done? Words cannot describe how he feels about what he did to Thomas Shaw.

'I killed a man,' he hears himself saying out loud, as he stares down at the headstone bearing his mother's name. 'Thomas Shaw,' he adds. 'I killed him to protect Katie, to defend the woman I love...' He takes a step back and looks around him. It's getting late, and the trees surrounding the graveyard are full of life, birds coming home to roost. 'But what about the others I've hurt? Thomas Shaw has a mum. What must she be going through right now? She was probably blind to his faults. The way I hope you were blind to mine and Christian's. And no matter the reason, no matter the justification, she'll blame me for his death. The way I can't help but blame you for doing what you did.' He can picture his mum slumped over the table in the kitchen, with the empty bottle of pills in front of her. Even now when he pictures that scene, there's a part of him certain that if he reaches out and shakes her he can bring her back. But he only needs to look down to see the grave, to see the name, to feel the reality.

'Maybe I should be blamed. I didn't have to shoot Thomas Shaw. I could have knocked him out. The problem is, I didn't want to hesitate.' Nathan does exactly that, drawing in a deep breath before moving on to the real reason he came to talk to his mum. 'I hesitated before,' he says, softly. 'I couldn't end Christian's life. He was part of me. He was part of you.' Nathan's eyes are badly blurred now, and he can't even make out the name on the headstone, or the dates of birth and death, far too close together. 'But it came at a cost.' Nathan holds his own stomach, as he'd seen Katie do so many times in Wales. He'd always thought it was because of the wound that his brother had inflicted; now he knows how little he'd understood of what she had been through. 'I cannot have a family,' he says, so softly that the words barely leave his lips. 'I cannot be the parent that you were.' He looks across at his dad's grave. A tough man, a frequently distant man, but always fair and supportive. 'That you both were.' He turns his gaze skywards, staring up at the encroaching dark. 'All I have is myself now.'

Several crows are startled in the field on the far side of the cemetery and they let out a series of low craws. He stares through the gloom, but sees no other movement. Looking back at the graves, he considers the feeling that's growing within him. He's not alone here. Someone is watching. He assumes it's the press. He'd done all he could to shake off any possible tails, but perhaps someone had put two and two together and figured he would come here. Nathan feels the desire to shout out, to scream at them to leave him alone, but they would only see it as more evidence of his madness.

He scans the treeline, glaring instead. There's no flash of late-evening light on a lens, no face peering out from behind a wall. If they are out there then they're hiding from him, in the same way he desperately wants to hide from them. For so many years he had managed to remain anonymous, working behind the scenes to earn the successes that Katie's bosses often took the credit for. How he wishes he could return to that simple and rewarding life, but to dream of that possibility, and to believe it might one day happen, is something beyond even his imagination.

The longer he stands staring out of the graveyard, out at the world of the living, the greater the fear building inside of Nathan. What if it's not the press watching him? He's thinking of the last time he'd been watched, at the place where Carl Watkins' body had been found. They'd discovered size eight prints at the top of the hill and Thomas Shaw had worn size eights, but the pressure of the feet hadn't seemed evenly distributed. Were they there to mislead? Were those prints the first steps leading him towards Thomas Shaw? Had he been tricked? Had he been used? And if so, why are they still hanging around? What the hell do they want from him now?

CHAPTER THIRTY-ONE

'What are you worried about?' asks Sam, as they pull up outside the address given to them for the mother of Thomas Shaw.

Katie doesn't know where to begin. First, they shouldn't be here, or anywhere near here; they should be letting the poor woman grieve, rather than searching for answers to questions that can wait. Katie's always pushed too hard for the truth, but increasingly she can see that she's being outdone by Sam. Worse still, Katie is growing concerned that the truth isn't what Sam is searching for. On the contrary, Katie's instinct is telling her that her superior is doing what she can to prevent elements of the truth coming out.

'This isn't right,' says Katie, quietly.

'Stay in the car if you want,' says Sam.

'Is it even necessary? I thought you were all about science, and so far science is telling us that Thomas Shaw killed Ben Peters. That being the case, Shaw is most likely responsible for the other crimes.'

'"Most likely" isn't science,' says Sam. 'Science is accuracy. Science is the eradication of doubt.'

'Fine,' says Katie, realising that's exactly what she wants, too, certainly with regard to Carl Watkins. She looks across at Richard, who has tucked himself in the corner of the back seat, out of view of the house. 'I take it you're not coming in?' she asks him.

'I can't have her see me,' he says. 'And I don't want to see her. I killed her husband.'

'You didn't *save* her husband,' says Katie. 'There's a big difference.'

'No there isn't,' says Richard. 'I'm also responsible in part for the death of Ben and Mike and Nigel Hartham. If not for that day in A&E twenty years ago, they would most likely still be here.'

Katie is about to try and ease the doctor's conscience again when Sam cuts in. 'And what about Carl Watkins?' she says. 'Do you blame yourself for that?'

'I suppose,' says Richard, curling himself up even tighter. 'Although I'd never even heard of the guy until a day or so ago, so his death can't have been intended to hurt me.'

'No,' says Sam, throwing open her door, climbing out and then slamming it shut. 'It can't.'

Katie is soon following Sam up the path to a property every bit as flash as Thomas Shaw's, with almost identical shiny white cars in the drive. Katie finds the similarity uncomfortable. Even approaching a front door makes her feel strange, reminding her of the last time, of the face of Shaw on the other side, just seconds from what could so easily have been her death. And when the door is opened Katie sees that face, or at least familial traces of it, with eyes as wide as those that had stared into hers as he gripped her neck.

'Oh Jesus, no!' says a deeply tanned woman with bleached-blonde hair who Katie takes to be mid to late sixties. Tears have washed mascara down her cheeks and she keeps gasping for air. 'This cannot be happening. You cannot be here.'

'You know who we are?' asks Sam.

'Hers is one of the only faces I see now,' says Vicky, jabbing an unlit cigarette at Katie. 'Every time I turn on the telly, it's there. Her and that murdering bastard.' She looks over their shoulders, clearly searching for Nathan, with a sudden anger. Then it just as quickly passes, her features folding in grief once again. 'And the face of my boy.'

'Your son's death was… tragic,' says Katie, struggling more than she ever has before to find the right words, 'but I'm sure you've been told the events leading up to it.'

'I know what I've been told,' says Vicky with another flash of anger. 'But there's no way my son would have had a gun by the door. Or all those drugs they were talking about. He was no saint, of course, far from it, but he was trying, and…' She lifts a shaking hand and squeezes the bridge of her nose as if to stem the flow of tears. 'He was succeeding.'

'Can we come inside?' asks Sam, glancing over her shoulder. Katie is also aware that the press might be around. In fact, she's amazed that they're not. There are neighbours watching, though, some from behind curtains, some peering over hedges, and it won't be long before what they've seen has been shared on the internet.

Vicky shakes her head in seeming disbelief at the stupidity of the question. Then she seems to see something through the tears and leans forward to consider Sam more closely. 'Where do I know you from?'

'Most likely the news as well.' Sam shows her identification. 'I'd like to hear why we're wrong about Thomas.'

'As if you'd listen. You lot want this neatly tidied up.'

'What I want is justice for my friends,' says Katie, hearing her voice rise. 'Ben and Mike Peters.'

'Now there's something he definitely didn't do!' says Vicky, with a high-pitched shout, close to hysteria. 'Absolutely no way he could have hurt anybody.'

'He was charged with attempted murder before,' says Sam.

'Wrongly accused,' says Vicky. 'And acquitted.'

'He was also going to kill me,' says Katie, turning her attention to her hands. She can't stop thinking of what she'd done with those hands, scratching at Shaw's cheeks, digging her thumb into the corner of his eye. She might even still have a trace of his skin under her nails, the steaming showers having failed to remove all evidence of that night.

'Because he was scared!' says Vicky.

'Of what?' asks Sam.

'I don't know,' says Vicky, lifting a hand to her mouth, a sign perhaps that she'd let something past her lips that she wishes she hadn't. 'He had a lot to lose.'

'What did he do for a job?' asks Sam. 'I mean, he clearly had money. Might it have come from drugs?'

'Of course not. He didn't need to sell that shit. Most of his money came from the same place this money came from.' She gestures towards a rather garish-looking vase and a gold-framed mirror. 'Paying me for what they did to Thomas's dad. Or rather, what they didn't do.' She crumples again, a wail emerging, as if the news of her husband's death has only just been broken to her. It takes a moment for her to speak again and Katie and Sam give her time. 'I know what the inquest said, I had to swallow that shit for months, but the truth is that geriatric doctor killed him.'

Katie fights the urge to look over her shoulder at the car where they might just be able to make out Richard moving around in the back seat.

'It really would be better if we could go inside,' she says. 'If you truly believe that your son was innocent, then I want to hear it. If you know about me, then you must know that I'm not scared of the truth. I'm not seeking to cover anything up. I'm not seeking to protect anyone.' Katie lifts a hand to her neck, running her fingers over the bruises left by Thomas Shaw's vice-like grip. 'I just want justice.'

Vicky looks at her long and hard, only breaking that look to suck in a shaky breath.

'You know, the crazy thing,' she says eventually, 'is that when I read about what you'd been through with the Cartoonist and with some of your other cases, I remember wishing you'd helped me with getting justice for my husband. I know you wouldn't have quit.'

'Nor will I here,' Katie says again. 'Not until we have the truth.'

Vicky wipes her cheek, nods and turns to walk down the hall behind her, taking the first right. Katie and Sam follow close behind and arrive at a brightly furnished living room, with almost as many framed photos of family members as they'd seen at Wendy Fish's flat. Although this time Katie doesn't doubt that here, the frames that look silver are the real deal. She moves across to them and picks up a photo of a young boy on the shoulders of his dad, both smiling broadly.

'They were inseparable,' says Vicky, snatching the photo from Katie and carefully placing it back on the mantelpiece. 'And he was a good dad to Thomas. She rubs at her empty wedding-ring finger. 'Bloody awful husband to me, sadly, but a good dad nevertheless.'

'Can you tell me about the crash?' asks Katie.

'What possible relevance could that have to what happened to Thomas?' asks Vicky, temper rising again.

'Are you willing to dismiss the chance that it might? At the very least it shaped who your son became, the same way my mum's death shaped me.'

'She died giving birth to you, didn't she?' says Vicky, confirming to Katie once again that almost every element of her life now seems to be public knowledge. 'Do you blame the doctors?'

'I think over the years I've blamed almost everyone. Now can you tell me about your husband's accident?'

Vicky sighs and turns her attention to the floor. 'Frank was pissed. Not unusual. He was driving like an idiot. Not unusual. Only this time he didn't get away with it.'

'Nor did the young lad whose car he hit,' says Sam, standing on the other side of the room beside a cabinet bearing a large number of different bottles. A glass has been poured and the top not put back on the bottle. 'From what I understand, the victim wasn't that much older than Thomas was at the time.'

Vicky looks up at the photos again and Katie sees one that shows Thomas in his late teens, the muscles already starting to grow, along with the look of menace.

'Again, what's this got to do with the murder of my son?' says Vicky, shooting a look at Katie.

'You believe Thomas has been framed for the murders of Dr Hartham, Carl Watkins and my friends,' says Katie. 'Therefore, should we not be looking at who might have had motive to do that?'

'I've met the family of the boy my husband killed in the crash. I've said sorry plenty of times, and they've accepted my apology.'

Perhaps it's the tiredness, or the delayed effects of very nearly having the life squeezed out of her, but Katie's feeling horribly dizzy and leans heavily against the back of a plush velvet sofa. 'Any other ideas, then?' she asks.

'Maybe it was a copper,' says Vicky, before lifting a hand to her mouth. Katie thinks it a strange reaction to an accusation that doesn't seem in any way out of character for the woman.

'What makes you say that?' asks Sam, rapidly crossing the distance between them.

'No reason,' says Vicky, slipping past Sam and moving to the glass of alcohol, which she dispatches rapidly.

'Do you want justice for your son?' asks Katie. 'Because if you do, you need to tell us everything.'

Vicky pours another glass and then makes it disappear just as quickly. 'I promised,' she says quietly.

'Promised what?' asks Sam, closing the gap between them again.

'Promised *who*?' says Katie, also moving closer to Vicky. 'Promised Thomas? Because you know exactly what he'd want you to do now. He'd want you to speak out, if it might prove his innocence.' As she says this Katie is thinking of Nathan, of the harm it would do him if she proved that the man he killed was not the monster the world now believed him to be.

'It's got nothing to do with it,' says Vicky. She's slurring her words now, the alcohol taking effect. 'Completely unrelated.'

'Was he gay?' asks Sam.

'Gay?' asks Vicky, looking first shocked and then offended. 'My boy? 'Course he wasn't. He had plenty of girlfriends.'

'Any recently?' asks Katie, sensing a discomfort in Vicky again, as if she's skirting a little too close to whatever it is she's hiding. Then the older woman's eyes narrow.

'You already know, don't you?' says Vicky. 'Of course you bloody do. You want me to keep quiet, to stop your pal getting in trouble.'

Katie is about to say that she doesn't have a clue what Thomas's mother is talking about, but realises at the last moment that this would be a mistake. 'On the contrary,' she offers instead. 'We want it confirmed so that we can investigate. I told you, I'm not looking to protect anyone here.'

'I don't know who she was,' says Vicky, pouring another drink and this time filling the glass to the rim. 'But then I guess I don't need to. You'll know her name. You'll know where she works. The only thing I was told was that she's a copper.'

Rather than say it out loud, Katie draws an internal conclusion: Thomas Shaw was dating a policewoman. She looks across at Sam, whose face remains frustratingly emotionless.

'Did you ever meet this policewoman?' Katie asks.

Vicky shakes her head. 'I only knew about her at all because I heard Thomas on the phone once. And it weren't his normal phone. It was one I'd never seen before. I asked him about it and he got angry, angry like he never did.' She lowers her head. 'Not with me. Not with his mum.'

'And there's nothing else you know about her?' asks Sam. 'No name? No words you might have overheard on that call?'

Vicky considers this for a moment. The effort of concentrating seems to challenge her balance in the same way Katie's is being challenged by her tiredness.

'Nothing,' she says, finally. 'I didn't really hear the words at all. I only knew it was a girl because he was smiling in a way that I recognised. And when I asked, he said it was a policewoman. And then he said I couldn't tell anyone. Made me swear to it.' She stops and considers the photos again, releasing a long, tremulous breath, before she speaks in a voice thick with emotion. 'He wasn't himself, not at the end. He was happy, excited. But at the same time he was…' She searches for the word and it comes with a face to match. 'Scared.'

'Scared of the policewoman?' asks Katie.

'I don't know,' says Vicky. 'Maybe he was just scared she was going to get caught.' This possibility seems to take her by surprise and again she lifts a hand to her mouth. 'I shouldn't have told you. Not if it's going to get her in trouble. It wouldn't have been what Thomas wanted. Not if he loved her.'

'If she's innocent then she won't be in trouble,' says Sam, making for the door. 'Thank you for your time.'

'What about my son's justice?' says Vicky, reaching out and grabbing Katie's sleeve. Katie can tell she's on the verge of breaking down again, unable to stop the tears, or the shaking of her hand. 'You promised me.'

'I promised you the truth,' says Katie softly, looking across at the departing Sam before locking her eyes on Vicky again. 'And I will get you that.'

CHAPTER THIRTY-TWO

Nathan walks back into the hotel room and finds Katie waiting for him, sitting on a chair, peering out of the window. She jumps to her feet and rushes across, about to throw her arms around his shoulders, when he holds up his good hand to stop her.

'That'll hurt,' he says, wondering if he should have let her anyway.

'I was worried,' says Katie, retreating fast. 'I thought you might...' She glances down at his wrist, at the scars that show how close he'd come before to taking his own life.

'So worried that you followed me?' he asks.

'What do you mean? I was with Sam and Richard. We went to see...' She hesitates, and Nathan realises in an instant where she's been.

'You went to see Thomas Shaw's mother, didn't you?' He squeezes his eyes shut, fighting his imagination, but the image of a distraught mother breaks through his defences. 'How is she coping?'

'As well as can be expected.'

'I'm surprised she let you in.' Now he's looking at the bruises on Katie's neck and reminding himself that things could be far worse than they are right now. 'She must have known who you were.'

'I think she let me in *because* she knows who I am, because she knows I won't stop till I have the truth.'

'Don't we have the truth?' Nathan asks, feeling his stomach drop.

'Not the whole of it,' says Katie, quickly. 'There are things I still don't understand. I still can't see the connection, especially with Carl Watkins.' She moves across the room and lowers her voice, even though they're alone. 'Thomas Shaw had a girlfriend. A secret girlfriend that he made his mum swear she wouldn't tell anyone about.' Her eyes widen and he can see the excitement that is so often there when possibilities present themselves during a case. 'He told her that she was police.'

'I see,' says Nathan, trying to control his own emotions. 'And you think it was Sam?'

'I don't know what to think with that woman,' says Katie. 'All I know is that she's not telling us everything. Not even close.'

'Where is she now?'

'God knows. Wherever she goes to at night.'

'Let's head over to the station,' says Nathan. 'We need to look through Thomas Shaw's personal effects.'

He sees the tension return to Katie's face. 'I'm not sure we can do that, given what's happened.'

'You mean you're not sure I can, given that I killed the guy.'

'I doubt either of us can.'

'And yet you got to speak to the mother.'

'I was with Sam. She seems to be able to do anything. It's like the rules don't apply to her.'

'Or she just doesn't care about breaking them.'

'The question is, how far does that rule-breaking go?' says Katie. 'So, what is it you're hoping to find at the station?'

'It's just a feeling,' says Nathan, moving over to the window and looking down at the street below. It's dark now, although there's still a stream of traffic. Under the street lights he can see dozens of people walking along the pavement on both sides of the road. A few aren't moving, but are waiting or watching at bus stops or in doorways, some clearly talking into their mobile phones or plugged into their music. Perhaps a few are the press, and have found out where Nathan and Katie are staying. Perhaps it was the press that had followed Nathan to his parents' graves, and he'll see the photos in the morning.

But Nathan is finding it hard to convince himself. 'It's not what I'm hoping to find,' he says. 'Far from it. I think you and I have the same gut feeling.'

Katie moves across to where he's standing and places a hand lightly on his elbow. 'Even if Shaw is innocent of the other murders, it wouldn't make what you did any less justified. He was seconds away from murdering me!'

Nathan turns to look at Katie and feels a wave of emotion crash over him. He's been holding it back, pretending that he can cope, that he doesn't need her, but the truth is he's never needed her more. As if reading his thoughts, she holds out a hand and he squeezes it tightly.

'No matter how painful,' he says, holding her gaze. 'No matter the damage. We just have to find out the truth.'

CHAPTER THIRTY-THREE

After yet another sleepless night, Nathan and Katie are up early and driving to Superintendent Taylor's home. Katie can't remember having gone there before. In all honesty, she can't remember giving much thought at all to the life her boss lived outside of the office. Everything was kept professional. Everything was about work. It was simpler that way. She looks across at Nathan and tells herself the same is true with him. They're good together, but only when their very different personalities combine to solve crimes. Beyond that, she's not so sure.

'I'm amazed Taylor's agreed to do this,' says Nathan, staring out of the passenger side window.

'He's doing it because he believes in us,' says Katie. 'Despite all the arguments, he always has done. We get results.'

'Sometimes they're not the results we want,' says Nathan, looking down at his hand again, the forefinger on his good hand bending slightly. She knows what he's thinking, the pull of a finger on a trigger; he's considering how that very simple movement has taken a man's life.

'You think this might prove Thomas Shaw was innocent?' says Richard, leaning forward from the back seat. The doctor has been much more engaged since hearing about the possibility that he might not have been the motivation for the murders after all.

'With regard to the death of Mike and Ben and your friend Nigel, perhaps,' says Katie cautiously.

'And Carl Watkins?' asks the doctor.

'I believe that's different,' says Katie.

'A different killer?' asks Richard.

'We're not discounting anything at the moment,' she says, remembering the doubts she and Nathan had expressed about the doctor himself. 'Or anyone.'

They're instructed to park at the end of a long residential street. It's barely a quarter past six in the morning, but there are still affluent-looking people walking dogs and healthy people jogging by. Katie, on the other hand, feels more unhealthy than she has in a long time, her body as worn out as her mind. She's so tired that Taylor's arrival takes her by surprise. He looks like he hasn't slept either. Katie suspects that he didn't even get the chance if he was hunting down what she'd asked him for. He's wearing a black sweater and a pair of jeans. She could never have imagined him so 'dressed down', and guesses that's the point. Taylor looks suitably uncomfortable as he looks up and down the street and climbs into the back seat.

'I always knew you'd get me the sack,' he says, sinking down in the seat.

'Or another promotion,' says Katie. 'But that's not really what we're talking about here. We're talking about catching a killer.'

'I was under the impression that we already had. DCI Stocks certainly believes that, as do the Forensics lab, who've found traces of Thomas Shaw's DNA at both Ben and Mike Peters' houses.'

'They've found what they were supposed to find,' says Nathan. 'I think Shaw was meant to be the fall guy all along. They knew we'd be coming back here with Dr Evans, and they wanted us to make the connection to the death of Shaw's dad.'

'But who are *they*?' asks Taylor, with a sigh.

'You might be holding the answer to their identity in your hands,' says Katie, having turned in her seat to face him. 'If you managed to get what we asked for.'

'It wasn't easy. I got a printout. But there were hundreds of images on his phone, some of which I would rather not have seen.' He swallows noisily, then dips his head forward as another runner jogs by. 'Shaw most definitely wasn't gay.' Taylor reaches in his pocket and pulls out several sheets of A4, folded over and creased very precisely down the middle. 'In fact, there were hardly any men on there, so I very much doubt you'll find who you're looking for.'

'You're assuming we're looking for a man,' says Nathan.

The superintendent does little to hide his surprise. 'You think a woman could have committed these horrendous crimes?'

'Let's see,' says Katie, taking the papers from her boss. With all four of them huddled round, they start to go through the images taken from Thomas Shaw's phone. She's looking for the girlfriend, afraid they might see someone very familiar to them. For fear of that same person tracking them down, Katie has taken the battery out of the back of her mobile. It's a slow process, and involves looking at images that are hard to figure out at first and then hard to forget when their blurred content has been determined. Looking at the dates, it's obvious that Thomas Shaw was involved with a lot of women for a period up until six months earlier. After that point, there are no women. There appear to be no people in his life at all, other than a few shots of Shaw's smiling mum. There are plenty of grinning and brooding selfies, lots of shots of Shaw shirtless down the gym, showing off the physique he clearly worked so hard for. Katie can't help but hesitate at the shots showing his arms and hands, that so very nearly took her life. And she's certain Nathan is looking at Shaw's chest, at the point where the bullet entered.

They're about to give up when Nathan tells her to stop. It's a close-up selfie of Shaw behind the wheel of his car.

'I think the woman we're after was with him then,' says Nathan, tapping the paper lightly with his forefinger.

'Because he's driving?' asks Taylor. 'It might be his mother taking the shot.'

'I doubt his mother would make him look like that. She can be aggressive,' says Katie, remembering her own confrontation with Vicky Shaw. 'But he looks properly scared there.'

'I thought you said it was a girlfriend? Would she scare him?'

'I don't know who she was to him. I only know she was supposed to be police.'

'Yes,' says Taylor, rubbing his unshaven chin. 'I don't know what I'm more upset about – the possibility that it's true, the fact that you didn't share that information with me immediately, or that you went behind my back to speak to Shaw's mother in the first place. Her son tried to kill you, for goodness' sake!'

Katie reaches for the bruises on her throat. 'I hadn't forgotten. And Vicky Shaw hasn't forgotten that her son Thomas was the one that died instead. And yet she gave us a crucial lead, so let's worry a little less about protocol and more about where this might be taking us.'

Taylor opens his mouth, no doubt to give her the usual dressing-down, reminding her of his rank and the need for respect, but he's also recognised the truth in her words, returning his gaze to the printout. 'So, what might this photo give us?'

'We know the date the photo was taken,' says Katie. 'And we know the car it was taken in.' She points at the distinctive black piping round the white leather seats of his Range Rover.

'But we don't know the location,' says Taylor. 'He took the geotagging off his phone.'

'He was with his mum just an hour before,' says Katie, pointing at the previous photo. 'At her house. And the following image, taken half an hour later, is from his house.'

'Taken in the hallway,' says Nathan, nodding. It's a location that Katie is certain he'll never forget.

'If he wasn't alone,' Katie continues, 'then Shaw must have picked the other person up between his mum's place and his own home. We can trace possible routes, get his car on the traffic cams, maybe get lucky.'

'It's a lot of work,' says Taylor.

Katie smiles. 'When have you ever been scared of that?'

'I can't get you in on the case,' he says. 'Not after what happened. But Sam Stone might be able to.'

'No,' says Katie quickly. 'We don't want her to know.'

'Why not?'

'I don't trust her,' says Nathan.

'Any reason for that?' asks Taylor, with a look that suggests he isn't surprised. Then he lets out a little gasp. 'You don't think she's Shaw's policewoman girlfriend?'

'I don't know,' says Katie, honestly. 'I don't think she's averse to mixing with criminals. In fact, I know she's not, but I'm afraid I can't say any more about that for the moment.'

Superintendent Taylor is used to this from Katie and Nathan, but this time he appears even more deflated than normal by their unwillingness to share. Nevertheless, he gives a reluctant nod.

'I'll see what I can do with tracking Shaw's movements.'

*

While they wait for Superintendent Taylor to get back to them, Katie drives Richard back to the hotel. He tells them he too hasn't been sleeping, and she's worried for his health. She leaves him in his room and then returns to the station to see exactly how involved in the case they're allowing her to be. Nathan, on the other hand, knows he'll be stopped from going inside, so he takes the car keys and drives off, telling Katie he needs more space to think. As she watches him go, she's gripped by a sudden and unexplained anxiety and wants to rush in and call him on the mobile she's given him. But then she's not sure what she'd say. Is there something she needs to tell him? She turns towards the police station, aware of faces up at the window, watching her arrival, witnessing her fear. But she doesn't see the face that she's most afraid of, framed by a perfect bob haircut.

CHAPTER THIRTY-FOUR

Nathan arrives at his destination after more than an hour on the road. He'd remembered the route from the first time. Still, it wasn't easy to drive with his broken hand and he's taken it slowly. Now that he's arrived, he looks out at what remains an idyllic scene, with the twisted oak up on the hill and the derelict farmhouse. The only evidence of the crime that's been discovered here is a sole police car parked up on the opposite side of the road from where Carl Watkins' body was found and plenty of police tape strung around the area. Nathan moves over to the police car and the two young officers, who have already climbed out having seen him approach.

'You can't be here,' says the younger of the two men. But he has a hand placed on his arm by the other. Someone who obviously recognises Nathan.

'Well done,' says the policeman, reaching out a hand. 'You've done the world a service getting rid of that bastard.' Nathan tentatively shakes his hand. The younger officer makes as if to do the same, then withdraws it. He's keeping his distance. On the dashboard of the car Nathan can see a folded newspaper with his name in a headline. He might be seen as some kind of hero now, but most people won't have forgotten what was written before.

'Anything we can help you with?' asks the older policeman.

'I just wanted to look around,' says Nathan. 'To try and understand a bit more about the murder.'

'I don't care what Shaw's reason was for taking out this one,' says the older policeman, nodding towards where Carl Watkins' body was found. 'He had it coming to him. Mike, on the other hand…'

'You knew him?' asks Nathan, hearing the catch in the policeman's voice.

'I came to this late,' says the constable, tapping his sleeve. 'Hence the silver in the hair but not on the arms.' He glances across at his colleague. 'It's not easy trying to keep up with these youngsters, and dealing with the flak. I met Mike at a couple of social functions. He gave me advice and support just when it was needed. And sometimes a kind word is all you need.'

The policeman smiles. 'I heard what you said about Mike to the press the other day. I mean, it was brave, you confronting them like that anyway, but to acknowledge Mike's contribution to all those cases you've solved…'

'He was one of the good guys,' says Nathan, half turning away from the two men. 'And both DS Rhodes and I will miss him greatly. Now, if you don't mind.'

The policemen return to the car, no doubt watching out for press, for weirdos, for people wanting to turn the site of a known criminal's death into a shrine. Nathan slips under the police tape and walks over to the edge of the ditch. He can see where they've dug the body out, a big hole for a big man. Or at least, he had been big before he'd started to rot away. Nathan looks at the tracks in the dirt where various vehicles have come and gone. There's not much room at the end of the lane, and most will have had to reverse a long way to be able to turn and get out. When he considers his surroundings, all the places that would have been perfect to hide a body, Nathan still can't understand why the killer chose here. Early on, at least, whoever it was had been trying to hide Watkins, and if they'd shifted him twenty feet into the undergrowth he probably wouldn't have been found at all.

Perhaps they simply couldn't do it, says Nathan quietly to himself. He's picturing the size of Carl Watkins, and can't help but picture Sam, and Katie, too. If it were either of them, could they have moved the body twenty feet? Could he?

Nathan closes his eyes with his back to the police car and considers what he knows. The answer to that question is simple: not enough. He pulls out his mobile and calls the incident room at the police station, hoping to speak to Katie. He has to wait a couple of minutes before she's finally put on the line.

'Are you okay?' she asks.

'I need detail,' he says. 'Has Miles Parker taken a look at Carl Watkins yet?'

'We've got an initial assessment,' says Katie. 'Of course, as ever Parker is reluctant to commit fully, but it looks like we might have been wrong about Watkins' killer being a different MO. It actually looks like a mix of Ben Peters and Dr Nigel Hartham.'

'You mean, he was given an overdose of drugs?'

'A mix of various. Heroin, tranquillisers and others that haven't yet been determined. Injected after a smack over the head.'

'But the smack over the head didn't kill him?'

'I don't think so. It was a hard hit, but not hard enough. And he'd been carefully positioned in the hole they dug him out of. In fact, he'd been arranged like he might have been if he'd been buried. Only he was upright.'

'A bloody big hole to dig,' says Nathan, looking down at the mud in front of him.

'Yeah,' says Katie. 'They certainly took their time.'

'Anything else found at the crime scene?'

'Photos don't show much,' says Katie, and Nathan can hear that she's moved across to the wall to look at them. 'If the killing took place close to when Watkins first disappeared, not long after the death of Steven Fish, then it's hardly surprising there's not much left for us to work with.'

'Can this really be the same killer as Fish's?' asks Nathan, working through a gallery of images in his own mind. They're images he'd avoided for so long, a crime that he simply couldn't bear to consider fully. But what has he got to lose now that he has finally taken a life?

'I still think we should be considering...' Katie lowers her voice. 'Well, you know what I think.'

'Is she there?' he asks, not daring to use Sam's name, worried that she might have moved across next to Katie to listen in on the call. She always seems to be close.

'No. I haven't seen her all day. What about you? Are you alone?' asks Katie.

'No, there are two policemen here.' As he says this he recognises the feeling that's been troubling him since his arrival. It's the same feeling he'd had back at his parents' graves. There's somebody out there, watching him. Of course, as with the cemetery, there's a chance someone in the press had guessed that he or Katie might come here, but there's also a chance it's not the press at all. And then there's the photo uploaded to the blogger's page. The killer had been at this very location, watching them. He considers sharing his suspicion with Katie, but he doesn't want to worry her. He's also not entirely sure this isn't what he was hoping for, the ultimate reason for coming back.

'I have to go,' he says.

There's a pause, a moment when he thinks Katie might say something to make his heart quicken, and maybe think again about the risk he's taking, but in the end all she offers is, 'Keep in touch.'

He feels the urge to say something more himself, as if the final words of their call might be important, but instead he hangs up.

He's thinking about the coldness that's developed between him and Katie as he stares down into the ditch, trying to figure out the emotions of a killer and what they were thinking as they brought an object down on the back of Carl Watkins' head. Dr Nigel Hartham's skull had been mashed to a pulp. Had that been with a different weapon? Or from a different motivation? And were drugs used because of who Watkins had been? Were they his drugs? Heroin would suggest as much. Or was the mix used because it meant that he would suffer less?

Nathan's thoughts return to his brother. If they were right that Christian had shared his life with someone, at least for a while, then what kind of person might that have been? It could easily have been a guy. It could have been Steven Fish. But Nathan is reminded of the houseboat, and just how much his brother had wanted to be like him. Wouldn't he have wanted a partner who looked like his own? Who did the same sort of job? In support of this is the evidence of Vicky Shaw. Her son had a new girlfriend, a woman he'd told her worked for the police, a woman Thomas Shaw was scared of. Might Christian and Watkins and Shaw have been seeing the same woman?

Sam. He keeps coming back to Sam. She's impossible to read, but not impossible to like. There's something about how closed she is that's drawn him in. Would his brother also have been attracted to that? Or was it the side of Sam that she's keeping hidden from Nathan what caught Christian's eye? She has so much control, but also the potential to lose that control completely. And she has no moral boundaries, not when it comes to Carl Watkins.

Nathan returns his focus to that very person, to a man whose avoidance of justice due had so angered Katie. He tries to picture his partner with some kind of bat, seeking out justice. It's not such a stretch. But then would she have held back at the strike? He looks down into the hole Watkins had been found in, and the darkness at the bottom seems to soak into Nathan. It's the place of burial, but not the point of attack. Where might that point of attack have been? How could a man as clever and careful as Carl Watkins have been lured out here and then clubbed over the head?

Nathan starts to walk, wanting to be away from the view of the police car, where he's sure they're watching him, judging him. He starts to climb the hill towards the twisted oak. He looks down to see if the mud from his previous visit is still on his boots, forgetting for a moment that he's been given a whole new outfit, that everything has changed since then. His other boots were covered in Thomas Shaw's blood. As were his other trousers. And when he looks hard enough at the boots and trousers he's wearing now – all brand new – he's certain he can still make out those bloodstains.

He passes the first tree with Ben Peters' initials carved on the other side, then the big oak with the 'C' for Carl Watkins. He keeps walking, right up to the top of the hill and over, continuing down the side of the farmer's field where they'd found the footprints, size eight, from whoever had been watching them last time around. Might they have come from the blond-haired man who had driven the two of them halfway to the school, then disappeared, only to appear again after they'd been attacked? Did Sam have an accomplice? Might Shaw have been her accomplice? Had she hung back, hoping that Katie or Nathan would attack him, silencing the only man who could identify her?

When he's walked for almost a mile, and he's well out of sight of the policemen, surrounded on all sides by dark woodland, Nathan stops and finally accepts what it is that he's doing. He hasn't come here to find things. He's come here to be found.

He lets his arms hang loosely by his sides and closes his eyes, just as he would have done when looking to find his way into a killer's mind. And that's the intention here, not to make that connection – he knows he can't do that anymore – but to give the appearance of making it. If he can play the part, if he can convince whoever is watching him that he's found something, that he's understood, then perhaps they will come out from wherever they are hiding. He has no weapon. He has no defence. And yet still he's happy to play this game. Is it a form of suicide? Is it a form of madness? Is it a desperate need to know the truth about the man he has killed?

Impotent. That's how Nathan feels, now he can't make the connection, now he can't use the gift that had given him his identity for so many years. He thinks back to the night that it had been lost to him, another night he had felt impotent. He had proved to his brother that he wasn't a killer when he'd failed to bring a metal bar down on his head, failed to protect the woman he loved. That single moment had cost him so much. In refusing to destroy the only family he had left, he had destroyed any chance of having his own family in the future.

'Family,' he says, quietly, his fingers twitching. The word has always carried such a weight of feeling, and even more so now.

His eyes squeezed shut, he tries to focus on his performance. He's supposed to be in a trance-like state, drifting into another person's mind, then playing out the crime in hideous detail. He's reminded of the smile that had spread across his face as he'd stood looking at the body of Steven Fish. He's not smiling now, not as himself or as the killer. The killer took no pleasure in the murder of Carl Watkins. He knows that much. There was rage and hate, but there was also confusion and restraint compared to the murders of Steven Fish and Nigel Hartham, perhaps even the same confusion and restraint that Nathan had felt standing over his brother with the metal bar raised above his head.

Nathan positions himself on the dirt track facing back down the hill, imagining himself standing behind the muscular figure of Carl Watkins. He flexes the fingers on his good hand, the right hand, the same hand that will bring a rounded object down on the back of Watkins' skull. And when he stops trying, when he simply allows his imagination to take over, he can feel that object, feel the weight of it, feel the intent. Way back at the beginning, when he'd first found himself losing his grip on his own reality and seemingly drifting into another's, he'd pulled himself back, petrified of where it might take him. Ten years on and he doesn't flinch, just relaxes his shoulders and lets go.

I can't do this. If I do this, then there will be nothing left. And he's waiting for me. He's willing to talk to me. Perhaps words will take us where we need to go. But then it didn't work before. There were only lies. I can't bear to hear any more of those. And look at him, look at the way he's standing. He knows I'm here, but he hasn't even bothered to turn around and face me. He's rejecting me. Again.

I have to do this. This is who I am. This will prove who I am, prove my independence. I don't need him. I've never needed him.

That didn't feel right. I've done this before, loved this before, but that was not the same. Steven Fish. Steven Fish meant nothing to me. He died only because of what he meant to Carl. With him it was easy, natural, fun. This is… This is… At least I hit him hard enough to knock him out. But he's not dead. There was too much tension in my arms, too much happening in that single second of contact. It was the past, the present and the future all coming together.

Oh, God! It's only now I'm able to stand over him that I can see what he was looking at, staring down at. I thought he was rejecting me, but he was looking at the hole, the hole I had spent so long digging. And he must have known what it was for. And yet he didn't move. Did he think he deserved this?

He does deserve this! And I can't stop now. If I let him live, then everything is over for me. And I'm not ready to give up yet. I'm still young. I'm still fit. But can I hit him again? Harder? Hard enough?

Drugs. Drugs are the answer. They're what brought us here. They're what's ruined everything. He has some with him. For me? To get rid of me? No. No, I don't want to believe that. I won't believe that. But I will use those drugs. And he won't feel a thing. He'll just drift away.

Nathan is back in an instant, his eyes wide, gasping for air as if he's been underwater for a long time. He hadn't expected to go there. He hadn't expected to be able to make that connection, but now that he has, he can see what's happened. *He* is a killer now. He had doubted it before. He had proved himself incapable. But Thomas Shaw has changed all that. And what has he learned? There's something important there. Something key. But it's frustratingly just beyond his grasp for now. He doesn't move, not an inch, for fear that it will take him away from where he was before, from that understanding. And he closes his eyes again, longing to return. But he's distracted by a sound from behind. He's been away from reality too long, and only now remembers his initial plan. He had come up here to bring somebody out of hiding. He had come here to be attacked.

The hands grab him before he has a chance to move, one round his neck, one pressed across his mouth. At first he wonders if they're trying to keep him quiet, to prevent him shouting out to the policemen down the hill. But before he can dismiss that as a ridiculous thought, with their car being more than a mile away, he smells the chemicals and feels the soft cloth on his lips and realises he's heading back down into darkness.

CHAPTER THIRTY-FIVE

'I can't get hold of him,' says Katie, fighting the urge to fling the mobile across the room in frustration. 'I'm going to have to go down there.'

'Down where?'

Katie spins round to see Sam entering the room.

'Where have you been?' asks Katie.

'I'll take that as "do you mind if I ask where have you been, ma'am?" If you must know, I've been investigating potential links between Carl Watkins' former suppliers and the cocaine found at Thomas Shaw's house.'

'Let me guess – there's a match.'

Sam raises an eyebrow. 'You seem surprisingly disappointed.'

Katie sighs and looks across at Superintendent Taylor. He's just come off several phone calls himself, many of which she's certain will have been showering his team with praise for solving a multiple murder, including that of Mike Peters, a serving police officer. She hasn't seen him so happy in a long time. One of the main reasons she hasn't yet shared her doubts.

'I'm just tired,' she says. 'And concerned about where Nathan has gone.'

'You think he might have done something stupid?' asks Sam.

'No,' says Katie, quickly. 'He just had a few lingering questions about the case.'

'And where did he go with these lingering questions?'

'Where Carl Watkins was found.'

'I see,' says Sam, with the faintest trace of unease, as she moves across to consider photos of that very scene. Although not, Katie notes, the photos of Watkins' exhumed skeleton.

A junior detective enters the room, her face a little flushed. 'Sorry, sir, and ma'am, ma'am,' she says, nodding at Sam, Superintendent Taylor and Katie, 'but I've just had a call from the two officers who were watching the location where Carl Watkins was discovered. They said that Nathan Radley had arrived to do some work.' The detective looks at Katie again. 'I'm sure you were already aware of his being there. It's just that he went up over the hill more than two hours ago and he hasn't yet come back to his car.'

'Tell them to get out there and look for him!' says Katie. 'Ring in instantly if they find him. We'll be there as soon as we can.'

'I'll drive,' says Sam, heading for the door, with Katie following close behind. The senior policewoman turns to look at Katie as they half walk, half run down the corridor. 'What do you think this means?'

'I don't know,' says Katie, considering Sam's blank expression again. 'But I have my suspicions.'

They arrive in less than half an hour, having weaved through the traffic with the sirens blaring. There'd been no lights and no traffic for the last few miles, just a near collision with an overly wide tractor and a scrape down the side of a hawthorn hedge.

Two policemen are standing at the top of the hill and Katie slips and slides in the mud as she runs up to talk to them. It reminds her of the hills she'd run up in Wales with Nathan. It reminds her that she could not bear to lose him.

'Any luck?' she asks, panting.

'We were just about to phone,' says one of them. 'We found this,' he walks them a couple of hundred yards ahead, close to the point where Katie had found the footprints and the broken mobile before. There are now more footprints and another phone,

not broken, a phone Katie recognises as the one she had given
Nathan, the one she had spoken to him on just an hour before.
The older policeman then gestures ahead at some flattened grass
and two intermittent parallel grooves in the mud.

'They stop a short distance into the woods over there,' he says,
pointing towards a dark mass of trees to their right. Katie starts
walking, following the lines herself. They lead her deep into the
wood. Sam has taken her time to catch up, but is alongside her
now, looking around.

'Looks like he was dragged here.'

'Yes,' says Katie. She doesn't make eye contact with Sam, focusing
instead on the footprints that have accompanied the drag marks.
They're not the size eights they'd seen before. They're smaller than
that, but slightly bigger than Katie's size four. Katie glances behind
Sam and can see she's left a virtual match to these new prints as she's
walked up to join them, but Katie keeps this to herself.

'Where next?' asks Sam. 'We never followed up on the possible
sighting before, did we, not after our attention was drawn to the
bottom of the hill.'

'No, we didn't,' says Katie, quietly. She's started moving again,
heading for an area where a little more sunlight is being allowed
through the canopy. She soon comes to a pile of logs, not freshly
cut, but probably from trees felled within the previous year. Next
to the logs is a poorly defined track, heavily rutted, but with
obvious new tyre markings. Katie and Sam follow the track for
half a mile until they come to tarmac road. There are no cars
passing in either direction, but it's well maintained, and from a
rough approximation of their position, Katie is reasonably sure
it leads back to the main road.

'You did well to find this,' says Sam, blankly.

'What's that supposed to mean?' Katie snaps back.

Sam folds her arms and takes a moment before speaking,
as if measuring her words carefully. The way Katie might in an

interview room, before going in hard. 'It's no secret you wanted Carl dead.'

'Whereas it was a secret that you and Carl were working together. Perhaps a secret he wasn't willing to keep. Or maybe he just betrayed you.'

Sam's arms are folded tighter still. 'I didn't kill Carl Watkins.'

Katie faces up to Sam. She's standing barely a metre away. The two women are a similar height and build, but only one is wearing an expression of rage. 'I don't give a fuck about Carl Watkins! The only thing I care about is finding Nathan. And if I discover that you had anything to do with Nathan's disappearance…' She's closed the gap and raised her voice, but Sam hasn't retreated.

'You're insane,' says Sam.

'Quite possibly,' says Katie. Nathan's disappearance has pushed her over the edge. She doesn't feel she can control her temper anymore. She certainly can't control her words. If this were an interview room, her boss would most likely have thrown her out by now, but there's nobody around to stop her here. 'Mike Peters doubted you. He told Ben Peters that just before he died.'

'And who told you that?' asks Sam, unruffled by the accusations. 'Would that be the oh-so-reliable witness, Ben Peters?'

'Don't you dare,' says Katie, the thumping at her temples seeming to urge her forward, to quit with the interrogation and launch the attack.

'I dare, because I'm still thinking rationally,' says Sam. 'You, clearly, are not. Why would I want to hurt Nathan? He's been helping me with the case, with the only thing *I* care about.' For the first time a trace of emotion colours Sam's voice, and Katie takes a breath and a moment to consider what this might mean. Was Sam's relationship with Carl Watkins more than just professional? And if so, what might she do to find out about his disappearance?

Suddenly Katie can see how alike she and Sam are. More than that; she can *feel* how similar they are. There is nothing Katie won't do to find Nathan. *Nothing.* Katie lifts a hand and draws in a breath as if about to ask a question before suddenly jumping forward. She takes Sam by the neck, twisting her round. From her instant reaction she can tell that Sam is strong, but Katie is strong, too, strong from running up and down hills, powered by her motivation. She has Sam's arm up behind her back in less than a second and lifts it upwards till she hears her groan.

'What the fuck are you doing?' Sam screams. She may be able to hide many emotions, but pain is clearly not one of them.

'The very thing I believe you did to Nathan. Only I don't have a knife to carve any skin from your back.'

'What are you talking about? Are you totally mad? You think I killed Steven Fish?'

'No,' says Katie, rapidly piecing it all together. 'But you believed that Nathan had. You were aware of the relationship between Fish and Watkins, and given the timing of Watkins' disappearance and the details in Nathan's journal, I think you came to an entirely false conclusion. You tortured my partner.' As she says the words, Katie can't help but give Sam's arm another lift, stretching the muscles further and threatening the bones.

'How the hell could I have done that?' says Sam, struggling and panting. 'I was knocked out.'

'I don't like coincidence. And it's quite a coincidence that you decided to go to the school where Steven Fish was attacked and that someone else was either already waiting or able to follow you there. I don't like that you sent away your colleague, the only potential witness, at the very last minute.'

'And how exactly did I knock myself out? Where did the brick go?'

'I imagine it went wherever your blond-haired colleague, or rather, accomplice managed to secrete it before you called him. Either that or you found somewhere to hide it yourself. A brick would be easy to hide. Maybe you went back and collected it later.'

Katie starts to nod, encouraged by how logical this sounds, despite Sam's protestations of madness. 'Yeah, I reckon that's what happened. You most likely don't trust anyone else enough to involve them in your crimes. I think you hit yourself just hard enough to make it look like you were out, but in reality you were able to hide the evidence before calling your partner.'

'Are you forgetting I saved *your* partner's life making that call?'

'Rubbish. The only thing that saved Nathan's life was the realisation that you weren't going to get what you wanted out of him. He didn't confess, and so you decided to try another approach, to keep him close and watch for signs of guilt. Well, I've decided to do the same but in a different order. And I've seen more than enough signs of guilt to convince me we should move on to the torture stage.'

'I could easily shout out,' says Sam, her face revealing panic for the first time.

'You could. But given the distance and direction of the wind, there's a good chance that nobody would hear. And if they do, well, then I'm going to tell them what I know about you. More specifically about you and Carl Watkins. I don't care what damage that might do to your career, or to mine. I only want to have Nathan back.'

'I haven't taken him,' says Sam.

'Nobody could have known he was coming here,' says Katie. 'And he would have been careful not to be followed. But you could have used the mobile I gave him to track him, the same way you used it to track me.'

'I said, I haven't taken him,' Sam repeats.

'But you admit that you did torture him before?'

A pause. Several pained breaths. And then finally the truth. Katie had seen this with so many criminals over the years, but there's no elation in hearing the confession, only horror, and burning anger. 'You don't understand what Watkins did to me.'

'You think I don't understand love?' asks Katie, her anger building.

'It wasn't love,' says Sam, and Katie can feel the struggle go out of the other woman. 'It was an obsession. He had control over me. Complete control. I needed him. For everything. For information. For my career. For strength. For a reason to get up in the morning.' She almost laughs, but there's no humour. 'He was like a drug.'

Despite her rage, Katie finds herself nodding freely, thinking of the relationship she has with Nathan. It's about work, about success, yes – but it's so much more than that. Her identity changes when he's not around.

'He kept saying your name,' says Sam, seeming to brace herself again.

'When?'

'When I was . . . when I was hurting him. He'd gone into some kind of trance and he kept saying your name over and over, and it was like he was immune, like he wasn't feeling anything anymore, at least not pain.'

Katie adjusts her stance in the mud, scared she's going to lose her balance, her grip. And not just on Sam, but on everything. Even in his darkest moments, when he must have feared he was close to death, Nathan had thought of her, had used her to bring him comfort. Katie can feel the desire to hurt Sam strengthening again. She pictures the look, the sound, the feeling as the other woman's arm snaps, and she's so close to getting there. She knows that she could, incredibly easily, like pulling a trigger, like giving a man on the edge of a building a push. It's that comparison that is holding her back. She's seen the effects of those crimes on Nathan and on her dad. With her dad she's certain it had played a part in his mental decline and ultimately in his death.

But then, she too has experienced the devastating effect of hesitation, and she can feel the strain on the muscles in her stomach, muscles that had been parted by Christian's knife on its way to denying her the chance of a child. In the end, what determines her action is Nathan. Just as he had turned to her in desperation, she now turns to him, picturing his face. It rises to the front of her mind so clearly that it almost makes her gasp. He's smiling at her broadly, an expression that speaks of contentment and trust, trust in her to maintain control and to remain on the right side of the law.

She lets go of Sam's arm and pushes her forward so that she falls into the mud. Sam struggles to get up, brushing the dirt from her knees, her stomach and the one arm she has managed to extend to break her fall. When she finally looks up, Katie expects to see Sam's eyes full of rage, but instead there are tears.

'I don't know who I am anymore,' Sam says, weakly.

'You're a detective,' says Katie, with the coldness that she's so often heard from the other woman. 'So rather than wasting time on self-loathing, why don't we do what we're supposed to be good at and solve this case?'

Sam straightens herself and nods, wiping a tear from her cheek, then rubbing her shoulder.

'Your attack on me might actually have helped.'

'In what way?' says Katie, not hiding her confusion.

'Well, you've revealed a few secrets. Mike Peters' suspicion of me, for a start.'

'A woman was following him, supposedly. And according to Ben, Mike was scared.'

Sam nods. 'Just like Thomas Shaw.'

'And then there was whoever was living with Christian. There's a good chance it was a woman.'

'So you think that's who we're looking for?'

'Carl always had a kind of sixth sense around men,' says Sam, 'a way of reading their intentions and keeping himself out of danger. But with women it was different. Maybe he simply didn't understand them. So yeah, I think I've always believed it was a woman.' She lowers her head and finds Katie's stare. 'I believed it was you for a while.'

'That's understandable,' says Katie. 'I can't say I didn't think about killing him from time to time. Because I knew he was guilty of those murders you helped him get away with. But this isn't about Carl. It's too late for him. Hopefully not for Nathan.' It's been a relief to find that Sam hasn't taken Nathan, but it also means she's no closer to finding out where he's gone. She knows what he went through with the torture before. She can't bear to think of it happening again. And this time at the hands of someone who most likely won't stop.

'So what does this woman really look like?'

'I guess there's a good chance she looks like you,' says Katie. 'Vicky Shaw thought she recognised you. Maybe the other woman had been following Shaw's mum, like she'd followed Mike Peters, making sure her identity was being kept secret.' Katie clicks her fingers, remembering something else she'd heard. 'And then Ben said something about a bob haircut.'

'There's also a good chance she looks like *you*,' says Sam. 'From what I understand, you used to have a haircut not dissimilar to mine. And if we're talking about a woman who was living with Christian, a man who was obsessed with being like his twin...'

'Have we had any more from Forensics on DNA left on the houseboat?' asks Katie.

'Nothing conclusive yet,' says Sam. 'And I very much doubt it will be. I think this person will have a clean record, much like Christian's was. So do you think the size eights were just to get us thinking it was a man?' Sam gestures back towards the location where they'd found the boot prints.

'There was something about the pressure within those prints that made me wonder from the start,' says Katie, thinking back to the size fours they'd seen today. 'And this last time she didn't bother with the pretence.'

'Why has she taken Nathan now? Was he getting too close? Had he figured something out when he came here, and they were watching him again?'

'Or was she running out of pages from Nathan's journal?' says Katie, swallowing hard. 'There were four missing pages. She's used three of them to inspire her killings.'

'But you said yourself, when you thought I was the one who had attacked Nathan, she can't have known he would come here. This can't have been planned.'

Katie closes her eyes and considers the possibilities. She thinks about how Nathan had been when she'd spoken to him on the phone. He'd sounded strange. He's sounded close to the way he had before he'd run away to Scotland. Had her distancing herself from him, or perhaps the killing of Thomas Shaw, led him to do something reckless?

'Maybe not planned by her,' says Katie under her breath, wondering if Nathan had allowed himself to be followed and had wanted to be taken. 'No,' she says, opening her eyes wide. 'Let's do this your way. Let's look at the science. And let's find the connection between Christian Radley and Watkins and Fish and Hartham and Shaw. I don't think they were killed randomly. I don't think anything about this has been done randomly.'

'I wasn't lying earlier,' says Sam, 'when I told you I was looking into the drugs link between Carl Watkins and Thomas Shaw. Carl had never spoken about Shaw.'

'Did he tell you everything?'

'What he didn't tell me I made sure I found out. I wanted to know all about his business, not only so I could try and keep him in line, but so I could keep him safe.' Sam lowers her head again, but only momentarily. 'What I'm saying is that I don't believe drugs are the connection. At least not in that form.'

'What about Shaw's girlfriend?' says Katie. 'Do you really think she's police?'

'I'm not convinced,' says Sam.

'I agree,' says Katie. 'I imagine Thomas was lied to, perhaps to ensure he kept his mouth shut, or, given that he didn't, as part of a long-term plan to get us suspecting each other.' Katie looks at the mud on Sam again. 'I guess it worked.'

'I'm also wondering about the gun and the drugs,' says Sam. 'It was far too convenient that they were there for us to find, and to escalate things when you went to call.'

Katie sighs, acknowledging the possibility that their actions have been predicted yet again. 'What about Ben Peters? I don't understand why he had to die. Whoever killed him must have known he'd already shared all that Mike had told him. And there's no evidence his house was searched.'

Sam continues to grimace and squeeze her arm and Katie wonders if she might have done some damage after all. There's dirt on her elbow, and when she lifts her hand to her face again, perhaps to remove any trace of tears, she leaves a muddy mark, a line not entirely dissimilar to the scar on Katie's face. Katie thinks about telling her, but it seems appropriate somehow, like a sign that they're in this together now.

'You think there might have been a personal connection to Ben?' asks Sam. 'Like Carl, he was killed in a way that was different. As though they cared about him.'

'It's possible,' says Katie. 'But then Ben didn't really have any personal connections. Although he was hospitalised a couple of times. Maybe it was another addict, someone he could have identified.'

'Maybe someone Dr Nigel Hartham could have identified, too.'

Katie is already moving as she recognises another line of enquiry, and another potential threat. 'Richard,' she says, sharply. 'We need to find Dr Evans now.'

CHAPTER THIRTY-SIX

Nathan opens his eyes. All around him is darkness and silence. He ends that silence with a groan, feeling the wound on his back and the ache in his broken fingers, and a headache which intermittently trumps everything else. He feels like he's lying on his side on a cold, hard surface. His limbs are tied, his arms and feet held behind him. He tries to work back through the events that have brought him here. It's taken a while, and concentration that seems to cost him some of what little strength he has, but eventually he has it all in order.

'Sam?' he calls out. There's an echo to his words. But no reply. He's not convinced that Sam's there. He's not convinced that it's her, but whatever it was that had just been eluding him before he was grabbed and drugged continues to remain frustratingly out of reach. He had seen something in his daydream, or at least made a vague connection that registered as true. He doesn't believe it will make much difference now if he figures it out, but it will still provide a crumb of comfort, the faintest sense of satisfaction.

'I know how important Carl Watkins was to you,' he says. He's starting to believe that he's alone – he certainly can't hear anything around him, other than his words bouncing back off the walls – and the statement is as much to get his thoughts out, to hear them and judge them and see what follows, as it is an attempt to start a conversation. But just as he's about to say something else, he feels a warmth on the back of his ear. He imagines it must be a draught, or perhaps it's his imagination, but then the words come:

'You know nothing.'

They are so gently spoken that once more he could almost believe that they've been created in his mind. But when the warmth comes again he realises it's someone's breath, so soft on his ear. Having come to this conclusion, he tries to figure out how they could possibly be low enough down to breathe on his ear, as he's lying on the floor. All he can imagine – it's the strangest image – is that they're lying behind him, mirroring his position, like a couple in bed. Only there's no contact. It reminds him, sadly, of the last few weeks in Wales with Katie. He'd convinced himself that it was all part of the healing process, that the distance between them would shrink again, but it turned out to be one of the many ways in which he's been proved a fool.

'Apparently I don't know anything,' says Nathan finally, hearing the tremor in his voice. 'Because you're not Sam.' Again, he doesn't know this for sure, the voice so quiet as to be impossible to identify. Although he is almost convinced that it does belong to a woman.

'Who am I?' the voice asks.

'Now there's a question I've been asking myself,' says Nathan. 'Ever since I took a life. I was hoping…' He feels his stomach sink as the reality of what he's saying hits home. 'I was hoping you were Thomas Shaw. Nobody wants to kill an innocent man.'

'I won't be.'

'Although,' Nathan continues, ignoring the chance to ask what it is this person thinks he's guilty of. 'I killed plenty of innocent people in my journal.'

'An inspirational work.'

'Not for myself. In fact, quite the opposite. It helped me to avoid acting out any of those fantasies. And now that I have killed someone, well, it was very different to how I'd imagined. But then I don't need to tell you that.'

'It's far better,' says the voice.

'So my brother told me. But then perhaps you're struggling to make the comparison. Perhaps you're lacking an imagination. You have, after all, needed to borrow from me. "The Plagiarist", isn't that what they're calling you?'

'People do what I want them to do,' says the voice. 'They always have done, and they always will.'

'Only if what you're wanting them to do is die,' says Nathan. 'Understanding, caring, *loving*, that might be a bigger ask.'

'Plenty of people have cared for me.'

'Thomas Shaw, you mean? I imagine he only ever really cared for himself. Far too many mirrors in the house, from what I remember. I also seem to remember that you were a policewoman, although I'm starting to doubt that's true.'

'And yet Sam was the very first name that came to you,' says the voice, with a soft chuckle. 'Of course, Katie would be disappointed that your first thought wasn't of her.'

'I'm sure she'll forgive me, given the circumstances,' says Nathan, shifting uncomfortably on his side.

'She hasn't looked to be in a forgiving mood when I've seen you together. I wonder what it is you've done to upset her?'

'The very thing that she won't be doing with you,' says Nathan, his throat tightening at the thought of what he won't be leaving behind. 'I hesitated.'

'Ahhh,' the word is drawn out, accompanied by more warm breath. 'I see. She's not a fan of the scars you allowed your brother to give her.'

'I'm pleased,' says Nathan. 'I was beginning to think you knew everything. Thank you for proving that you don't.'

He is half expecting the pressure on his shoulder wound, but that doesn't stop the contact making him gasp. There's light, too, behind his eyes, like lightning, and he could almost believe he's been struck.

'I could always make you talk,' says the voice behind him.

'Didn't you try that before?' says Nathan, thinking back to the bars of the gym and the source of the wound that's now causing him so much pain.

'Levels of ignorance,' says the voice, with another little chuckle. 'I'm pleased to know yours are far higher than mine.'

'Is this serving any purpose?' asks Nathan. 'I mean, if this is a competition to see who knows more, then well done, you win, give yourself a prize.'

'You are the prize. You've always been the prize.'

'Excellent. Now, again, shall we get on with this? I mean, I know you like to take your time...'

'Not always. The doctor was quick.'

Nathan guesses they're referring to Nigel Hartham, and he instantly pictures the poor doctor's head pummelled by a hammer.

'Even though you missed the nail,' he says. Beyond survival, he's not really sure what he's trying to achieve with this conversation, but something is telling him not to be himself, but to be more like his brother, or how he imagines his brother might have been when acting like his true self.

'I achieved my goal.'

'And what was that?' asks Nathan.

'A little bit of revenge. There's plenty more to come, of course.'

Nathan can feel his body tense in anticipation of more contact, more pain, but this time the short distance between them remains. 'So there is a reason to all of this?'

'If I simply wanted to randomly kill people because I'm crazy, that would be a reason, would it not?'

'So you're not crazy?'

'Who am I to judge? Admittedly there have been others who have judged, but they're not around anymore.'

Nathan's headache is worsening again, clouding his thinking. He feels like he's being given clues, but he can't pick them out.

'I'm afraid you're going to have to spell things out for me,' says Nathan, 'because whatever drugs you knocked me out with, along with the smack over the head you gave me the other day, are doing little for my reasoning.'

He feels the firmer breath of a laugh on his ear. 'I really am going to have to spell it out for you. And I will, because I'm miles ahead in our little knowledge competition. S-A-M. That's who took a knife to you in the school the other day. I'll admit I felt a bit sorry for you when I saw you on the news, all that pain you suffered because you were getting the blame for one of my crimes.'

The processing time is slowed by his discomfort again, and by the fear of where his conclusions are taking him. 'Carl Watkins…?' he asks tentatively.

'That is correct. Quite emotional, that woman, despite all appearances. Seems Samantha Stone believed you'd messed up the good thing she was on to, a hugely immoral professional partnership that had helped to take her so high. Or maybe she wanted to check it wasn't you before she moved on to Katie, a far more obvious candidate for taking out poor Carl Watkins.'

Nathan feels the tension return to his body worse than ever, as he considers the possibility that Sam might turn her attentions to Katie. There's still the possibility that Sam is talking to him right now; he cannot determine enough in the whispered voice to confirm or deny this. 'You knew him?' he asks.

There's a pause before the answer comes, and it's even quieter than before. 'Not as well as I would have liked.'

Despite it already being dark, Nathan closes his eyes and tries to return to the place he'd been as he'd stood over the burial place of Carl Watkins. He can just about feel the moment of impact, the spade on the back of the head. Delivered with force, but also with hesitation, with the same hesitation he'd felt as he'd stood over his brother with a metal bar.

'It's about love,' he says. It's not a question but a statement, and he's suddenly confident it's true. 'It's always about love.'

'We had a connection,' says the voice. 'And it should have been love, but it wasn't.'

'Did Sam love him?'

'You need to ask her that yourself. Not that you'll ever get the chance. I imagine she'd tell you it was strictly professional between them, but from what I observed it was more than that. Well, it was from her perspective. Of course, Carl was using her all along. He had no time for love. No time for anything other than work.'

'What about Steven Fish?'

'What about him?' The question is snapped back with such speed and aggression that Nathan flinches. When there's still no contact – and he can so vividly imagine the knife being slipped beneath his ribs, or drawn across his throat – he considers the significance of this reaction. First, he's now certain that this isn't Sam. The increase in volume, adding shape to the voice, is sufficient to convince him of that. Secondly, he's spotted a potential weakness, something he knows he's going to have to be extremely careful in trying to exploit.

'They were together?' he says. 'Watkins and Fish?'

'They were yet another lie,' says the unidentified woman, her emotions seemingly back under control. 'Carl was never true to himself. But then you can probably sympathise with that, because up until a day ago, when you finally allowed yourself to take a life, you weren't living up to your own promise.'

'I killed Thomas Shaw protecting the woman I loved.'

'You're right, it *is* always about love,' says the voice, seemingly even closer than before. 'Protecting it. Avenging it. Or simply loving what you do.'

'And that,' says Nathan, 'is the problem for you. You're up against two people who love what they do. Whatever happens here, Sam and Katie will track you down. And as I said before, there will be no hesitation when it comes to delivering justice.'

This time the laugh is far freer than before, and there's no breath on his ear to accompany it. That's because there's distance between them. He hadn't heard her move, not a sound, but she's clearly several metres away.

'You have too much faith in them. I've made sure to lay down a few distractions, to keep them away for just long enough. If anything, I imagine they're busy suspecting each other, and there's no way they'll be able to get here in time.'

In time. Just two words. Two words that seem to tell Nathan everything. He can see those words etched out at the front of his mind, lit up by the pulses of pain from his wounds. He hears a screech of metal and realises a door behind him is being opened, but his muscles seem slow to react, and before he can stretch his neck towards the sound, the door has been slammed closed.

CHAPTER THIRTY-SEVEN

BLOG: Seeing Red
The anonymous, unfiltered truth about crime
and the criminal justice system

Here's an exclusive for you: Thomas Shaw is innocent!

I thought it was over. It was supposed to be over. That's what the police and the media were saying. I don't trust either of them as a rule, but on this occasion I think I was desperate. Thomas Shaw certainly seemed perfect for the role, with those muscles and tattoos and the look in his eye that spoke of violence. But I guess I must have read him wrong. I guess we all did. And I think we were meant to. I think whoever has been committing these terrible crimes has been playing us, making us think things, making us doubt. Right back at the start there were lots of you believing it was Nathan that had killed DS Mike Peters. I never believed that, because I believe in him. Katie, on the other hand – well, I was always slightly less sure about her. She seemed so on edge during the inquest. Understandable, I suppose, given what she'd been through, but nevertheless there was something about her posture and the way she moved, the quick-fire way she gave answers in court, that made her kind of frightening.

That's not to say I think Katie's killed four people – and I can't believe that's how many we're up to now – but I do reckon she's hiding something. I also reckon she's not good enough for Nathan. He deserves somebody who properly understands him, understands the darkness in him, rather than just using his gift to get results. And that's what she's always done, in my opinion, she's *used* him. I bet she'll keep using him now, even though he must be a broken man reading this and finding out that Thomas Shaw is innocent.

Maybe I'm just anti-Katie because she's police. You know me, I'm not exactly a fan. I always think they're hiding something. I can't stop thinking about why Samantha Stone, a top dog at the National Crime Agency, is involved. They know something about this case, and they're not telling us, the public, stuff that we have a right to know.

Maybe what I'm sharing isn't such an exclusive. Maybe they never believed that Thomas Shaw was guilty. Or maybe he was guilty but was working with somebody else. I know people think that serial-killing is the kind of thing you do on your own, but there's Bonnie and Clyde, Rose and Fred West, plenty of examples of couples who've worked together, sharing their passion, sharing their sickness. *A couple*, now there's a possibility. I wonder if Thomas Shaw had a girlfriend? Hell, for all I know it could have been Samantha Stone – she looks the type to want her men rough. Maybe that's the big cover-up here.

I'm cheating a bit in my amateur detective work, because while I reckon the police know something we don't, I can absolutely guarantee I know something the police don't. And this brings us back to my big exclusive, and the thing I probably should have mentioned at the start, but I got a bit carried away. I have another page of the journal. The last missing page from Nathan's journal! Well, here it is, the big finale:

It seems appropriate that I'm running out of room. Because it doesn't feel like this is working anymore. Putting my fantasies down on paper isn't enough. I need to talk to someone, to see their response, to understand just how bad things are. I've thought about Mum, but I couldn't do that to her, especially given what she's going through with Dad. But who else? I find myself walking down the street sometimes, and staring at people a little too long, wondering what's going on in their heads. Is there anybody out there struggling like me? I mean, I watch the news, I know there are plenty of sick people in the world, but are these fantasies, are these urges only felt by crazy people? I wish I could talk to someone and rather than see a horrified expression, have them tell me it's okay, that they're the same as me.

The same. It's an odd thing for somebody to dream about who's already a twin. I have thought about speaking to Christian, of course, but there's no way his thoughts are like mine. I know him well enough, I can see how untroubled he is. The last thing I want to do is make him think that he might be like me, to put that doubt in his head. No, Christian must never know, and that's why this journal will be burnt or at least very carefully hidden away.

What would I do if I did find somebody to talk to? Would we hold each other back, or might it give us the confidence to act out our thoughts? That has to be a danger, to see and feel that excitement shared.

I think a lot about the perfect crime. And it's not just getting away with it that would make it perfect – it would be a crime that I wouldn't feel guilty about. I guess they'd have to be guilty of something themselves; maybe they'd done some hideous stuff and got away with it, no evidence against them, no chance of justice. I could deliver that justice. I love vigilante movies. And I do love to act. Maybe the vigilante is a role I could play.

Or maybe I should be the director. If I can't kill somebody myself – and God, how I hope that I never do – then maybe I can satisfy these terrible urges by manipulating somebody else. A killer as guilty as the victim. If I plan it right, I could be there, watching one of the murders I've dreamt up being played out. Maybe seeing the reality would be enough. Maybe hearing the victim's screams would cure me.

It was dropped into my inbox not more than half an hour ago. I keep thinking about the bit about staring at other people and wondering what they're thinking. I'll admit I do have a few dark thoughts of my own, and it gets me worrying about my mental health. I'm sure it's natural to think about death, yours and those you care about, yours and those you don't care about. It's probably even natural to stand behind somebody at a railway station just as a train is passing through and think about how easy it would be to give them a push. *Easy* – I suppose that's the word that sums it all up. It's all far too easy – to lose a life, to take a life, accidentally or otherwise.

The life I'm worried about right now is Nathan's. I haven't seen or heard anything from him. And what if this endgame – and I imagine it must be that, with this having been the final page torn from his journal – involves him? Is he going to be the last victim of The Plagiarist? Do they think he's partly responsible for all these crimes, because they came from his mind? Is that what he thinks? Is that how he ended up letting the journal that was supposed to be burnt or carefully hidden away get into someone else's hands? Was he genuinely hoping that someday, somebody would act out one of his crimes, that the reality of seeing it would 'cure' him? I'd love to have a chance to talk to Nathan, to find out the truth about what he was thinking and what he's feeling now. And maybe I'm not alone in that. Maybe that's exactly what the killer wants, now that they've used his thoughts as inspiration. Have they taken him? Are they talking to him now? Are they hurting him now?

My mind feels like it might just snap. God, I never thought I'd feel emotions as strong as these. Perhaps it's the drugs, perhaps it's just what following Nathan's story has done to me, like I'm a part of his life, but I'm warning you, whoever you are, that if you do have him and if you do hurt him in any way, I'm going to track you down and I'm going to kill you. That's an absolute promise. And I won't have to steal somebody else's imagination to come up with how I'm going to do it: I've got plenty of ideas. In fact, they're bursting out of me.

CHAPTER THIRTY-EIGHT

'They still don't know who this blogger is?' asks Katie, staring down at the computer screen where she's just read the latest post, a fist pressed into the tabletop.

'We've got half a dozen people working on it,' says a sergeant standing behind Katie. 'But the connection has been rerouted and bounced around the world many times. They're unbelievably good at covering their location, which in itself might be a clue as to their identity, because I'm sure the security services must have a list somewhere of the most capable and dangerous—'

Katie cuts him off with a look. 'Are we going to find out their identity?' she asks.

'Maybe soon.'

'Soon might not be fast enough,' says Sam.

'If we find the blogger I think we'll find the killer,' says Katie, trying to keep her thoughts on the job. 'They're making too many good guesses. There's no way they could have figured out that Nathan would be taken. And as for that stuff about Thomas Shaw's girlfriend…'

'A clear sign of insanity,' says Sam. 'But not necessarily of guilt.'

Katie looks across at the other woman. Katie had believed for a while that Sam could have been Shaw's girlfriend, but that was based on many things, including the evidence of Thomas Shaw's mum, things that until very recently hadn't been shared with Katie's bosses, let alone the public. Despite events, Sam appears to have retained control over the people in the room, evidenced perhaps by the fact that not one of them has mentioned the mud on her knees, elbows, stomach and face. Her bob haircut still somehow looks immaculate, and the expression on her face has returned to one of complete calm.

'We've been made to look like prize idiots,' says DCI Ken Stocks. He's standing in the far corner of the incident room, running his fingers through his hair, leaving great chunks of it standing up on end.

'Who gives a damn what we look like,' snaps Katie. 'I want to find Nathan before it's too late.' She spins round, taking in the other faces. There's Sam Stone, Taylor and Stocks and several other detectives. There's also Dr Richard Evans. He'd come to the station the moment he'd seen the news about the blogger's latest posting and Katie had thrown her arms around him, relieved to find him safe. Now, with Nathan the one in danger, all she feels is frustration, as nobody is offering any answers.

Dr Miles Parker enters the room. Normally he's the last person Katie wants to see, but today she's anxious to hear from anyone that might be able to help.

'DNA on the houseboat,' he says. Even he's not trying to be clever now. Just the facts, delivered straight. 'Only two samples. One male. One female. Male is Christian Radley. As for the female, we have no matches on the databases so far. There'll be more to come soon enough, but most likely not a name.'

'It might not even be the killer,' says Taylor. 'He might simply have had a girlfriend who never knew what he was like.'

'But when it came out in the news...?' says Stocks.

'Then he might have killed her.'

'She came back and removed things from the houseboat,' says Katie, annoyed at having to explain things that she sees as obvious.

'Perhaps she was ashamed,' says Taylor. 'She might not want to be publicly associated with his crimes. Or maybe she thinks we'll believe she was involved.'

'Trust me, it's her,' says Katie firmly. She points at the material that surrounds them. 'All of this is her.'

'There's something we're missing,' says Sam, leaning against a wall, seeming not to notice or care that, pinned to the same wall, are photos of Steven Fish's decapitated corpse.

'Carl Watkins,' says Katie, seeing Sam flinch out of the corner of her eye. 'Whoever is doing this, most likely a woman, has a close connection to Carl Watkins.' She points up at the photos of his body. 'He was killed with a restraint that we haven't seen with the others.'

'Other than Ben Peters.'

'It's drugs,' argues Ken Stocks. 'That's what connects those two.'

'Perhaps that's the connection,' says Katie. 'But I'm not sure it's the motivation.' She's good like this normally, when the pressure is high, but this is too high; this is Nathan's life, and she can't stop thinking about that. It's clouding her judgement. What will she do without him? 'Love,' she says quietly. 'I think somewhere in among all this horror is a crime of passion.'

'You don't think the killer found another partner?' asks Taylor.

'I'm willing to bet the killer has had several. Thomas Shaw being one of them.'

'The secret girlfriend,' says DCI Stocks with a grunt. 'Secret from us until a short while ago.'

'It was the police connection,' says Katie, glancing at Sam. 'I don't believe it now, I think we were being misled with that, but at the time that intelligence needed to be limited distribution.'

'Agreed,' says Stocks, his face starting to flush. 'But I should have been part of that small group.'

'I ordered her not to involve you,' says Sam. 'I'm not at liberty to share the details, but there remains the possibility of corruption at the highest levels within the force.'

'Are you looking at me?' says Stocks, jabbing his chest so hard with his finger he forces out a noisy breath.

'Everybody,' says Sam, stretching her arms wide, before wrapping them around herself. Katie can't help but admire the front of the woman, to stand and all but accuse the others without showing a trace of her own guilt. 'But those are questions that will have to be put on hold for now. Our focus is on finding the killer.'

'Our focus is on finding Nathan,' says Katie. She clicks her fingers and then points at the sergeant. 'Have we had any luck with the traffic cams, trying to track Shaw during his journey from his mum's house to his home?'

'Limited,' says the sergeant, shifting his balance from one foot to the other. 'We were able to track his car for part of the journey, but the images weren't good, and while there's a chance he wasn't alone, it's impossible to tell.' As he speaks, he moves over to a desk and hunts through a pile of printouts. 'Shaw pulls over at one point, perhaps to make a call, although we haven't been able to tie it into his phone records.'

Katie sighs. She realises she'd pinned her hopes on getting lucky, a freak shot of a passing car with a freeze-frame sharp enough for a positive identification. A trawl of social media has provided them with plenty of potential shots of women wrapped around Thomas Shaw, but nobody that's given him the same look of excitement and fear that can be seen in the selfie taken in his car. She moves across the room, unable to stand still anywhere for long, unable to stop looking up at the clock on the wall by the door, which keeps screaming at her to *get on with it!*

'Why don't we go public?' she says. 'Nathan's face is well known.'

'We might not need to go public after the blogger's latest post,' says Taylor. 'He or she more or less said they were worried about Nathan being taken.'

'It's a she,' says Sam. 'And they've definitely got a crush on Nathan. An obsession, even.'

'Does that stop them being a he?' asks Stocks.

'Of course not,' says Katie. 'Nor does it stop them being the killer. In fact, if we are looking for Christian's old girlfriend, then she's more than likely to have an obsession with the twin that's still alive.' As she says this, Katie finds herself desperately praying that Nathan *is* still alive.

'So the blogger is also the killer?' says Taylor, looking at Katie, then up at the printouts of the blogger's posts.

Katie shrugs. 'It would certainly explain why we've got six officers failing to track down their location, and yet the killer is supposedly able to drop the blogger an email at their private address whenever they see fit. Plus, the blogger, in addition to sounding increasingly unstable...' Katie draws in a breath and hopes she's not starting to do so herself, '...has gone out of their way to make us believe the killer was a man. I think that was all part of the deception in the build-up to taking Nathan. That's not to say there haven't been truths in there. In fact, I'm sure I'm missing something important.' Katie looks at the printouts again, but the words seem to swirl in front of her.

'But why send this final message, if that's what it is?' says Sam, gesturing at the blogger's post that at present is only on the computer screen. 'Are they trying to tell us something with this? Are they giving us clues? Or are they enjoying the game too much?'

'They're enjoying mocking us,' says Stocks, with another thump on the desk next to him.

'I don't know,' says Katie. 'On the other pages of the journal Nathan was able to identify locations that his brother had written down. But there doesn't appear to be anything on this last one.' Katie looks away from the computer screen and stares up at the ceiling. 'Maybe she's not playing anymore. Maybe that really was the finale, as she's called it.' She feels her stomach sink. She's never felt so empty, so hopeless, so lost. 'Christ, I wish I knew what she looked like. There's a chance she's got, or at least once had, a bob haircut, a bit like...' Katie casually gestures towards

Sam, who's grabbed the pile of social media hits, flicking through them for the second time. She drops them heavily back on the table in front of Richard.

'There's nothing jumping out.'

'We're clutching at straws,' says Stocks.

'Of course we bloody are,' Katie snaps back, looking up at the clock again. 'But you're going to have to go out and face the world's press soon, tell them how we've got it all wrong and that one of our team has been taken. Wouldn't you prefer to be able to tell them, and with an element of truth, that we're already pursuing leads? Or would you rather just tell them that we've given up?'

The look on Stocks' face tells her that there's still plenty of fight in him.

'Just do what you have to do,' he says.

Sam moves over to the wall on the far side, this time looking at the images of Dr Nigel Hartham.

'Who is meant to be suffering the most here?' she asks.

Katie wants to tell her she knows exactly who's suffering the most: Nathan, who's probably being tortured right now, who is perhaps already dead, but then she reminds herself of what Carl Watkins had meant to Sam.

Katie is pulled out of her musings by a voice behind her. She turns to find that Richard has moved over to the pile of social media photos that Sam has just dropped on the table.

'I might be wrong,' he says, pointing at the image on top, 'but I think I know this woman.' Katie and Sam rush across and find the old doctor's crooked finger picking out a woman in the background. The shot is taken in a crowded bar. Thomas Shaw is at the front of the image, but the face Richard is pointing at belongs to a woman right at the back. Everyone else in the photo is smiling and appears lost in their little groups, but this woman is looking in the direction of Shaw with a focused stare. She has a pale face and shoulder-length hair.

'How do you know her?' Both women rush to ask the question at the same time.

'She was a patient, or rather someone I helped for a while. Maxine something. I'm not sure I ever knew her surname. She was not well. In fact, she was terribly troubled. And she was an addict.'

'Like Ben Peters,' says Taylor, joining the group and registering a similar level of excitement.

'But she's not even with Shaw,' says Stocks. 'Aren't we supposed to be searching for a girlfriend?'

'And maybe that's what she became,' says Katie. 'If you look at the date from the metadata, this was taken months ago. Maybe she was checking him out, choosing the perfect man to use. Just as described in Nathan's journal.'

'I might be wrong,' says Sam, lifting the photo up and holding it close to her face, 'but there's something about her face. I reckon I might have seen her before too.'

Katie grabs the printout from Sam and searches for recognition herself, and while there's nothing definitive, she agrees that there is the faintest hint of familiarity. Perhaps it's simply in the stare. She's seen that stare from so many criminals in so many interviews. Normally it's big men trying to intimidate her, but this time it's a woman in a photo who can't be more than five and a half feet tall.

'Do you have an address, Dr Evans?' asks Ken Stocks.

'I'm afraid not – it was more than ten years ago. And she didn't have an address back then. She was homeless.' The doctor nods. 'Yes, I remember now, she was living on the streets. She overdosed and I managed to bring her back from the brink. This was just before Thomas Shaw's dad, before I failed to save him.'

'How long were you in contact with her for?'

'Several months. I wanted to make sure she was doing okay. The problem was, I was far from okay by then. My PTSD had taken over, and I needed to get away. I admitted to her that I couldn't cope and that I had to make a clean break.' The old man seems to crumple and Katie grabs hold of his arm and sits him on the table behind, ignoring the papers that fall to the floor. 'What if I'd stayed?' he asks, looking up at the images of the victims on the walls around him. 'Could I have helped to avoid all this?'

'Might she have known Ben Peters?' asks Sam, ignoring the doctor's question.

'Perhaps,' says Richard. 'She might have seen him briefly when he was hospitalised. But they wouldn't have interacted. He didn't interact with anyone.'

'Would that have given her motivation to kill him?' asks Taylor.

'Perhaps his death was supposed to be an act of compassion,' says Katie. 'An end to his suffering. Or perhaps it was just envy.' She turns to Richard. 'You kept on treating Ben, didn't you? After you'd left her, when you said you couldn't cope, you kept treating him.'

'She wouldn't have known that. Not unless she'd come to Wales. It was a secret.'

Katie considers this, and the answer comes to her almost instantly. 'Coincidence,' she says, rubbing her stomach. 'If there's one thing I don't believe in, it's coincidence. Everything happens for a reason. If she holds some kind of a grudge against you and me and Nathan, then she would have wanted us together. She would have created a situation where we had to come together. She must have known I already knew about you, about where you lived, because of Ben. All she had to do was find a motivation for me to go to you, to a doctor.'

'Food poisoning!' says Richard. 'You think she did *that*?'

'I'm sure of it. And then she killed Mike Peters to bring us back to London, to start all this,' Katie gestures to the photos behind her, 'this madness.'

'And we're going to make sure she doesn't get her finale,' says Sam, grabbing Katie's hand. Katie is so surprised by this, she doesn't struggle as she's pulled towards the door. 'We are not going to let Nathan become another victim. Don't share her photo with the public!' Sam shouts back to the others, with her familiar authority. 'Not yet. We'll call you soon.'

CHAPTER THIRTY-NINE

Nathan is getting used to the dark. He has no watch, and therefore no way of knowing how long he's been tied up, but he reckons it must be at least two hours. There are aches and pains beyond the injuries he already has, and although some time has passed, if anything the effects of the drugs that had knocked him out seem to be getting worse.

His fear now is for Katie. Might she be the next one to be attacked? Worse still, might she be putting her life on the line to come and save him? Or is some complicated plan being acted out, which will bring Katie here to find him? If there is a connection between the unidentified woman and Christian, and if she's the one who has been stealing scenes from Nathan's dark imagination, he can't bear to think what she might have planned for her final act.

In time. He still can't forget those words. Nathan is trying to cling on to the hope that what he'd said to the woman is true: that Katie and Sam have time to hunt her down, that they will try something unexpected and not fall into another one of her traps. Perhaps there is also something he can do. Of course, physically there's nothing, not tied up with knots on his wrists and ankles that he's tested over and over, but then almost all of Nathan's successes have resulted from what he's been able to do in his mind. And what better place to be able to concentrate than in a dark and silent room.

He shuts his eyes and tries to summon up all the memories that he's been pushing down for the past twenty years. Can he figure out what's on the final page that was torn out of the journal? Would that help him? Or might that merely give him a description of his fate? Nothing comes.

He rests the back of his head against the door. It's cold and hard. Metal. Every wall he's found is metal, and given the dimensions, the echo from his words and the screech of the door being opened, he's pretty sure he's in a shipping container. That would explain why he's sweating and struggling to breathe, along with whatever drugs are still in his system. He's tried pressing his mouth up against the tiny gap between door and wall, to draw in more air and to shout out for help, but there's been no response. There's been no sound at all. What if this is it? What if he's heard his attacker's final words? What if these metal walls are like the walls of a coffin, *his* coffin? He may never see daylight again.

CHAPTER FORTY

'I'm going to kill her,' says Katie, as Sam accelerates hard down an A-road headed out of London. 'When we find her, I am going to kill her.'

'You'll have to get there ahead of me,' says Sam, barging her way between a lorry and a white van. The van driver screams something out of the window and for a moment it looks like he's going to give chase, but Sam is travelling far too fast. At first Katie had found it frustrating they were in Sam's private car, no blue light, no siren, but with such aggressive driving it's made little difference in the end.

Not that she knows where they're heading at such speed. In the ten minutes that have passed since they left the police station, Sam has refused to reveal this information. Katie knows it's a question of trust, and while that's the last thing she's ever felt for this woman in the few days they've been together, she's now starting to think that Sam represents her only hope. There's a level of single-mindedness and determination in Sam that Katie recognises in herself. After the discovery of Carl Watkins' body, Katie had seen some of that drive and energy disappear, but it's back now, in full force.

Katie spends the next twenty minutes silently checking her phone, waiting for the guys back at the station to call, looking for a new post on 'Seeing Red', looking through the thousands of comments about it on other sites for clues.

She looks up when the engine stops, and finds they've pulled up to a set of high metal gates. When she peers through them and down a twisting drive, she can just make out a beautiful stone cottage with a pale blue door. It reminds her of the sort of house she's dreamt about living in after she and Nathan had left Wales and returned to London. Something on the outskirts of the city, within commuting distance if she wanted to go back to work, something she could start a family in. Perhaps she could picture it without a child, in time, but without Nathan…

'Who lives here?' Katie asks, desperately trying to get her mind back on the job.

'You'll find out. I doubt he'll be long.'

'Do we even know if he's in?'

Sam points up at a little camera halfway up a tree, behind the gatepost to their right. 'That just moved,' she says.

'So we aren't trying to surprise him.'

Sam smiles. 'Oh, I imagine we'll still be able to do that.'

A couple of minutes later and a side gate, surrounded by thick ivy, is pushed open, revealing not only a series of unfastened locks, but a tall, slim gentleman in gardening gloves, holding a sharp-looking pair of shears. His long grey hair is slicked back from his handsome face, and piercing blue eyes behind a pair of spectacles seem to dance with intelligence.

'Can I help you ladies?' he asks in a refined voice.

'I hope so,' says Sam. 'We're looking for Tristan Hunter.'

He raises one eyebrow. 'Can I ask what it might relate to?' As he asks, the man lifts a hand to his cheek, touching the point where Katie realises Sam still has a muddy mark. Not very professional, but then Katie doesn't believe this is an entirely professional visit.

'Past business,' says Sam. 'Business that will have dried up for you a couple of years ago.' She leans out of the open window and peers down the drive at the house. 'Although you still seem to be doing okay.'

Katie can see the flash of fear on the man's face, but it's quickly hidden and he offers a smile. 'I think you might have the wrong address.'

Sam reaches into her pocket and pulls out her identity card. 'I'm Samantha Stone from the National Crime Agency. This lady with me is…' Sam stops and sits back, allowing the man a better view of Katie. 'If you've been following the news at all recently, I think you'll be able to figure out for yourself who she is.'

'Indeed,' says the man. There's a trace of sweat on his top lip. 'I'm still not sure what you're doing here. You're right, my name is Tristan Hunter, but I gave up my business not two, but almost ten years ago, and yes, I was fortunate and it was profitable, as legal work tends to be, but—'

'I'm afraid we don't have time for this,' says Sam, cutting him off. 'I know exactly what you've done for the past decade, and I know exactly who you used to do it for. I'm not here to arrest you. I just want you to answer a few questions for us about Carl.'

The name Carl seems to send a shiver through Tristan and he stumbles slightly before correcting himself, pushing his shoulders back and narrowing those remarkable blue eyes.

'Look, I'm sorry if you've driven a long way, ladies, but there really has been an unfortunate mix-up. I don't know this Carl you're referring to.'

'I've changed my mind,' says Sam sharply, before popping open the door. 'I think I will arrest you. Money-laundering will do for now. And I can easily track down those accounts in the Cayman Islands. Carl gave me the numbers for safekeeping. Don't worry about your family – Christina and Seb, was it? – you can give them a call from the station, explain to them… Well, I think you might have quite a lot to explain to them. Carl told me you'd never let them in on your little arrangement. It appears he didn't let you in on ours either, but then that's hardly surprising – you don't last as long as he did in the drugs game without being strict on who you share your secrets with.'

Tristan opens his mouth and then closes it again. He's taken two steps back and Katie wonders if he's going to try and escape. She reckons he must be in his mid to late fifties, but is in good shape and would probably be able to keep up a good speed for a while.

'I've spent the last six months running and up and down mountains in Wales,' says Katie. 'There's absolutely no chance you'll get away.'

'Nor is there any need to run if you simply answer a few questions for us,' says Sam, pulling her door closed again. 'You can return to your gardening and your family and nobody will ever know we had this conversation.'

'Do you promise?' asks Tristan, eyes widening.

'I try not to make promises. I tend to break them. But you're a clever man, very highly regarded by Carl for your careful reasoning and weighing up of risk. Surely you can see what the correct course of action is here?'

Tristan's shoulders sink, and after glancing back at the house a couple of times, he asks quietly, as if those within the house, more than a hundred yards away, might hear him, 'What was it you wanted to know?'

'I want to know about the women in Carl's life.'

Tristan almost laughs at this, but his features still seem too tight to allow him to. 'Clearly he was careful with his secrets. I was starting to think you knew everything about him.'

'He wasn't gay, if that's what you're suggesting,' snaps Sam.

'He wasn't? Well then, I must have got confused when he told me he'd fallen in love with a man. I must have been misled when I saw him cry when he told me that the relationship had ended, just a week before he disappeared.' Tristan looks down and considers the dirt on the toes of his boots. 'They are saying on the news that they've found his body. Maybe he died of a broken heart, but my bet would be suicide.'

'Then you'd lose that bet,' says Katie, leaning across to get a better view. 'And you'll lose your freedom if you're not careful about what you say.' Katie can feel the heat coming off Sam with the revelation about Carl's sexuality. 'Just tell us about the women. This one, for example.' Katie reaches into her pocket and pulls out her mobile, scrolling through to the photo she'd taken of the social media image from the bar. She uses her thumb and forefinger to enlarge the photo, focusing on the woman in the background behind Thomas Shaw.

Tristan takes the phone and holds it up close to his face to inspect it. Even with glasses on he's still clearly struggling. Or at least pretending to do so.

'I'm sorry,' he says. 'I can't make her out properly.'

'I warned you before about wasting our time,' says Sam, grabbing back the phone and tossing it onto Katie's lap.

Katie looks at the picture herself, the nagging sense that the woman looks familiar somehow instantly returning. She also has the feeling that she's just read something online that could connect the dots. In the background she can hear the conversation between Sam and Tristan continuing, threats and protestations, but she manages to drown it all out as she breathes deeply and allows herself to sink into her thoughts. Her inspiration for this is of course Nathan, watching him slip from reality into fantasy so successfully. She makes her way through the things she's just read on the blogger's site, the comments from others, the pages from the journal and the words from the blogger herself, a person that Katie is now a hundred per cent convinced is the killer. And it's when she accepts this possibility that the significance of one sentence in particular leaps out at her with such startling clarity that she lets out a gasp which instantly silences the other two.

'What's wrong?' asks Sam.

'The blogger,' says Katie. 'She said, *I lost my dad coming up for two years ago and I know how much it hurt.* If she is the killer, then who do we know who died around then?'

As she says this Katie is considering the photo on the screen again and finally she's seeing the reason for the familiarity. It's in the eyes. Many times Katie had stared into Carl Watkins' eyes, as they'd weighed each other up, as he'd stared her down and then offered a wink on his way out of the interview suite. He'd been accompanied by various lawyers on those days who'd seemed competent enough, but Katie knows that the two people she's with now were the real reason Carl was able to escape conviction time and again.

'Carl Watkins didn't have a daughter,' says Sam, 'if that's who you're thinking of.'

'Actually,' says Tristan, 'he did.'

Instantly the fight seems to leave Sam again, with further confirmation of how much Carl had been keeping from her. But in Katie it's growing, along with the belief that they're closing in on a solution to the case. But will it be too late to save Nathan?

'You met his daughter?' she asks, quickly.

'I'm not even sure Carl ever met her. He only mentioned her once, right at the end, when he'd told me about losing his boyfriend. He was drunk and out of control. He said the baby was a mistake, the result of a relationship with a woman he'd known thirty years ago. A junkie.'

'No names?' says Katie, before remembering what Richard had told them about his patient. 'Maxine, for example?'

'It might have been Maxine, or Max. I can't remember, I'm afraid. I'd had a few drinks myself. Carl was so down. I mean, over the years he'd dodged a few bullets. Literally on a few occasions, and certainly with the cases I was involved in. I'd be advising him to plead guilty, to make a deal, when he'd suddenly come up with information that there's no way he should have known and he'd walk out of there scot-free.' Tristan looks in at Katie. 'I was never there, for obvious reasons, but I believe you were.'

'Just focus on what information *you* can suddenly come up with,' says Katie, sharply, 'if you're wanting to walk away scot-free.'

Tristan pushes a hand through his hair, his long fringe falling across the front of his eyes, but Katie can still see the moment when the revelation comes to him. 'The mother was a policewoman.'

'I thought you said she was an addict,' says Katie.

'I think that was after. He said he'd used this woman, tricked her into giving him stuff, then he'd walked away. She'd kind of lost it, I think. Maybe there were mental health issues. I really don't remember.'

'And that's all?' asks Katie, glancing across at Sam again. To the casual observer Sam would appear untroubled, but Katie has been around her long enough now to know when she's badly hurting.

'I have nothing else,' says Tristan. 'I promise you.'

'Then get back to your family,' says Sam, pushing the car into reverse.

*

'I think I should drive,' says Katie, as they clip the verge on a country lane, having avoided a tractor at the very last second.

'I think you should answer the phone,' says Sam, nodding at Katie's lap. When she looks down Katie can see that the screen has lit up.

'Hello?' she says.

'Where the hell have you been?' asks DCI Ken Stocks. 'No, scrub that question, I know exactly where you've been.'

'What do you mean, you know where we've been?' asks Katie, checking her side mirror, wondering if they'd been followed all along. But then, given the speed they'd been travelling, there's no way anybody could have kept up.

'Check our favourite blogger's site then phone me back,' says Stocks, before hanging up.

CHAPTER FORTY-ONE

BLOG: Seeing Red
The anonymous, unfiltered truth about crime and the criminal justice system

This is getting properly crazy. I thought it was over, at least for me, because the last page torn from Nathan's journal had been sent. But now something else has arrived, and I can see we've barely even started. It's a photo, but the internet here is too slow and uploading it will take time we don't have. It seems I was right before: Nathan is in trouble. So all I'll say is that this photo, supposedly taken just a few minutes ago, shows DS Katie Rhodes and Sam Stone from the National Crime Agency chatting to a man outside the gate of his home. He's a grey-haired guy in glasses who I wouldn't have recognised if it wasn't for the text accompanying the photo:

A retired solicitor arguing with a senior figure from the NCA. What, or rather who, could possibly connect these two? Drugs? Corruption? The answer to this and so much more is with our friend Nathan Radley, along with the antidote to the drugs he's taken. To find him, go to where my mother was killed. I suggest you get there fast, because poor Nathan is rapidly fading. I wouldn't get there too fast, though, or you might bump into my gun and me.

I told you it was crazy. If you can help, please do, because I'm not convinced that everyone on the police force will be trying their hardest. It seems to me that with all this talk of corruption, they have far too much to lose.

CHAPTER FORTY-TWO

'We can't go back,' says Sam, dropping the phone on which they've read the blogger's web page back into the centre console.

'We have to!' says Katie. 'We have to find Nathan. I know it doesn't help you, but please.' She can hear the desperation in her voice and feel the tears of frustration in her eyes.

'I didn't say I wasn't going to help,' says Sam, starting the car. 'Clearly I am.'

They've been parked on a roadside verge, not too far from Tristan Hunter's home.

'Whether there is evidence or not, there's no way I can get out of this. I'm not even sure I want to anymore. But while I have lost, there's no fucking way I'm letting this woman win.' Sam jabs her finger at the mobile screen, at the same time revving the engine loudly, before pulling out onto the road and accelerating hard. 'But we can't go back to the office. They won't let us work this case, not in the way we need to. We have to trust them to do what they can while we do our thing out here.'

'But what are we going to do? We can't look through the whole of the journal, not in three to four hours.' Katie swallows hard, considering the time. She thinks of Nathan slowly struggling with his breathing, and her own breathing becomes strained.

'We don't need the journal. Leave that to others. If there was an obvious connection to a crime, I think somebody out there among the thousands that have read his journal would have already spotted it. Maybe it's just meant to throw us off track. We have to stop playing by her rules.' Sam makes a sudden adjustment to get the car back in line, her attention obviously not on the driving. 'The point is, we already know quite a lot about this woman, based on what Tristan told us.'

'You're right,' says Katie. 'We have a photo of her. And we have what Richard and Tristan were able to tell us.'

'It's also likely, given that the blogger and killer are one and the same, that she was nearby ten minutes ago. That's most likely why she couldn't download the photo quickly, because she's working on her phone.'

Katie looks in the mirror, then scans their surroundings – open countryside, hardly any cars. 'Might that make it easier to track her?'

'I don't know. I'm sure the guys back at the station are already on it.'

Katie nods. 'Let's check.' She draws in a long breath, composing herself and finding her focus. Then she reaches for the mobile and presses redial.

'What the hell is going on?' asks Ken Stocks, having answered on the first ring. 'What's this about Sam and the solicitor?'

'It's not important,' says Katie. 'Not right now. All that matters is finding Nathan.'

'You sure Sam wants us to do that?'

'Just listen!' she cries, allowing the emotions she'd successfully suppressed to get the better of her for just a moment. 'We've confirmed that it is the woman in the photo behind Thomas Shaw that we're after. She's Carl Watkins' daughter. Although I don't think she played much of a part in his life.' Katie pictures the pale white top of the drug dealer's skull in the ditch. 'Only his death. Her name may be Max, or Maxine, as Richard suggested. We should be able to get the rest if you share the photo with the press. In fact, get it out to everybody.' Katie closes her eyes and in an instant works her way back through the conversation with Tristan. 'We believe her mum was a policewoman, who will have given birth about thirty years ago. The mum suffered from mental health issues and was more than likely a drug addict. If her death was newsworthy and made it into Nathan's journal, then it must have been unusual. A suicide, perhaps? Although it might just have been the local papers, and we do believe we're looking at London or close by.'

'How do you know all this?'

'Get a car out to the solicitor's house. His name is Tristan Hunter.' Katie gives the address. 'He won't be a happy man at the moment, and will no doubt be reluctant to share, but see if he knows anything else. And check whatever cameras are around, because there's a good chance Max, as I guess we'll have to call her for now, was close, and given the lack of traffic around here, we might be able to identify her car.'

'Are you coming back to the station?' asks Stocks.

'No. We'd be a distraction. And I want to know you're focused on the right things.'

'But I can't just ignore these corruption allegations.'

'Point proved,' says Katie firmly, looking at the clock on the dashboard, the hands of which seem to be moving far too quickly. 'Let's just concentrate on Nathan. For now. Ask all the question you like about me and Sam when this is over. Now call me back as soon as you have anything.'

Katie hangs up and turns to Sam. 'This isn't going to work,' she says. 'We don't have the systems they have, the databases, the links to the cameras.'

'We do.' Sam indicates, taking them away from the A-road back into London. 'Thanks once again to Carl.'

*

Fifteen minutes later, and they're pulling up outside a block of flats in an area on the outskirts of London that Katie doesn't believe she's ever been to before. Once more Sam has ignored all her questions, and so Katie has given up asking them, choosing instead to focus on an internet search on her phone. The trawl of news items from thirty years ago has offered little, and again she starts to wonder if anything they've been given is true. That is, apart from the threat to Nathan's life. About that she is in no doubt.

The two women are quickly out of the car and heading for the block of flats. An old lady holds the front door open for them, and her gaze lingers a little too long on the scars on Katie's cheeks. Still, she doesn't have time to worry about being recognised.

Bouncing off the walls as they run up four flights of stairs, they arrive panting at a door that Sam starts to beat her fist on. It seems to take forever before the door is opened and a ghostly white male in his mid to late twenties, wearing colourful shorts and nothing else, stares wide-eyed at them.

'Who the hell are you?' he asks. 'And what the fuck happened to your face?'

For a moment Katie thinks he's talking to her and instantly moves to cover her scars, then she remembers the muddy mark on Sam from their fight in the woods. Sam lifts her hand and finds the now dried mud, licking her fingers and quickly rubbing the mark off. Then she barges past the man in the doorway, calling back, 'Don't you watch the news, Danny?' before he can protest. He hurries after her down the hallway, with Katie left to close the door behind them.

In the living room, computers are stationed everywhere, cables snaking across the floor, all of the monitors on and giving out information. One of them is showing a twenty-four-hour newsfeed.

'There you go,' says Sam, pointing up at the monitor, where a picture of her and Katie is behind a scrolling feed. 'Now we need to utilise your expertise.'

'Are you police?' asks Danny, not daring to look up at the screen for too long, where the answer to his question is written in bold.

'We are. But I am also a friend of your former employer. Somebody who is sadly no longer with us.'

Danny opens his mouth, revealing his disbelief and yellowing teeth.

'That's right,' says Sam. 'Carl Watkins. I know exactly what you used to do for him and I need you to do the same for us now.'

This time Danny manages to get a single word out. 'Why?'

Sam gestures towards the newsfeed again. 'Because if you don't, then you will be in just as much trouble as we are!'

CHAPTER FORTY-THREE

Nathan is rolling around the floor of the shipping container, inching his way across to each wall. He finds nothing new, but deep down he knows that he's just trying to distract himself from his thoughts. Even thoughts of Katie haven't eased his discomfort the way they usually do. On the contrary, he's started to picture her life without him, blaming herself, hating herself. He's tried to scratch some words into the floor with his nails, some way of letting her know that it's okay, that he didn't suffer, and that she has to go on without him, but the floor is too hard and his nails too short, and all he's succeeded in doing is open up the breaks in his fingers.

The pain seems to be everywhere now. His head is spinning violently and the whole of his back feels like it's on fire. He wants to cry, but it seems he's too dehydrated for that. His throat is parched and his skin feels like it's being sucked into his bones.

Exhausted, he finally stops moving, unable to take it anymore. He hasn't felt this drained of energy since he lay on the kitchen floor of his family home, cradling his mother's lifeless body. She had taken her own life, but he doesn't even have that option. Still, the part of him that has been scared this might be his life for days or even weeks to come, while he starves to death, is now content that the end is coming far sooner than that.

In time. The answer is there, in those two short words. It had also been in the confidence with which his captor said them. She had known, even as she departed, what his fate would be. He lies perfectly still, trying to feel the movement of blood around his body. More specifically, he's trying to figure out what might be in that blood. He knows he was drugged before; he can vividly remember the hand being placed over his mouth and the sweet smell of chloroform and whatever else was in the mixture before he slipped into darkness.

He can picture the scene where that had happened. Discounting the glimpse of light as his captor slipped away, the view of the countryside on top of the hill with the twisted oak will most likely be the last view he will ever have of this world. Not bad, as things go.

Certainly better than his twin had managed, slicing his own throat in an abandoned warehouse. Better than his dad, staring at the ceiling in the family bedroom. Better than his mum, looking down at the carefully arranged table in the kitchen – a meal for the children, a photograph and the briefest of notes. Better than Ben Peters, in a derelict house that spoke of his tragic life. Better than Dr Nigel Hartham, propped beside a bin down a rubbish-filled alleyway. Better than Thomas Shaw, staring at the floor in the hallway of his home, watching his blood pool around him.

Nathan knows that they will all be equal soon, though. He knows for certain that he will be joining them, because as he's been thinking, he's carefully worked his way around every inch of his body and he's come to the beginning of the end. There's hardly any part of his body that isn't in pain, but at the centre of the inside of his elbow that discomfort is tellingly focused. Like a pinprick. Like the point of a needle.

CHAPTER FORTY-FOUR

'That's more than fifty different names for Max we've been offered now,' says Sam, staring up at one of Danny's screens as he scrolls through a social media feed. 'Why would people make stuff up, when they know somebody's life is at risk?'

'I imagine there's a few of them they're not making up,' says Katie. 'I have a feeling Max has been living several lives.' She looks down at the list she's started to compile of details that people have been sharing not just with the authorities, but with the internet. Some have even posted photos with the same woman, but she's never centre frame and her appearance is remarkably different in each.

'She's not been charged under any of the names I've tried,' says Danny, rolling his chair between different keyboards, his fingers dancing across the keys. 'Not by the police. Not even for buying anything online.'

'She must have inherited a few of her dad's tricks,' says Sam, sadly. 'Certainly for deception.'

'Her name probably isn't going to lead us to Nathan, anyway,' says Katie. 'Maybe if a landlord, or whoever sold her the place where Nathan is being held, sees her photo.'

Sam turns away from the screens. 'Even if he does, it's probably going to be lost in the avalanche of information. There's no way of sifting this. Even if there were fifty of us on the job.'

'They'll be having the same problem back at the station,' says Katie, checking her phone again. She's not missed any calls. There have been no calls. Clearly no breakthrough, and it's been more than an hour since the blogger's message came in. Exactly how quickly was Nathan fading? How much longer does he have? She looks down at Danny, who seems to be enjoying the challenge, and she wishes she could be so emotionally detached. 'I take it there's no way you can find out who the blogger is, or where they're blogging from?' she asks him. 'We've had plenty of our guys try, but they say she's too good.'

'From what I've seen, they're right. No way even I'm getting you anything of value within the next few hours, even putting all my effort into it.'

'Then let's focus elsewhere,' says Katie. 'What about the death of the mother? It was thirty years ago. Maybe twenty-five. Maybe twenty. We don't know.' This time Katie considers the list of deaths that she's made from their searches. It seems endless. So many people have died in remarkable ways, in terrible ways. This is not news to Katie; she's had a better view than most of the injustices and misfortunes of life. But the scale of it seems overwhelming. Of course, they can narrow it down to former policewomen, but still there's nothing that jumps out at her, and anything they've pursued has quickly led to disappointment.

'Questions,' Katie continues. 'Questions will bring us the answer. Why did she kill her dad, for example? What had Carl Watkins done that was so unforgivable?'

'He deserted her mother,' says Sam. 'Left her to suffer. Maybe even introduced her to drugs.'

Katie is surprised to hear Sam talk so negatively about a man she's always defended. But then Katie imagines Sam had never been blind to the truth; she'd just accepted that truth, learned to live with the man, perhaps even to love him.

'But how did Carl meet the mother? Might she have arrested him?'

'Would that be too long ago to be on the database?' says Sam, spinning round.

'We can give it a go,' says Danny, dragging up records from well before he was born.

'There,' he says, pointing up at one of the screens. It takes Katie a moment to follow his finger, but eventually she can see the names. 'Two arresting officers for possession. One a bloke. One—'

'Margaret Ames,' says Katie, breathlessly, bouncing on her tiptoes as a surge of adrenaline seems to lift her up and off the floor. 'Can we search for what's happened to her?'

Danny is on it already, hunting through news databases and the death register. The three of them are scanning the text that pops up, searching for the name Ames, looking for confirmation that they might have found the right person.

'That's it!' says Sam, reaching up to jab the screen so hard that for a moment it looks like it's going to fall from its support. It's an article from a local newspaper, describing the overdose of a former policewoman, leaving behind a young daughter.

'The body was found in a scrapyard,' says Katie, reading quickly as her heartbeat rises. 'The same scrapyard where she arrested Watkins.'

'Does that mean he killed her?' asks Danny.

Sam doesn't answer, but Katie can see the acceptance on her face. She imagines Sam has now realised what Carl Watkins really was. She thought she'd known the truth, found something under the surface that she'd been unable to resist, but several more layers have been stripped away, and now Sam can see, as Katie had always been able to see, what a hideous, manipulative man he had been.

'Let's ring it in,' says Katie, lifting up her mobile as she heads for the door.

'No,' says Sam. 'That's not far from here. We can get there first.'

'But it might be a big place,' says Katie. 'We need as much backup as possible. And Nathan will need medical assistance.'

'Put the phone down,' says Sam, as she lifts the car keys. 'You're wasting time. Agree we go alone, or find your own way.'

The coldness has returned to her face, and Katie knows exactly what she's thinking. After realising what a monster Watkins had been, Sam has shifted rapidly from seeking revenge for someone she'd cared about, to a desperate need for self-preservation.

'There might not even be any evidence of what she knows,' says Katie. 'Or there might be far more than you could possibly destroy. And don't forget, the police are already talking to Tristan.'

'There's no connection between me and him. I was careful.'

'But not so careful as to not admit your collaboration with Carl Watkins to me, or to Nathan. And Danny here is now a witness, too. Are you going to get rid of us all?'

The young man instantly turns and rolls back on his chair. Katie is staring straight at Sam, but she's already had a good look for potential weapons, something to disable her. Something to get those keys. But then part of her is convinced that she doesn't need a weapon, because her desperation is at a level where nothing is going to stop her if she takes that step forward.

'Don't be as bad as him,' says Katie. 'And don't give the bitch behind this what she wants. And you know this is it. We might have done some bad things. We might have told a few lies, but we're still on the right side. The same side.'

For a moment, Sam remains just as she had been the first time they met, when she walked into the interview room and sat silent and emotionless. But then her features twitch and twist, and Katie sees the kind of transformation she's seen so many times on the faces of criminals bombarded by the facts she's so carefully collated, confronted by the truth she's revealed. It's too late. There's no way out. The past is the past. But it will also inevitably shape the future.

'Call them,' says Sam, turning for the door.

CHAPTER FORTY-FIVE

Nathan knows he's slipping away and that he won't be coming back. He knows because of that tiny prick on the inside of his elbow. He knows because his decline is far too sudden. It's not normal. It's not natural. There's something in his system that's dragging him down. The squeeze on his chest is constantly tightening. It's robbing him of oxygen. It's robbing him of hope.

There will be no more light. There will be no more Katie. The only question is, what comes next? He's given this a lot of thought. He had a whole year up in Scotland to contemplate his death. Although most of the time all he longed for was nothingness, there had been days when he'd convinced himself that there was a heaven and he was going to make it there, because actions, not thoughts, were what counted in the end. Now he's surely heading to hell. Might Thomas Shaw be waiting for him there? Or might this be hell already – a continual reflection on what he's done?

The answer to that is as sudden as it is unexpected. With a screech, the door to his right is opened, and silhouetted in the doorway he can make out a small woman.

'Katie?' Nathan calls out, weakly.

'Not long.' The words are not whispered now, but it's not Katie; it's the voice of his captor. 'It seems I underestimated the two of them. You were supposed to be dead already.'

He feels the weakness in his body again. 'Have you drugged me?'

'With the good stuff this time,' she says, tapping her pocket 'Slow-acting, but irreversible in the quantity I've given you. I had a little left over from Dad.'

'Your dad?' he asks. Even though he knows his time is running out he wants to keep her talking, hoping that Katie will be here soon, trying to ignore that word, *irreversible*.

'Not scientifically proved, but I certainly believed him to be. Mum never got a chance to tell me his name, and when I finally tracked down the most likely candidate, well, sadly he didn't have long to live. Still, I think we both saw enough of each other, saw the similarities in our features, and our personalities.'

Nathan can't see those features himself, the woman remaining in silhouette, but he no longer has any doubt who she was to Carl Watkins.

'You held back,' he says. 'When you hit him. Was it with the spade you used to dig the hole?' He doesn't wait for an answer. 'I think you were intending to kill him, but you hesitated. Which is why you had to use his drugs.'

'Drugs that he had probably brought to finish me off. Unlike you, he didn't have the balls to use a gun. This gun.' She adds to the silhouette by holding out her hand and the unmistakable shape of a pistol. 'So he'd have injected me with something, made me look like a junkie, despite all I'd done to try and kick the habit. Then he'd have dumped my body somewhere. Treated me like scrap.' She laughs and turns to look over her shoulder at the partly open door. 'Just like he did with Mum.'

'He killed your mum?'

'Several times. She was a good policewoman before he got into her head. He was like a poison. It seemed appropriate in the end that I used the poison that had made his fortune to finish him off.'

'But the spade was what you'd intended,' Nathan says. His voice is still weak, and his body weaker, but he's finding the strength for this from somewhere. 'You wanted to hit him with the same frenzy you'd used on Dr Hartham. You'd dug the hole and led him over to it. Maybe you told him you had something buried there.'

'Evidence,' she says. 'And that's exactly what it turned out to be in the end. Evidence of what he'd done to my mum.'

'You found killing Steven Fish easy?' says Nathan, thinking back to pictures of the headless corpse.

'The so-called boyfriend? That was nothing personal. Not in relation to him, anyway. It was just a way of sending a message to Dad. Let him know what was coming his way.'

'But you couldn't kill him how you wanted to. It's not easy killing family, is it? No matter who they are. No matter what they've done.'

'Whereas you found shooting Thomas Shaw easy enough. I hoped one of you would lose the plot over there. You, Sam, Katie, you all had so much potential.'

'You planted the drugs at his house? And the gun?'

'I made sure they were there. Made sure he was high. And scared. And ready to attack anyone who came for him. You supposedly know all about getting into people's heads. Well, his was extremely easy to get into. Via his bed, that is.'

'What about my brother?' asks Nathan. 'Did you understand him?'

'We understood each other,' she says. 'He was the only one. He will always be the only one.'

'How did you meet?'

She laughs at this, and he can just make out a crossing of her arms. 'He caught me. He did what you were scared to do. He looked at the evidence from Steven Fish and he tracked me down. He would have been a far better detective than you.'

Nathan sighs. 'For a long time I thought he was a far better person than me.'

'And you were right, he was. He was because he was true to himself.'

'And what a world it would be if we all gave in to those instincts,' says Nathan, sadly. 'So did you live on the houseboat with him?'

The woman takes a few steps back to the door and peers out through the gap. Nathan can hear sirens in the distance.

'For a while,' she says. He can see part of her face now. She has shoulder-length brown hair and attractive features. She has none of the physical strength that Carl Watkins had. But all of the casual menace. And it's not just in the way she's leaning against the doorway of the shipping container while half of London's police force is no doubt racing towards her; it's the gun that's now swinging from the tips of her fingers. 'It was never going to work,' she says, finally, leaning her head back and tapping it slowly against the door frame. 'Christian and I had so much in common, but we still weren't the same.'

'Like a twin, you mean?' says Nathan. He's been straining to lift his head from the ground to get a better look at her, but now he lets his head fall. At the same time, he can see the gun turning towards him.

'All he ever needed was you. And yet you walked away.'

'I didn't want to infect him with the darkness that was inside of me. I had no way of knowing it was in him, too.'

'Perhaps if you'd hung around. Perhaps if you'd talked.'

'You're right,' says Nathan. 'I deserted him. I left him alone to become a monster. The same way your dad left you. And then there's Richard Evans. Was he helping you with your addiction?'

'Until he did exactly the same fucking thing all men do. They start thinking too much about themselves.'

If he had the strength Nathan might argue that, because all he's thinking about at the moment is the gun and about Katie, who will no doubt be at the head of those racing to try and save him.

'Do you have a name?' he asks.

'Several. But seeing as this is probably the end for both of us, I'll give you the one that means the most. The one that my mother gave me. It's Max.'

'Does anybody else need to die here, Max? Haven't you got your revenge?'

'Maybe when you've stopped talking.' She moves quickly across from the door and presses the barrel of the gun to his temple. 'And stopped breathing.'

The cold of the barrel is soothing in a way, and he strains to keep his head against it. 'So if I'm dead, then you won't hurt anybody else?'

He feels the barrel tap twice against his head. 'Ah. I see what you're asking. Now isn't that sweet. You're worried about your little detective friend. Well, I'd love to tell you that I'll leave her alone. And in truth, she means next to nothing to me. But you see...' Max moves back over to the door, this time cautiously peering out from behind it. 'It's not just revenge for me that I'm seeking.'

CHAPTER FORTY-SIX

Sam and Katie had believed they would get to the scrapyard first, and Sam had driven recklessly in trying to do so, but when they arrive they find half a dozen officers are already at the scene. Armed police have been called, and have started to position themselves around the site.

'Impressive,' says Sam, sullenly. 'I shall miss being part of something as efficient as this.'

'Let's just focus on getting Max.' Katie rubs her wrist, wishing she had a watch. 'And Nathan.'

'We're not getting in there,' says Sam. 'Not till they've secured the area. And even then…'

'But we have to,' says Katie. 'He might not have long.'

'We don't know that for sure. That might have been another lie.'

'I'm not willing to take that risk.'

'And they,' she gestures towards the police teams rushing around, 'aren't going to take a risk with you. Besides, they've not even got the gate open yet.'

Katie looks over at the scrapyard gate, where two men are struggling with bolt cutters to cut through several thick chains. Hearing a noise behind her, she turns and can just make out some press crews arriving in the distance, being shepherded to the side of the road by police officers.

'They're going to crucify me when the truth gets out,' says Sam, rubbing at her cheek as she stares back at them, finally trying to remove the last of the muddy mark. 'They won't understand why.

Nobody will. And I don't want to be remembered as being like Carl. I'm not like Carl. I was trying to do some good, trying to make a difference.'

'You could help save a life here,' says Katie. 'That would be making an enormous difference.'

'Do you love him?' asks Sam, turning her back on the press. 'Or is it just an obsession, a need that has to be answered?'

'I'm not sure I know what the difference is. Certainly not at the moment.' Katie places a hand on her stomach. 'We were supposed to be there for each other. He was supposed to protect me.'

'I was supposed to be there for my little sister,' says Sam. 'I didn't even know about her drugs problem until it was too late. I'm not sure my parents ever forgave me. Or themselves. And I know for sure that I've never stopped wishing I'd been a little less wrapped up in my own world and seen what was right in front of my face. It's given me drive in my life, and it's given me desire, but it's also pushed me into making some unforgivable decisions.' Sam pulls at the collar on her mud-covered shirt, dragging it away from her neck as if she's struggling to breathe. 'Maybe I'm a fool, still blind to people's faults after all this time, but I don't think I'm a bad person.'

Katie watches the final chain fall away on the gate. Then she reaches out and grabs Sam by the elbow, gripping her hard and staring into the senior policewoman's eyes. 'We've all fucked up in the past. This is about the present. Now I need to get in there, and there's no way I'm going to be able to unless you do your thing.'

Sam looks at her for a moment, her emotionless face threatening to crumble. Then her features set solid again and she nods, before shaking off Katie's hand and striding forward. 'Come with me.'

The head of the armed response unit is at the gate, barking orders into his radio. Katie strides up and matches his no-nonsense tone as she holds out her identity card.

'DS Rhodes, and I need to get inside.'

'That's not going to happen, I'm afraid, ma'am,' he says. 'I have strict orders not to let anyone in. I also have very specific orders in relation to the two of you.'

Katie tips her head back and groans. She should have predicted as much. The accusations against them have been out in the world for more than an hour now. They have already been stripped of their powers. And yet at the same time Katie feels something else growing inside of her. It's not the gift of life. She will never have that. Instead, it's the gift of not caring about her own life. Or rather, being willing to give it up for another.

With this in mind, she starts to run. The policeman reaches out and tries to grab her, but she's too quick and is through the open gate in less than a second, sprinting deep inside, waiting for a shot to ring out, perhaps from Max, or perhaps from one of those who are supposed to be on her side.

Fifty paces in and Katie realises she doesn't know where she's going. It's a big yard, and it isn't obvious where Nathan is being held. She looks frantically around, her heart banging in her chest. She runs ahead, going around and behind hundreds of stacked cars, abandoned diggers, twisted sheets of metal, rusting old white goods. She's so focused on trying to spot which direction she needs to head in that she only hears the footfall at the very last second. She spins round, lifting her arms in defence, ready to be bundled to the ground by someone trying to protect her, or flattened into oblivion by someone looking to kill. In the end neither of those things happens. It's Sam, and she passes right by, calling out, 'This way!'

Katie catches up quickly and they find themselves zigzagging between more stacks of cars that look precariously balanced. They round a corner, mud splattering up the backs of their legs, their hair flattened to their foreheads with sweat, and they see the rusting blue shipping container in the distance.

'That's it,' says Sam. 'I'm sure of it.'

'How do you know?' asks Katie as they start to run again, this time at a slightly slower pace, ready to throw themselves out of the way of a bullet.

'I waited behind just that little bit longer,' says Sam. 'The armed response lead had downloaded a map of this place. That container is perfect for hiding someone.'

They slow to a cautious jog as they draw close, and they can see that the container's door is partly open.

'I'll go first,' whispers Sam, but Katie doesn't allow her to push in front.

'We go together,' she says.

On the ground in front of the doorway is a three-foot-long, hollow metal tube. Katie bends down and picks it up. She doesn't believe it's a coincidence that it looks so much like the metal bar that Nathan had failed to bring down on his brother's head. It's been left there for a reason, but she's not about to give up the chance of having something to fend someone off with or, better still, of starting an attack.

'Come in,' calls a woman's voice. 'I hope you're not too late.'

Any sense of self-protection Katie might have felt has vanished. She drags back the heavy metal door, before lifting the bar above her head. Sam is alongside her. A faint, occasionally flickering bulb hanging from the roof reveals Nathan curled up motionless on the floor at the far end of the container. Sitting in front of him, with her legs crossed, like a little girl in a school assembly, is a woman of about thirty years of age, with shoulder-length brown hair and eyes that seem to cut through the semi-darkness.

Katie looks for the gun and waits for the bullet, but as her eyes adjust she can see the woman has her arms down by her sides, palms flat on the floor, just behind two syringes – one full and one empty – and a gun. She looks perfectly relaxed, and yet at the same time everything about her is a threat.

Katie draws in a breath and readies herself to rush forward.

'Not just yet,' says the woman, placing a hand lightly on top of the gun. It's obvious to Katie that she could lift it and fire it long before Katie could cover the distance between them. 'I was joking before. Nathan will still be with us for a while. Let's have a chat first. I've wanted to speak to the two of you alone. I mean, so much of our conversation up until now has been done on the internet or in the press, or in the messages I've left for you. By messages, I mean bodies. I should probably be specific, to avoid any confusion. Anyway, it's nice to make it more *personal*.' She draws out the final word with a grin that Katie would love to wipe from her face. 'So we should probably start with introductions, shouldn't we? My name is Max.'

'I know who you are,' says Katie. 'And you know who I am. You also know what I'll do if you don't hand over that antidote in time.'

'And I'm sure you'd take great delight in it. The same way that Nathan told me he enjoyed taking another person's life. He might have acted all upset about it, but it would hardly be the first time he's put on a performance for you. We were talking, and with the sort of honesty that people save for the end of their life, he told me it was the greatest thrill, like finally becoming who he was supposed to be. I imagine you'll feel the same, which is why you two are perfect for each other.'

'And were you perfect for Christian?' asks Katie, not taking her eyes off the syringe, her fingers curling by her side as if she already has it in her grasp.

'We had our moments,' says Max. 'He could be very sweet.' She grins again. 'But I forgave him that in the light of all his other, far more positive traits.'

Sam is leaning forward, peering into the dark corners of the container. Katie knows what she's looking for. She wants the evidence of her relationship with Carl. She wants it so that she can destroy it.

'How much did Christian tell you?' asks Katie, wondering how many of her own secrets were shared by Nathan's brother.

'About your night of passion?' asks Max. 'About the night Christian, post some rather dramatic plastic surgery, persuaded you to sleep with him? I imagine I know more about it than you do, given how much you'd had to drink. Christian was very specific, you see, and had a great facility for words. He didn't write them down like his mum and his brother, but he passed them along when he knew they'd give pleasure.'

'How could the man you supposedly cared about sleeping with someone else have given you pleasure?' asks Katie, pushing back the images of that night that were flashing up in her mind.

'Because of the pain that followed for you,' says Max, taking on a softened tone, as if she's talking to a child. 'Because of the horror. I knew you wouldn't understand. You don't get it. Just like Thomas Shaw didn't get it.' She rolls her eyes. 'All muscle. All surface. But when it came down to it, when I pushed him to see how much he could achieve, he got pathetically scared.'

Katie's own fear is continuing to gather. She needs to find a way to help Nathan. She's even started to consider which way to twist and turn her body to increase her chances of surviving the bullet that will get to her before she can get to the antidote. But above all this careful contemplation, Katie keeps returning to the same word, again and again, the word that has haunted her since she first looked at the scars on her cheeks and since the doctor told her that she couldn't have a child: *hesitation*.

'You've talked,' says Katie. 'And I've listened. And if bringing pain and horror is what you've been trying to do, then you've certainly succeeded. But I don't think you brought us here to see Nathan die.'

'What makes you so sure of that?' asks Max, raising an eyebrow.

'Because of who he is. Because of his twin. If you kill him, that will be like killing Christian.'

'You're forgetting that thanks to the plastic surgery that managed to fool you, Christian didn't look at all like his brother.'

'Surface,' says Katie, stealing Max's earlier word.

'But Nathan proved himself different on the inside, too. He couldn't kill. He was all talk. Or rather, all words. It was down to me to take those words and make them mean something.'

'He's still the twin of the man you loved.'

Max opens her mouth to answer, but Sam cuts in.

'Maybe she didn't love him, not at the end. I think maybe Christian gave her up for his brother.'

'Who cares what you think,' snaps Max. 'Oh, everyone thinks you're super-smart, bringing down drugs gangs, climbing the ladder, but you needed my dad for that. And he played you all along. You got him off a couple of murder charges, helped put his rivals away, and he even managed to make you believe that he cared about you, when all the time he loved Steven Fish.'

'He wasn't so clever when he let you walk up behind him and smack him over the head,' says Sam.

'He underestimated me,' says Max. 'Most people have. They see a small woman and they make their judgements. He came to kill me.' She lifts the gun in front of her, tapping the barrel with her other hand. 'He had this very weapon to shut me up. But I think in the end he wanted to finish me off like he did Mum, making it look like another drug addict overdosing. Problem was, he lost his focus, convinced himself the little girl couldn't be a threat. He must have forgotten whose DNA I was carrying.'

'Or maybe not,' says Sam. 'I doubt he'd forgotten what you did to Steven Fish, to the man he *loved*. And maybe it all finally dawned on him when he came face to face with his past, with the monster that he had helped to create, that he couldn't escape justice anymore. Maybe he didn't want to.'

'That's just shit!' says Max, her face flushing, the gun lifted and pointed directly at Sam. 'Shit that's been costing Nathan

precious time. So let's get down to it before it is too late.' She
turns to look at Katie. 'You were right. I don't want Nathan to
die. I want you to save him. And you can, very simply. I will let
you come and take the antidote and I will hand myself in if you
do one simple thing.'

'What?' says Katie quickly, sensing more than ever that her
hesitation might cost her everything.

'Bring that bar down on Ms Stone's head with enough force
to kill her.'

'*What?*'

'I don't think I need to repeat myself. What I will say is that
you have two minutes to make your decision.'

'And if I won't?' says Katie, although she believes she's already
figured out the answer.

'Then I'll shoot you both, before crushing the syringe containing the antidote.'

Perhaps it's the anticipation of the bullet, or the memory of
the last time blood had been spilling out of her, but Katie's free
hand moves to her cheek and then to her stomach.

'Why two minutes?' says Katie.

'Less than that now, but it's more fun with a bit of pressure
on. Now to help with your decision, not that it should be all that
difficult, let us consider once again what Sam did for my dad.'

'Do you have any actual evidence of that?' says Sam.

'Of course. And that will come out, in the fullness of time. But
I wouldn't worry about it, because time is something you don't
have, Ms Stone, not in any of the scenarios I've just described.
Besides, you helped my dad get away with murder. Twice. Your
death will be nothing less than you deserve.'

'You're probably right,' says Sam, taking a step forward. 'I
should be punished for my crimes. So why not shoot me yourself?'

Max's eyes widen, then she recovers her outward calm. 'Because
that's not the deal. Not yet. I want to see what Katie is made of

first. Stronger stuff than her former boyfriend, I think. But then she only has about twenty seconds left to prove that, or she'll be ending up every bit as dead as he will.'

'Then do it,' says Sam, turning to look at Katie. Katie doesn't return her stare. 'Close your eyes and fucking do it! There's no other option. You have to. My career is over. I have nothing left to live for.'

Katie looks over at Nathan, at the one thing she has left, and that will soon be gone if she doesn't make a decision.

'Save yourself and save Nathan,' says Max.

'By becoming a killer?'

'It's exactly what Nathan did with Thomas Shaw. That's how he saved you. Are you not willing to do the same in return?'

Katie feels the weight of the bar, knows she has to do something, to come to a decision that she'll either regret for the rest of her life, or that will bring about the end of her life. And it's not that she's panicking, far from it – her mind is doing what it's always done under extreme pressure: it's processing information even quicker. She's working through the words she's just heard, judging them, interpreting them. *Hesitation*. She keeps returning to that word again. What's the real reason Max is so keen to have this finished? Is she only interested in achieving what Christian was unable to – making someone a murderer? Is she really so desperate for Sam to die? Katie takes another step forward. She's only inches from the barrel of the gun now. She can see the speed with which Max's chest is rising and falling. She can also more clearly see two syringes either side of the younger woman on the floor. One is full and the other not quite empty.

'You didn't give him all of it,' says Katie, nodding down at one of the syringes. You couldn't. It's like your dad, when you wanted to kill him with whatever you hit him with, but you held back.'

'I gave him enough,' says Max. 'And you're the one that's holding back now. You're the one that's killing him.'

'What will you do once this is over?' asks Katie. Sam remains close behind, seemingly determined to keep within striking distance of the bar.

'I'll be taken away by your colleagues,' says Max. 'I'll spend the rest of my life in jail.'

Katie continues to stare at the syringes. 'I don't think that's what you ever intended.' The words are coming out before the thought is fully formed, but she goes with it anyway, trusting her instinct.

'In truth, even I'm not totally sure of my intentions,' says Max. 'I've been confused for quite some time now. Perhaps ever since I discovered a man could toss the mother of his child away like a piece of scrap.' She places one hand on the floor to her side, and Katie is certain Max is sitting almost exactly where her mother's body was found. 'But I do at least understand the situation here. I hope you do too. Unless you do what I've asked, you're not getting the antidote and Nathan will be every bit as dead as his brother.'

'There is no antidote,' says Katie, her hunch having grown to a terrible certainty. 'Whatever mixture you gave Nathan is also in the second syringe. That syringe was for you, for you to die in the same way and the same place as your mum. Only you bottled it, just like couldn't give Nathan everything. And now you're hoping that I'll be partly to blame for his death, by hesitating.' As she speaks, Katie lifts the bar high above her head. At the same time, Max leans forward and presses the gun into Katie's belly, close to the point where Christian had thrust the knife. For a moment, the two women stare at each other, frozen in that position. Then Max pulls the gun back and lifts it, before grinning and saying, 'Time's up.'

Katie tries to bring the bar down, not waiting any longer, not caring about the consequences for herself, but there's a sudden flash, soon followed by a deafening bang and she's falling backwards, dropping the bar. Katie crumples to the floor. Squeezing her shoulder, she can feel the hot blood pumping out. It's not a fatal wound. Not yet. But she doesn't have long.

In the mayhem, Katie's missed Max turning the gun on Sam. The senior policewoman looks ready to leap forward, but at the same time Katie can see the focus on her face. Careful calculations are taking place.

'You most likely thought the gun wasn't loaded,' says Max to Sam. 'Were probably still trying to convince yourself my dad only took it along to scare me off. You were so wrong about him.' Max turns to look at Katie, her eyes burning bright. 'And I was wrong about you. I really thought you had it.' She shakes her head and sighs. 'But you couldn't even do it to save your own life.'

'The game's over,' says Katie, through gritted teeth. She's certain she's going to pass out at any moment, but she knows that if she does, if she enters that darkness, then she's likely never to come out.

'Not quite,' says Max. She takes a step forward and points the barrel of the gun at Sam's head. 'Now it's Ms Stone's turn. It's up to you, Samantha, to see if you can be sensible, and not quite such a coward.'

Katie sees Sam look down at the metal bar on the floor to her right, a horrified expression on her face. 'You mean, use that on Katie? I can't.'

'You can't?' Max says, with a laugh. 'You were quite happy to torture Nathan. Quite happy to sleep with my dad, with a drug dealer and murderer. Have you suddenly found morals?'

'But it's not—'

'It's all right,' says Max, cutting Sam off. 'Just relax. You've got it far easier than Katie. Forget about the bar. The only thing you have to do is walk out of here and tell your friends the story. Leave out the stuff that incriminates you, if you want. You see, there is no physical evidence of your dealings with my dad. I lied about that, just like I lied about the antidote. The only thing you need to worry about is what is in my head, and the drugs in the other syringe here are going to rapidly remove any trace of that. Simply step out of this container into the sunlight and you'll be okay. If you choose to stay, on the other hand, well…'

Still slumped on the floor and through partly closed eyes, Katie can see Max's finger twitch on the trigger with the gun held up towards Sam.

'Go,' says Katie, weakly. A new wave of pain takes her, and rather than flinch and try and hide away from it, she brings it into focus, at the same time remembering what she'd been told about Nathan as he'd been tortured at the school. He'd thought of her. It had got him through that nightmare. She does the same, picturing his face, his smile, and somehow the pain starts to recede.

'There's nothing else you can do.' She's aware of Sam looking at her as she takes a small step towards the door. She can see what will happen. Once Sam has gone, Max will move across and bolt the door shut. A lock has been placed on the inside, and there's no way anybody will be able to break in in time. This will become a coffin for them all.

Katie looks across at Nathan. He's not moving. He most likely won't move ever again. She'll never get the chance to tell him how important he is to her. To say sorry for the way she's treated him. More than that, she's thinking that they'll never get to work together again, and of all the injustice that will pass because they're not around.

As she starts to drift towards unconsciousness, she stares at Sam. It appears the other woman is not going anywhere. She cannot bring herself to walk away and leave her to die, the same way Katie hadn't been able to bring the metal bar down on Sam's head. Katie finds herself smiling; then, with a pain so intense she can barely breathe, she rises slowly to her feet. She finds Sam's stare again and the two women exchange a look that tells Katie her intentions are understood. There is no other option.

'No hesitation,' says Katie, before turning to face up to Max. With whatever strength Katie has left, and with her thoughts focused purely on Nathan, on this faint chance of saving him, she charges forward at the barrel of the gun, with Sam beside her.

CHAPTER FORTY-SEVEN

'I had gone,' says Nathan, looking out of the window of his hospital room at the tops of trees gently swaying. 'I was right there…' He stretches a hand out. It's not really directed at anything. But then, where he's trying to get back to isn't in any location that he could place, or that he understands. There had been no bright light at the end of the tunnel, no booming voice, no gates at the top of the stairs; it was just a sense of nothingness laid out before him like an endless ocean, and he'd wanted so much to dive in, to give up all thought, all feeling. A blessed relief. The only thing that had held him back was what he's looking at right now: Katie's beautiful face.

She's lying in the neighbouring bed, hooked up to just as many machines as he is, her shoulder patched up and held in a sling.

'I know what you mean,' says Katie. 'I think I was there too. And to be honest, it wasn't such a terrible place.'

'No, it wasn't.' Nathan came back for Katie, to be with Katie, and to be with Katie, he knows that he has to play a professional role. 'But we've still got stuff to do here.'

'Plenty,' says Katie. 'Although I guess we'll have to see where we stand after all the formal questioning.'

Nathan tries to calm himself as he thinks of another inquest, another no doubt very public inquiry into his behaviour and that of those he cares about, because he knows any distress will instantly register on the machines monitoring his heart. It's not easy, but he's got enough drugs – and good drugs, this time – in his system to help suppress any panic.

'I still don't fully understand what happened,' he says. 'Why did you both rush forward at the same time?'

'It was simple maths,' says Katie, remembering the calculation she'd been able to make in the middle of the fog of pain. 'The only way we could possibly save more than one life was to give Max two targets at the same time. The chances were that between me and Sam, one of us was going to survive.'

'But why did Sam take that risk, for me?'

Nathan can see Katie flinch, before her features twist in pain. 'I keep hearing that gunshot ringing out in the metal container. In that moment, I believed it could have been me that was hit for the second time, but looking back I can see that Sam knew exactly what she was doing. I couldn't move fast, not with my injury, and Sam was always going to get to Max first. She also crossed in front of me before diving forward on Max. The doctors reckon the bullet in her chest should have killed her instantly, but she was still able to get in a couple of strong blows that knocked the gun from Max's hand and left her barely conscious. I landed a punch of my own before being dragged away by armed officers rushing in.'

'Sam could have walked away,' says Nathan, wiping a tear from his cheek. 'Kept her life. Kept her career.'

'I think she wanted to prove who she really was,' says Katie. 'To us. To her colleagues. To herself.'

'I owe her so much,' says Nathan. 'Both of you.'

'And you'll repay us,' says Katie. 'By doing what you do. Every murderer we track down, every victim we find justice for, will be in the name of Sam Stone.'

Nathan falls back on his pillow, releasing a long breath. 'And Max? Do you think she'll talk?'

'Who knows? And who knows what she might have to say?'

'I'll be honest,' says Nathan. 'I would like to find out more about my brother. He might have been a monster, but I've spent most of my adult life trying to understand those like him, and him more than any…'

'Let's worry about ourselves first,' says Katie, straining to reach out from her bed. Nathan stretches out his own hand towards hers, but with their injuries, they don't even come close to touching. Still, it's a start, and their excitement at what the future might hold registers instantly on the heart rate monitors between them.

*

Two weeks later and Nathan, Katie and Richard are standing in the middle of a graveyard. The body of Ben Peters has just been lowered into the ground in front of them alongside the grave of his brother Mike, and although the few mourners who attended the service have now departed, Nathan's certain that there are still people watching from a distance. He and Katie are big news, and will remain so for quite some time. But this time, he's not going to run. There is no hiding, not from the press and not from the authorities. They will ask their questions and he will answer as best he can. The early signs are good for a return to work, with Superintendent Taylor and even DCI Ken Stocks willing to act as character referees. Nathan knows that they don't really trust him, but what he and Katie bring they value highly: results.

'I must head back to Wales,' says Richard, lightly pressing a hand on Nathan's good shoulder. The pain of his injuries is lessening now, but he knows it'll take a long time before he's fully recovered.

'We'll come and visit,' says Katie. 'If you don't mind?'

The old doctor smiles a broad smile. 'The door of my yellow house is always open for you.'

It seems so long since Nathan arrived panting on the doorstep of that house, fearing losing Katie to the pains in her stomach. In the end, those had been the first signs not only of food poisoning, but of the poisoning influence of Max.

'It's been a pleasure,' says Nathan, holding out his hand. Richard takes it and shakes it firmly, before turning to Katie. She pulls him into a tight hug, her face pressed into his shoulder.

'You take care,' she says, tears forming in her eyes. 'And call us if you need anything.'

'What I need is for you two to stick together,' says the doctor. 'What you have, whatever it might be, is something special.'

Nathan feels his face flush and looks across to see the same has happened to Katie. It's highlighted the scars on her cheeks, but also the awkwardness that still exists between them.

They wave goodbye to the doctor, and then return their attention to the graves, of two brothers who deserved so much better. Nathan hasn't visited his own brother Christian's grave – hidden away, with no name on the stone – nor does he imagine he ever will, but he can't help reflecting on the importance of family. He will most likely never add to his. He is the last of the Radleys, as Katie is the last of the Rhodeses, but while he's with her, while they're working together, sharing their experiences, making the most of whatever abilities they have, it somehow seems enough.

A LETTER FROM NICK

Hello,

Thanks so much for choosing to read *The Goodnight Song*. If you enjoyed it, and want to keep up-to-date with all my releases, please sign up at the following link. Your email address will never be shared and you can unsubscribe at any time:

www.bookouture.com/Nick-Hollin

It hardly seems five minutes since I was starting out on book 1, *Dark Lies*, and here we are with a sequel. I've loved returning to Rhodes and Radley. I now see them as close friends. Given what I've put them through, they might not be so keen on me.

I hope you enjoyed their latest adventure, and if you did I would be very grateful if you could write a review for *The Goodnight Song*. I'm very keen to hear what you think, and it makes a huge difference in making other readers aware of my work.

Whilst I'm not the greatest with social-media – work and family rarely afford me the time – I would be delighted to hear from you over at Twitter @vonmaraus.

Best wishes,
Nick

ACKNOWLEDGEMENTS

Family, friends, agent and editor. Same people. Same support. Same sacrifices. Even more appreciation.